April
in the
Back of Beyond

APRIL IN THE BACK OF BEYOND
By p.m.terrell

Published by
Drake Valley Press
USA

This novel is a work of fiction. Any resemblance to actual persons, living or dead, is entirely coincidental except as noted under "A Note from the Author". The characters, names, plots and incidents are the product of the author's imagination. References to actual events, public figures, locales or businesses are included to give this work a sense of reality.

Cover photograph of The Old Gates of County Westmeath, Ireland, copyright 2019, Willie Forde Photography of Ireland (https://www.facebook.com/williefordephotography/).

ISBN 978-1-935970-46-0 (Trade Paperback)
ISBN 978-1-935970-45-3 (eBook)

APRIL IN THE BACK OF BEYOND
by p.m.terrell

With Special Thanks to Mary Lewis

1

I arrived in what the Irish refer to as the back of beyond, a remote western region of the island, before the village had fully awakened. Having landed in Dublin on the red-eye from Newark, I discovered us to be the first airplane to arrive at the terminal, and we were quickly whisked through the international process with barely a line. It was early April, too early for the tourist season to have begun with its noise and congestion, and by the time I collected my luggage I found to my amazement that the other passengers had already disappeared into the Irish mist. A short time later I had my rental and driving directions on my tablet and had set off toward Galway.

Traffic along the M6 was brisk; even rush hour traffic was no match for the States and before I had reached the city of Galway, I veered off the motorway onto a local road, which twisted and turned around Lough Corrib until I at last reached the tiny village where I was to pick up the keys to the cottage I'd rented for the remainder of the month.

It hadn't occurred to me to compare the time of my arrival with the normal hours of a pub so I wasn't at all surprised to find the front door locked. I stood for a moment and attempted to peer through the adjacent window but the mists were clearing as the sun rose so it was lighter outside than in. I turned about and studied the single lane that wound through the village. There were shops on either side for two blocks before the narrow road disappeared around an upward slope, presumably leading to my rented cottage.

As I stood there contemplating my next move, the village began to stir in a leisurely sort of way, rather like myself on a sleepy Saturday morn when I've no good reason to rise. A man in a heavy jacket and a flat cap exited a vehicle across the way, unlocked the butcher shop and set out a blank easel upon which he carefully printed the days' specials in bold letters. A woman in a flowing pink cardigan wheeled a cart from the adjacent hardware store and arranged it along the sidewalk where the wind chimes for sale jingled in a steady breeze made chillier as it crossed the lough. I felt weariness and hunger descend over me, having traveled all night with only the occasional uncomfortable snooze in a constricting airline seat and an unappealing snack that went half-uneaten.

I caught sight of a corner grocery and before I knew it, my feet were taking me there, hoping for a hot cup of coffee and perhaps a packaged Danish or croissant. As I stepped off the curb to cross to the next corner, a door opened alongside the pub and a young couple walked with energized purpose into the alleyway. I caught wind of their banter but didn't understand their words. Norwegian, I surmised, and no doubt they'd speak English as well but they were quite obviously tourists and engrossed in their conversation. Then my eyes fell on the gently closing door and I found myself making a beeline for it before it had the chance to latch.

The grocery forgotten for the moment, I stepped onto a landing adjacent a stone staircase. On one side lay a flight that curved upwards, perhaps to rooms above the pub. On the other side, a shorter flight swept downwards and that's the one I took, following the distinct aroma of fresh brewed coffee.

I held onto the wall as I took the uneven steps, the light so dim I was having second thoughts before I spotted the light peeking around a doorway. I swung it open to a large bright industrial kitchen, spotless except for two plates of half-eaten food set beside the ample sink. I caught a glimpse of my image in the polished stainless steel refrigerator, my layered brunette hair appearing rather unkempt and my skin pale against enormous brown eyes. My clothes were rumpled due to the red-eye, accentuating a body I'd often considered to be too thin, a product of high metabolism. To my right I heard the clinking of glass and I pushed onward through another door and into the pub itself.

A man was busily unpacking a box of liquor behind the bar, oblivious to my presence. An oblique light from an adjoining room snaked its way inside and played off thick silver hair that teased the top of his collar. As he bent down to pick up another bottle, his eyes fell on me and for the briefest of moments, the color drained from his face.

"Mister Cassidy?" I asked. When he didn't respond, I continued, "I'm Hayley Hunter—"

"The author," he said, interrupting me. "From America."

"Yes."

He set the bottle on the bar and came round to take a closer look at me. "My, but I thought you were a ghost when I saw you standing there."

A chill breeze drifted through the room though I could detect no clear source for it. "Are ghosts common around here then?" I joked.

He met my gaze with sharp blue eyes that twinkled as one side of his mouth curled upward. "It's Ireland. No pub worth its liquor would be without one."

I chuckled. "I hope it isn't too early for me to get the keys to the cottage, Mister Cassidy?"

"Fergal," he corrected. "Call me Fergal. Not too early at'al." He reached across the counter to remove a set of keys from a hook. I noticed there were probably a dozen hooks and all but one had keys still dangling from it— two, now that he'd gathered the cottage keys. He caught my scrutiny and added, "You sure you want to be staying in the carriage house?"

"Is there something wrong with it?"

"Oh, nothing wrong at'al. In fact, it's just been renovated this past year with all the modern comforts." He started to hand over the keys but grasped them a bit tighter as his hand steadied itself in midair.

"Then why wouldn't I want to stay there?"

He glanced toward the adjoining room where the sunlight was growing brighter as it continued to find its way through the window. "Well, it's a bit removed, you see, where if you stayed upstairs in one of our rooms above the pub—"

"I'm sure they're just as nice, but as a writer I tend to like something more secluded."

"Breakfast is part of the deal if you stay here," he cajoled.

"I'm sure breakfast is delicious," I said just as my stomach decided to answer as well.

"You have had breakfast, 'ey?" His astute eyes narrowed.

"I was going to the grocery next door—"

"The grocery." He spat the words out though his smile broadened. "No. You'll have a proper breakfast before you leave here you will." He tucked the keys into his pocket.

"I couldn't possibly put you out—"

"No bother at'al. I'd just prepared breakfast for a young couple staying with us here. Though," he added, rubbing a five o'clock shadow, "they unfortunately only wanted porridge and fruit. I've a good Irish breakfast for you—sausage, rashers, white and black pudding, eggs and fried tomatoes—"

"Oh, no, no. It all sounds very good but I couldn't possibly eat all of that," I protested. My words grew louder as he turned to walk away from me until I found myself nearly shouting at his back until I had no other recourse than to follow him into the kitchen.

⋇⋇⋇

In the end, he talked his way into cooking me two fried eggs and more bacon—rashers—than I had any business eating along with some homemade soda bread. He was quite the chef, too, and more capable around the kitchen than myself. We chatted as he cooked and I ended up eating at the butcher block counter in the kitchen on a stool perhaps meant for the help though at this early hour I saw no one else.

"So you're here to write a book, are you?" he said as he poured us both a cup of tea.

"Mostly research a book," I answered between bites. "I've traced my family genealogy back to an ancestor that left Scotland for Ulster in 1608."

"Did you now?"

"Honestly, I hadn't expected to find any record of him but as it turned out, I discovered quite a bit in my online research."

"Ah. Online."

"You did say the cottage has wifi?"

"Oh, absolutely. Couldn't live without it myself for sure. And there's a satellite dish and solar panels on the rooftop; all the modern conveniences, as I said." He picked up his teacup but hesitated as he held it halfway to his lips. "So you're here to follow up with what you've learned online are you?"

"Yes. I'm meeting with the historians and genealogists that helped me. And I also want to go to the places I'm writing about. There's nothing quite like standing in a spot, getting the lay of the land... though I suppose a lot has changed in four hundred years."

"Nonsense. That's not so very long ago." I must have looked at him quizzically because he continued, "Four hundred years is nothing in Ireland, while four hundred miles is the journey of a lifetime."

I felt a rush of excitement, becoming quite animated despite my tiredness. "I'm planning to go to the Inishowen Peninsula, Burt Castle and Derry—"

"The Inishowen, 'ey? Are your ancestors the O'Dohertys then?"

"No, but I'll be writing about Cahir O'Doherty and O'Doherty's Rebellion. It forms the backdrop for the book."

"Ah yes. The last Gaelic King of Ireland. Rich history it is. So your ancestor came here during the Plantation of Ulster, did he now?"

"That's right."

"Then the Ulster American Folk Park should be one of your first stops. They've a library there to rival any genealogy center in the world."

"Yes," I said. "I've been corresponding with a genealogist there for quite some time—Michelle

Mitchell. We've become good long-distance friends of a sort."

"Don't recall the name but then I don't get up that way much at all these days. Say, don't misunderstand me, I'm pleased you're here renting the cottage but it's a wee bit far from your research. Why not stay closer?"

I hesitated. "I've been in Ulster before—stayed there, actually—but, well to be honest…" My voice faded and I hoped he would fill in the blanks but he didn't. He only continued to peer at me with those arresting blue eyes, obviously waiting for me to continue. "I've read," I finally said, "that tensions are high in Ulster—with Brexit and all."

"Ah. In some pockets, yes. Not for the tourists, you see; they're perfectly safe if they stay to the touristy places. But you'll be off the beaten trail, I presume. Most likely, you won't hear much if anything at all about the tensions between those that are seizing the moment to try and unite Ireland and those that wish to remain with the UK. That is," he added, his eyes growing darker, "unless you go looking for trouble."

I laughed rather nervously. "No. That's not me at all. I'm not interested in present day politics; my interest lies in the 17th century."

"Well then, since you're staying down this way, there are universities—Galway and of course Dublin—where meticulous records have been kept, some dating—oh, I'd say a thousand years or more. Though," he added rather wistfully, "much was burned on Easter Sunday, you understand."

Though he said it as though it had happened just last week I added, "In 1916."

"Aye." He switched course. "And should you need directions—or even a guide—I can help to arrange that for you I can."

I finished my breakfast as another wave of exhaustion settled over me. "Thank you for the offer, though I think if you don't mind, I'll get those keys from you and head out to the cottage? I'm afraid today might be a day for ridding myself of this jet lag."

"Oh, of course. Of course." He quickly tidied up the counter, stacking the dishes into the sink. "I'll take you out there myself, make certain you're satisfied with the arrangements."

"I don't want to be a bother—"

"You won't be. Now, it might be just a couple of miles from the village so we can leave your rental here and walk it—"

"I'd rather drive, if it's all the same to you." I hastily added, "I've brought my luggage and computer equipment and it's a bit heavy to carry that far..."

"Of course. I hadn't thought of that." He walked into the hallway and returned with a neck warmer and jacket. "I'll ride along with you then, and walk m'self back. It's a fine day for a stroll, it is."

As it turned out, his offer to ride along with me meant he would drive and I would ride, which suited me perfectly fine. It was turning into a beautiful day now that the mists were dissipating and the sun was beginning to break through the clouds that rolled in steadily from the Atlantic like mirror images of the ocean waves. He took the single lane out of the village, turning at the slopes I'd spotted earlier and winding through fields that even in this early month were already green and lush, broken occasionally by centuries-old hedgerows or ancient stone walls.

We didn't get far before we were brought to an abrupt halt by dozens of cattle being herded right down the center of the lane. Fergal rolled down his window and called a greeting to the farmer, his words coming so quickly that with his heavy accent, I only caught a word here or there—something about an author staying at the Auld Carriage House. The farmer looked more than a bit surprised at this and marched toward the car, gaping into the window at me.

"Why would you stay there?" the man demanded. He appeared to be in his late 60's. His hair might once have been an orange-red but strands were turning white and his bloodshot lavender eyes were framed with pale lashes. Even from across the car, I could tell he reeked with alcohol and I fought the urge to cover my nose.

Before I could answer, Fergal retorted, "It's a grand spot, Danny, and don't you be scaring her off from it. She wants the peace and quiet out there to write her book."

Danny stared harder at me. "A romance novel?"

"Historical," I corrected politely.

"Her family's from Ulster and she's here to document it," Fergal explained.

"Who's her family?"

"None o' your business, that's who," Fergal answered again before I barely had the time to open my mouth. "Now get your cattle out of our way before the woman falls asleep right here on the road. She's come a long way from America, she has, and she doesn't want to spend even longer to go the last mile."

Danny turned away as I caught the word "American" spoken in none too gentle a fashion.

We poked along behind the herd as Fergal said out of the corner of his mouth, "Danny's in his cups again but he's a harmless one, he is. His land butts up to mine, and as you can see, he moves his cattle from one graze to another." He pointed off to my right. "His house is that one over there."

I followed his line of sight to a one-story stone house with a sharply steeped roof. I couldn't see much of it from the lane, as it was partly obscured by the rolling terrain, but what I saw put my heart instantly at peace for it was a white-washed cottage with a brilliant red door that looked remarkably similar to the pictures I'd seen online of the carriage house I was renting.

And I wasn't to be disappointed. My own cottage was similar with an aged whitewashed exterior and a deep blue door instead of the neighbor's red. Fergal stooped to remove a weed from the flower garden, which appeared to have been recently planted and already in bloom despite a dogged spring chill. I took in the deep-set window sills with imperfect vintage glass as he unlocked the door. Then standing back, he ushered me inside.

I stepped into a large room that was almost dwarfed by a sectional sofa set in the middle that was clearly angled for full advantage to the fireplace and above it, a flat-screen television mounted on the stone. Off to one side and situated in front of a large window was a round table that seated four and in the far corner was a quaint kitchen, set apart from the rest only by an island that angled outward from one wall.

Fergal crossed the room to another door and flicked on a light. "The bedroom is here," he said. As I followed him inside the room, I caught a glimpse of him leaning to smooth out imagined wrinkles in the quilt before passing to another door. "And the bath and closet is here in the back."

"It's perfect," I said, taking in the modern glass shower and separate soaking tub. "Absolutely perfect."

"I took the liberty of stocking a few foods for you," he continued, moving back to the main room. "But there's a restaurant joined to the pub as well, and you'll find good food and craic there, if I do say so myself." Now that I had seen the rental, he seemed to grow a bit anxious. He held out the keys and dropped them into my hand. "You have a mobile, I take it?"

"I do—and international service."

"Good. Good. You'll find decent reception here and as I mentioned before, the rental is outfitted for wireless too, in case you have a need to pop on the Internet. The password is taped to the wall beside the table."

"So it is."

"Well then, I'll get your luggage in for you."

"Oh, don't bother. I'll get it later."

He nodded his head so slightly I wondered if I'd imagined it. "So you see to get back to the village, you only need follow the road. You're quite certain you want to remain out here?"

I waved my arm to encompass all that I'd seen. "I'm positive. Everything is absolutely perfect. I can't imagine it being any better."

2

I awakened with a start at the harrowing sound of a woman's scream. I bolted upright and then immediately froze as I attempted to clear the brain fog and orient myself to my surroundings. I had fallen asleep on the sofa, intending only to lie down for a moment to rest my eyes. The last I remembered was placing my head on the decorative pillow and pulling a cozy throw over me. In the time that I'd slept the room had morphed from the cheerfulness of the sunrise to something else entirely, long shadows having crept into the corners where they lay like lumps that swayed ever so slightly.

It was then that I realized the walls had taken on the color of fire—the red, orange and yellow of a fireplace stoked to a full flame. My eyes instinctively raced to the fireplace, which sat as it had that morning with tinder in the grid ready to be lit and a larger log atop the kindling base. It was cold and as I cleared the cobwebs from my head I realized the room had grown chilly as well.

I whirled about to discover the drapes still open and I crossed the room to determine the source of the colors that danced upon the walls. The window faced to the west and there my eyes rested on the setting sun which had set the room ablaze with color. Puzzled, I glanced at my watch; it was half past seven and I had slept the better part of the day away.

My heart calming now, I gazed for a moment at the idyllic view. In the distance upon which the sun rested was the lough that led to the Atlantic. Black cliffs rose on either side of it at varying heights, the only factor that served to distinguish the water from the skies as it reflected its glory. As my eyes began to focus on the ground between the cottage and the water, they fell upon a hulking shadow set atop a hill. It couldn't have been more than a five minute stroll from the cottage and I marveled that I had not noticed it upon my arrival. As I attempted to identify it, the last vestiges of the sun appeared to reach toward it, engulfing it in a final bolt of sunshine. The rays shot through two stories of windows, revealing the ruins of a manor house. It did not appear to have a roof and there were fewer windows on the second floor than there were on the first, leading me to believe that over the years parts of the upper floor had caved in. In fact, as I narrowed my eyes to focus more clearly, I wondered if the only thing that remained was the front wall.

A sound traveled across the fields and the sunlight vanished as if the noise had snuffed it out. A whistle. Remembering why I had awakened so abruptly, I wondered if I had heard a whistle and in my deep state of slumber, I had mistaken it for a woman's scream.

I turned on the lamp beside the window, instantly bathing the room in a warm glow. Then I recovered my car keys from the table where I'd laid them that morning and stepped outside to retrieve my luggage from the rental car.

The vehicle was parked directly outside and a lamp mounted beside the door illuminated it nicely. I rubbed my arms against the chill as I made my way to the boot and opened it, hauling out my single piece of luggage as well as my laptop case.

I heard the whistle again and I turned to look to the east where a flashlight was swaying from one side of the road to the other, occasionally turning behind to illuminate cattle trudging toward the neighbor's barn. The whistles were apparently intended as instructions to two dogs, their figures barely visible as they crested the hill but their barks carrying through the open expanse and their bodies discernable from the cattle by how quickly they moved and how much closer to the ground they crouched.

The flashlight stopped abruptly. It wasn't far from the cottage to the road but in the darkness I could not make out the man's outline. Rather, I felt his presence more strongly than I could see him and my heart began to thump wildly. I realized I was probably fully illuminated by the light from the rental's open boot so, having been caught watching him, I raised my hand in a wave. The flashlight did not move, and I could find no evidence that he had waved back.

Self-conscious now, I turned back and closed the boot, picked up my two pieces and made for the door. Once inside, I closed the drapes against the night sky and began to unpack.

As I set my toiletries in the bath, I found myself gazing out a port window at the neighbor's cottage and barn. The cottage was barely visible, hidden by the same rise that had sheltered it from the road on the drive in that morning. But the barn was more prominent and I watched as the flashlight swung from side to side as the cattle were brought inside an adjoining enclosure.

Somewhere on the other side of that structure was the village. Fergal had said it was only a couple of miles and perhaps it was as the crow flies, but now it seemed a long distance away, the lights not even visible from this vantage point. Realizing I was once again standing in the light, I closed the blinds before the neighbor jumped to the conclusion that I was spying on him.

I unpacked the remainder of my things, choosing the table beneath the window for my laptop and portable printer. The hearty breakfast I'd consumed had remained with me and I thought momentarily of driving into the village to check out the restaurant Fergal had mentioned that adjoined the pub but quickly decided to explore the kitchen instead. It was, I decided, a hot tea kind of evening and if I was lucky, I would discover some delectable groceries.

As the clock struck midnight it found me in front of my laptop, my plate picked clean beside it. Gone was the mouthwatering boneless breast of chicken and every last drop of sauce it had marinated and cooked in, along with creamy colcannon potatoes and an assortment of steamed vegetables. Fergal had laid in so much food, in fact, that even though I intended to stay the month, I feared I wouldn't be able to eat it all—so I was giving it my best shot.

In between bites, I'd begun reading through the first draft of my next book. Like my other historical work, I had begun with Internet research, taking great care to limit myself to libraries, historical societies and universities. I had also contacted a variety of descendants which I referred to as 'distant cousins' for copies of any information they had on our common ancestor. I had pieced together through family records that he had hailed from Wigtownshire, Scotland and had joined King James' call for British and Scottish Lowlanders to immigrate to Ulster in what would become known as The Plantation Era.

I had then contacted the various descendants and institutions as well as the places in question for additional information, which had primarily been provided via email, but unfortunately some of the sites no longer had curators. Now I was 'on the ground' to verify my facts and see the sites firsthand, to get the flavor of the land and discover previously untold stories from a variety of characters' descendants.

Not wishing to remain awake all night and sleep the next day away, I reluctantly closed the laptop and pushed my chair back from the table. I was just about to rise and gather the spent dishes when something caught my eye and I leaned in closer to the window, gently brushing a drapery to the side. Hastily, I shut off the lamp beside me, casting the interior into darkness. As my eyes adjusted, I recognized a herd of cattle similar to the one Danny had been leading home in late afternoon. Puzzled, I stood and crossed to the door, stepping outside. This new herd had been in the opposite direction in the field furthest from my neighbor's so, shivering against the brisk wind, I made my way to the corner of the house to peer beyond.

The entire herd of cattle was stark white as if the moon's glow was reflecting off their bodies, though I could not see the moon in my present location. It must have been blocked by the steep pitch of the cottage roof, but I quickly lost interest in that and focused instead on the hour. Who on earth would herd their cattle homeward at midnight? The thought of the witching hour was enough to send my heart pounding and yet I felt transfixed to the spot I stood within, in the darkness barely out of reach of the outdoor cottage lamp that glowed like a beacon just beyond the corner.

Each cow must have worn a bell because they rose in an eerie cacophony as if in answer to a set of whistles and the excited barking of a dog which I only occasionally spotted as it must have been a black and white border collie. In any event, the rather large dog weaved and bobbed through the shadows until it became part of the shadows themselves. Gradually I made out the shapes of two men; their shirts were light colored, the moon also appearing to seek them out so that they glowed with an eerie luminosity. They began at opposite ends but as they neared a gate halfway up the hill toward the ruins I had spotted earlier, the herd became tighter and the men joined one another. I could not see a wall on either side of the gate so it seemed to me the cattle could simply be driven upwards, but they were herded through the gate as if the walls were still there on either side.

Then one of the men abruptly halted and turned toward me. He couldn't have been more than a hundred yards from where I stood and less than that by a crow's flight. I instinctively froze, the friendly wave I had offered Danny hours before immobilized as if time itself had stopped. His shirt continued to billow in the wind and now as I stared back at him, I realized his face and hands were so white they appeared to blend into his clothing. Yet oddly, I could see nothing below his waist—not the telltale shape of trousers or of any particular stance.

A gust of wind swung round the corner, catching me and nearly sending me tumbling off my feet. I must have cried out for my voice felt like it was ringing in my ears. Afraid for some absurd reason that I had given away my position, I turned back toward the man but he was gone. In the blink of an eye, the two men, the dog and the cattle had simply disappeared.

I blinked and strained my eyes. It was not possible for them to have reached their destination in so short a time; there was no barn in sight and besides, they had been crossing open fields on their way toward the ruins. The gate swung as though caught by the same gust of wind as I, the metal glinting in the same peculiar light that had reflected against the herd only a moment earlier.

My breath caught in my throat and I bolted around the corner toward the door when I ran directly into a man's rock hard body. Caught off balance, I began to stumble but he caught me, his strong hands holding onto my arms to steady me.

"Are you quite alright?"

"Fergal," I breathed, my teeth beginning to chatter. "Whatever are you doing here this time of night?"

His hands dropped away from me though his piercing blue eyes continued to examine me, his brows knitted. "The pub is open," he said haltingly, which gave me the impression he was carefully choosing his words. "Danny just came in, yeah? Told me the lights were on in the carriage house, and since I hadn't seen you about since I dropped you off this morning—yesterday morning, I suppose now—I thought perhaps I should come by to check on you."

"I'm fine," I managed to say. "Just getting a breath of fresh air."

"Did I frighten you so badly?"

"Yes; yes, you did," I admitted. "I didn't expect anyone to be wandering around in the dark out here."

"Forgive me please. It's just—well, you're out here by yourself and—I suppose I'm feeling responsible."

I hugged my arms against my torso in a futile attempt to ward off the chill. "I often write at night. There's no need to worry."

"I see."

"I'm freezing out here," I said at the same time as I noticed his short sleeves. "Apparently I'm unaccustomed to the cold."

"Oh, aye," he said, stepping out of the way and gesturing toward the door. "I'll leave you to it then."

I reached the door and turned the knob, stepping inside. "Thank you for your concern," I said.

"If you should need anything—"

"Yes. Thank you." I politely closed the door and crossed to the window, where I made certain the heavy drapes were closed. I had forgotten to thank him for the food he'd left me and now that I was safely inside the cottage, I hoped I hadn't appeared rude by my abruptness. I left the plate on the table and headed toward the bedroom, where I reached upward to make certain the drapes were drawn tight there as well. And there, in the midst of a layer of gray clouds was the thinnest of moons, the barest of waxing crescents, incapable of illuminating anything at all.

3

I snapped a photograph of the open pages that listed another set of ancestors at yet another era in Ulster history. I had several dozen documents already saved on my phone just from this trip alone, records which would later be added to an ever-growing stack of documentation. I had originally intended to write a book about three ancestors—all brothers—that left Ulster for America in the early 1700's but I became increasingly inquisitive regarding their desire to leave Ireland. After all, who would want to leave the Emerald Isle voluntarily in a specific era not known for a famine? Following their trail had led to their parents and all the way back to one Scottish ancestor, who departed Scotland and all he'd ever known to move to Ulster and pledge allegiance to King James I of England. My ancestor's loyalty to the English monarchy would set in motion a chain of events that would alter the course of generations of descendants.

I met Michelle Mitchell, a historian and expert on Ulster history, at the Ulster American Folk Park in Omagh, Northern Ireland. She had been a treasure trove of information in a correspondence that began a year earlier, becoming long-distance friends of a sort. It was good to finally meet her in person, though she was not what I'd expected. I'd seen a black-and-white photograph of her online but had not expected a woman of nearly six feet tall with large bones and a shock of red hair which brought to mind the old Irish adage, *Red on the head where the Viking tread.*

Having served as a museum volunteer, she suggested we meet at the Folk Park for further research. I had been there twice before, spending hours upon hours in the comprehensive museum as well as their outdoor recreation of Irish life through the centuries. Now I'd spent a long morning in their library and with Michelle's capable assistance, had compiled enough background not only for my current book but for several generations after. It was exactly the gold mine I'd hoped for, as a London publisher was interested in an entire series that would transform historical dates and events into action and adventure.

I'd left the cottage before daylight, traveling the N17 for more than two hours before veering off to the east and from the Republic into Northern Ireland just as the mists were clearing and the sun was persistent enough to peek through. It's said that every day on the island contained all four seasons so I was fully prepared with layers of clothing and a rain jacket to boot.

As a child, I thought the two countries were one and the same, much as one referred to the North or South in the States. It was only when I'd begun my research into family history that I'd discovered my ignorance. The island had been divided into two completely separate countries in the early 20th century and I was only now beginning to appreciate the Republic's status as a country independent of England.

Though a treaty between Ireland and Great Britain had been signed on December 6, 1921, Michael Collins would not take possession of Dublin Castle for Ireland until January 1922. When he stepped out of his motorcar seven minutes late to the ceremony, the Lord Lieutenant and last British Viceroy of Ireland, Lord Fitzalan, reportedly noted, "Mr. Collins, you are seven minutes late" to which Collins replied, "We've been waiting over seven hundred years; you can have the seven minutes."

Ireland's repeated conquests by other countries was a complex history that included my own ancestors harkening back to a time in which King James was colonizing Ireland at the same time as Jamestown, Virginia was founded in his name and the colonization of America was underway. But unlike America, who fought and won her independence in the 18th century, Northern Ireland was still fighting for hers.

King James, like a stream of monarchs before him, saw the island as a threatening back door into a possible conquest of England, especially when the Spanish Armada sank off Ireland's coast in 1588, raising an alarm of an invasion when in fact the ships had blown off course during heavy storms. To control Ireland meant protection to the British, no matter the island had been inhabited for thousands of years already and had been divided into a myriad of kingdoms already controlled by Gaelic chieftains. The country then became the bread basket for England, largely agricultural except in the northeast near Belfast, raising livestock and planting crops to feed England's growing population.

"You see," Michelle said in a rapid-fire melodious accent that sounded at times to be equal parts Irish and Scottish brogue, "the Plantation Era which your Scottish ancestor joined pitted native Irish against the English and those that pledged allegiance to her. And because King Henry VIII had left the Catholic Church and anointed himself the Supreme Head of the Church of England in 1531, Ireland was to become ground zero in a religious war."

"So the native Irish were overwhelmingly Catholic," I said, "while the Scots and Brits were largely Protestant."

"Precisely. It was a looming reason for King James to colonize it; by bringing in Protestants, he hoped to convert the Irish population. Spain was an enemy at the time and overwhelmingly Catholic. The English monarchy hoped to keep the kingdom together through religious fervor as well as political reasons."

I stood from the table and stretched my arms and back. "Can you believe we've been here for three hours?" I said, glancing at my watch. "It doesn't seem possible."

"Time flies when you're pouring over scores of documents. Fun stuff this; land grants, declarations of possessions and wealth and your ancestors' roles in defending this conquered land for the British monarchy."

"You're kidding, right?" I laughed.

"Precisely." She closed some of the books we'd finished perusing, placing them in the queue to be returned to the shelves. "So where are you staying this trip? Same as usual?"

On my prior trips I had stayed in the beautiful, quaint village of Ballygawley in County Tyrone, which just happened to be the closest village to my ancestral home at Glencull. It also would have made this excursion only a few minutes' travel with time to spare. "Not this time round. I'm glad you told me about the growing tensions in Northern Ireland," I said, my voice instinctively dropping to a hoarse whisper though others in the library were immersed in their own research and weren't paying any attention to us at all.

"Brexit," she said as if that explained everything. Her voice had also dropped. "It's mucked up what peace we had."

"I'm staying near Galway in the Republic."

"Ah, fine call. It will be convenient for your drive into the National University of Ireland as well."

"Yes and the place I'm renting is delightful."

"You found a cottage then?"

"Yes, and newly renovated. In fact, everything feels so new there that it can't have been open long... Tell me, just why is Northern Ireland part of England instead of united with Ireland? I mean, I know they were separated in the treaty but I never understood why Ulster was set apart from the rest of the country." It was a question I'd wanted to ask in our email exchanges but thought it better to wait until we were face to face, especially with new political tensions brewing. After the Good Friday Agreement of 1998 which President Bill Clinton had negotiated, the bombings and guerrilla warfare had either stopped or gone more deeply underground. Talk of Brexit had revived the debate about Northern Ireland and hostility on both sides was peaking again.

"Ah, you're asking for a history lesson there," she said, her green eyes sparkling. "When Ireland was divided in 1921," she continued with renewed passion, "the majority of counties voted in favor of a country independent of England. However, due to the massive influx of Scots and Brits into Ulster—including your own ancestors—six counties in Ulster voted to remain with Britain, which became known as the United Kingdom in 1922. Only Donegal, Cavan and Monaghan, the three remaining Ulster counties, voted to become part of the new Republic, because the Irish

Catholics outnumbered the Protestant immigrants in those counties."

"Ah. That's why Northern Ireland doesn't stretch all the way across the northern end of the island."

"Precisely."

"And now I've heard there's a debate whether to join Northern Ireland with the Republic?"

"Debate is a kind word for it, I'm afraid. With the referendum of 2016 to withdraw from the European Union—which has become known as Brexit, as you know—predominantly Catholic Irish Republicans have been pushing for uniting Northern Ireland with the Republic of Ireland. We've seen recruitment rise in Sinn Fein and the Irish Republican Army—"

"—the Irish political party and the paramilitary—"

"Exactly. Consider them to the far left while to the far right, Protestant Loyalists—descendants of the Scots and Brits we've been researching here today—are preparing for a civil war to keep Northern Ireland part of the United Kingdom."

"A civil war?" I sucked in my breath. "Do you think it will come to that?"

"I should hope not."

I nodded and avoided her eyes as I closed and stacked more of the reference books we'd completed. Perhaps I was being overly cautious but I knew that unlike the United States, here one rarely asked outright what religion one belonged to. Instead, a series of questions identified one as either a Catholic or Protestant and therefore as a Republican or Loyalist and doors either opened or slammed shut as a consequence. "So, were your ancestors—?" I began hesitantly.

"Scots. Same as yours," she whispered conspiratorially. "What most people outside Western Europe don't realize, though, is that Scots and Irish have been intermingling for centuries before Britain as we know it today even existed, dating back to the Celts and beyond. The east coast of Northern Ireland is only ten miles from the Scottish west coast, you know."

"I didn't know," I marveled.

"What is fascinating to me," Michelle went on, "is while your ancestor had been Calvinist when he entered Ireland, there is ample evidence here that the family had protected Catholic priests from certain torture and death and had even donated land for both a Catholic church and a Catholic school in Ulster."

"That makes my heart sing," I admitted. "There seems to be so much animosity between the two religions that I'm proud my ancestors saw people as human beings regardless of which church they attended."

"Ah, the 'my Jesus is better than your Jesus' syndrome. Well, many did not believe in that. Now it's my turn to ask something of you?"

"Go right ahead. I'm an open book."

"Your eyes are very nearly black."

"Yes."

She studied my complexion. "Your skin tone is olive, your hair is dark. Has anyone ever told you your ancestors are most likely Spaniards?"

"I've heard that. Some of my ancestors were known as 'Black John' or 'Black James'—"

"Ah. That proves it then. That's what they called those from Spain."

"I wonder if that's why they were more tolerant of those in the Catholic faith?"

"It's entirely possible. So, and have you discovered everything you were searching for today then?"

"For now, I believe I have," I answered. "More than enough. I can't begin to thank you sufficiently for all you've done."

"I've enjoyed it. Just let me know what else you need—any time at all."

I glanced at my watch. "Do you have time for lunch?"

"I would love to, but I have another appointment this afternoon. Besides, you have a long drive ahead yourself, you know. Unfamiliar roads can get dicey out that way."

"Good point."

Michelle walked me to the parking lot and gave me a quick hug before saying good-bye. I pulled up my navigation app on my tablet, accessed the cottage coordinates that I'd saved in the driveway earlier, and as the artificial intelligence voice began to direct me, I pulled out of the space and headed for the main road. With any luck at all, I'd reach the village by dusk.

4

The motorway was nearly empty as I made my way toward the southwest. The skies had turned a beautiful blue with hardly a cloud in sight, though I knew things could change in the blink of an eye. It was an island in the North Atlantic, after all; the first landfall the weather would encounter as it reached Western Europe. As I drove I thought of the Atlantic, the waves vacillating between placid and choppy like a fickle child, the storms that brewed over the open waters, and of the numbers of Irish that immigrated to America or elsewhere across those capricious seas. One of my ancestors had been discovered to be a ship's captain that transported people from Ireland to points beyond and I wondered what those journeys must have been like and whether his passengers had been desperate to leave their homeland due to famine or war or if they were, like my own ancestors, in search of a greater fortune.

I reached the village as the first vestiges of nightfall descended, coming through the roundabout to the exit onto the lane that had already managed to feel like home. I parked in front of the pub as I had before and entered this time through the front door. It was dimly lit inside, the stone walls trying their best to absorb the yellow lights cast by the occasional sconce.

There were two men at the far end of the bar nursing their drinks and three older ladies sitting round a table by the fire peering over maps. I recognized the young couple from the day before, now focused only on one another's eyes in a darkened, romantic corner.

"What have you?" the barmaid asked. She finished drying off a glass and set it on the shelf behind her before making her way over to me. She appeared quite young—perhaps all of 18, though I supposed she might be older, working in a pub and all. Her hair was auburn, her skin scattered with freckles, and her vivid blue eyes met mine as she placed a bar napkin on the counter in front of me.

"Guinness," I said. "Is Fergal about?"

"Aye; do you need him then?"

"If he's not busy."

She eyed me curiously as she poured the draft, taking care to move the glass under the dispenser in such a way as to create a shamrock in the foam atop. Then she set it before me and stepped to a door at the far end of the bar where the two gentlemen still sat silently observing me. "Da," she called, "there's a lady here to see you. It's the American."

I was equally surprised at her name for him and the moniker for me. He appeared curious as he rounded the corner of the doorway, his brows high and eyes wide. "Ah, Nora," he said to his daughter, "this would be the author I told you about. She's renting the carriage house."

"I knew who she was on account of her accent." Nora smiled and made as if she was planning to say something else but the women at the table called to her and with an apologetic smile she stepped toward them instead. Fergal came around the bar, sliding onto the bar stool beside me.

"How are things at the carriage house then?" he asked. "Are you quite comfortable there?"

"Oh, everything is wonderful," I answered. "I dropped by to apologize for last night."

"Apologize?"

"I'm afraid you caught me by surprise. I wasn't expecting anyone out there in the middle of the night."

"Ah, it's I who should apologize, 'ey? I should have phoned first, I suppose."

"No, you have every right to check on things. I meant to thank you for all the food you left me, and in my surprise, I forgot. So, thank you. It was thoughtful of you to do that."

"Oh and sure it's part of the service it is. If you had stayed in one of the rooms upstairs here, I would have cooked breakfast each morning, part of the service, you see. As it was, with you staying out there, leaving you with some hearty fare seemed the right thing to do."

I took a sip of the Guinness stout, the foam tickling my upper lip. It might have been my imagination—of which I knew I had ample supply—but the gentlemen at the end of the bar appeared to be straining to catch our conversation.

"So all is right out there?" he asked.

"It's wonderful. It's the best of both worlds really— the old world charm and such modern conveniences. It feels like a brand new home meant to appear like an old one. I could almost smell the paint on the walls."

"Ah. Well, you're right on the one count. It isn't a new property for sure but a very old one but it's been only recently renovated. You're the first to stay there, you are."

"Really? It wasn't a rental before the renovation?"

"Oh no. No. It was empty for some time, fell into disrepair it did. I decided on gutting the thing and fixing it up, spent a bit of time there and a lot of elbow grease and must admit, I was rather pleased with the result."

"So you did the work yourself?"

"Every bit of it, I'm afraid."

I chuckled. "Why are you afraid?"

He shrugged and despite the dim light I could have sworn he was blushing. "Just a figure of speech. It was… rather difficult to find the help I needed on it."

One of the men guffawed and Fergal's face flushed a deeper crimson.

"That's quite admirable of you," I said, a new appreciation forming. I tried to lower my voice but without much sound in the background, I knew my words continued to carry. "Had it been your parents' home?"

"Oh, goodness, no." His eyes widened as though I'd suggested something quite shocking. "No. Not at all."

"Then you bought the property?"

"No…" he glanced at the far end of the bar and caught Nora's eye. She promptly cranked up the volume on the flat-screen television mounted behind the bar and while I didn't hear her words, she must have said something to the two men about the sports game. They began to converse among themselves as they turned their attention to soccer. After a moment, Nora strode to a pot of coffee and began readying three Irish coffee mugs on a tray.

Apparently having satisfied himself that no one was continuing to listen in on our conversation, he said in a soft voice, "My grandfather purchased the property, oh I'd say nigh on a hundred years ago now."

"Then he lived in the carriage house? Or did he live in the big house?"

"Oh, no, neither one. The big house you're referring to—the house on the hill? The one in ruins?"

"Yes. I wondered about its history."

He avoided my eyes as he swept non-existent dust off the bar counter. "Burned to the ground, it did, shortly before my grandfather purchased it. He wanted the land, you see."

"But he never lived there."

"No. His house is at the end of the lane here. My mother lives there now."

"Oh, how nice." I took another sip of my drink as my mind began to form a mental image of his family: his daughter Nora perhaps somewhere between 18 and 22, his mother, perhaps a woman in her 70s or so, and Fergal himself. Despite his silver hair, he might have been in his late 40s or early 50s. "And you and the missus—"

"My wife's up in Derry," he said bluntly.

"Oh. I'm sorry. I shouldn't have pried."

He shrugged and absent-mindedly touched the stack of napkins in front of him, half-heartedly straightening them. "No bother. She's happier without me and I'm..." His words hung in the air for a moment. "So the carriage house suits you, you say?" Abruptly changing the subject, his attention riveted back to me. "I've long had plans to turn it into a holiday rental."

"It's wonderful. It's everything an American imagines when they think about Ireland—the rolling hills, the fresh air, the countryside, the cattle in the fields—"

"Ah," he chuckled. "Danny's cattle."

"And the others, too."

"What others?"

"The two men on the other side." He gasped almost inaudibly but I plunged ahead. "Though I was very curious last night why they waited so late to herd their cattle home. I assume they live on the other side of the ruins?"

He stood and for a moment, I thought he was prepared to either faint or bolt. Instead, he hurried around the bar, poured himself water from a tap and drank it in one long swig. He refilled the glass and slowly returned to the counter in front of me. He placed both palms on the bar and appeared to be quite interested in the back of his hands. "There's nothing on the other side of the ruins."

"Nothing?" I asked quizzically.

"Oh, there's a steep cliff on the other side, mostly rock. I suppose if you're into rock climbing, there's that."

"But no more fields?" My own voice had grown softer as I contemplated this. "Another house, then? A barn?"

He shook his head and eyed his water glass. "From the cliff side, one can see British barracks in the distance—of course the British abandoned them when Ireland became independent back in 1922. But it isn't possible to actually reach the barracks from the cliffs; not possible at all."

"I see. Then the two men were herding cattle on *your* land. Maybe that's why they were out in the middle of the night—"

He downed the second glass of water and then poured himself a Jameson's. "There have been no cattle—or animals of any sort—on that property for nigh on a hundred years now. My grandfather bought the land to expand his own herd but cattle are spooked there and animals—even birds—give it a wide berth. They panic, you see, and my grandfather told of one time a herd he'd just placed there stampeded for the cliffs—" He stopped to wipe beads of perspiration from his forehead.

"Surely they were stopped in time," I said, my voice revealing my shock.

He shook his head. "One time was quite enough. So you see there hasn't been any livestock there since that time." Before I could respond, he asked weakly, "Was there anything else you wanted then?"

"No," I answered. "Everything is perfect." The words rolled off my tongue automatically and without conviction, but he didn't seem to notice.

"I wouldn't mention what you thought you saw to anyone else," he added uncomfortably. "People around here wouldn't take kindly to such an active imagination."

His words sent alarm bells through my body and I found myself uncharacteristically tongue-tied. But I needn't have felt obliged to respond, as he quickly downed the shot of Jameson's, poured another and turned his attention to the others, calling out to each of them as he quickly made his way to the room in back of the pub.

I sat quietly as I nursed my drink, my cheeks blazing as I replayed the conversation. Then I reached into my bag, set what I knew was way too many euros on the counter, and left.

5

I awakened to the sounds of a woman sobbing. My mind sprung fully awake while my body remained immobile as if I was still under the influence of sleep paralysis, the down quilts piled atop of me. It took me a moment before I realized I was wide-awake. As the crying continued, my eyes adjusted to the dusky light in the bedroom, my mind consciously identifying each object I saw, ticking them off like so many items on a list: the dresser, the chest of drawers, a chair... The corners were overcome with shadows while blue-gray fingers of light crept from a slight part in the draperies, too weak to cast adequate illumination.

Then a man's weary voice added to the sobs. "It will be alright, April. No one is coming for you." His accent was different than any I'd heard thus far; while most definitely Irish, it was also cultured like one might expect to find in the halls of London's upper establishments.

I slowly willed my body to awaken, drew back the bedcovers and slipped out of bed. On silent bare feet, I made my way to the open bedroom door and peered into the living room. Thanks to two modern skylights, this room was bathed in more light, the twinkling of the stars tenaciously finding their way through gaps in the fast-moving clouds. The room, like the bedroom, was not large and I easily came to the conclusion that I was alone.

Then who was crying?

Despite the man's reassurances, the woman sounded panicked and inconsolable. "We'll be away from here soon, April," he was saying, his own voice heavy with mental exhaustion.

She murmured something in return but I could not make out the words; they came fast and clipped similar to Michelle's Ulster speech pattern, requiring me to concentrate on each word as though it was a second language. All I could decipher was, "They are here." Midway through her murmurings, she was wracked with sobs that sounded as though they were bursting forth from a broken heart. Simply hearing it was enough to cause me to wipe a tear from the corner of my eye.

I ambled back through the cottage, peeking into the bathroom and pausing at a vantage point where I could see all three rooms. There was only one explanation: despite their clarity, they were outside.

As quickly as the thought occurred to me, my mind debated with itself as I considered the solitude of the cottage and the distance between me and the nearest neighbor. That would be Danny, I thought, and while no one had mentioned a wife, I could only surmise that they were outside of his house and their voices were carrying across the open expanse. Yet even as the possibility entered my mind, I knew it had not been Danny's voice I heard.

Since I was up anyway, I switched on the bathroom light and as I stepped inside it, the voices abruptly stopped. I waited, expecting at least a sniffle or one more escaped sob, but it was as if a radio had been playing and it had been hastily switched off, leaving nothing but utter silence. Not even an owl hooted in the distance. Once again, I walked back through the house, checking window and door locks.

Puzzled, I returned to the bedroom to curl up in bed, pulling the warm covers back over me. I was trembling now from a mixture of chilled air and apprehension. There was another explanation, I thought: it had all been my imagination.

Fergal's words came tumbling back to me. He was not the first to suggest that I had an overactive imagination. My earliest recollection of the accusation was before I'd even been old enough to start school. We had been living in California and I'd been playing hide-and-seek with my sister and two brothers. I chose a spot in the darkened garage amid furniture and boxes that had not yet been unpacked and placed into our new home when everything began to sway. I had watched in horror as a floor lamp appeared to move toward me as if it had grown feet and come alive.

I'd flown out of the garage, found my mother—as all small children do—and she convinced me that it had been only my imagination. It was decades later before I found the gumption to bring up the incident to her again. Only then did she admit it had been earth tremors, the kind that California was famous for. She'd been afraid to tell me the truth so she'd instead convinced me that my mind was unstable and I could not trust what I had seen or heard. The circumstances would be repeated throughout my childhood as I heard voices that were supposedly not there, or footsteps walking the halls when everyone was presumed to be asleep, or I witnessed luminescent figures no one else admitted seeing.

And now Fergal had accused me of the same overactive imagination. And in this instance, perhaps he was right. After all, in the hours before I'd climbed into bed, I'd been writing about the burning of Derry in 1608, an incident that touched off O'Doherty's Rebellion and led to the fateful demise of the last Gaelic King of Ireland, ending over a thousand years of O'Doherty rule—nearly five times longer than America had been an independent nation. The scene I had been writing was filled with women's and children's cries, most of whom would have been terror-stricken, panicked, and inconsolable as they watched their homes burn to the ground and O'Doherty's men rampage through the town with no one to stop them. The woman's words, 'They are here' could very possibly have been conjured by my own imagination, spurred by the images of O'Doherty's men on attack. Perhaps more than one man sought to console them, promising them they would be away soon. Away from what? I wondered. Away from Ulster, perhaps? Away from warring Irishmen seeking to drive English and Scottish invaders from their island?

I was wide awake now, and I knew no matter how I tried to twist and contort into different positions, sleep would remain elusive. I found my phone on the nightstand and checked the time. It was nearly 4:30. I'd gotten roughly two hours' sleep.

Still, I rose and wrapped my housecoat about me and slid my cold feet into fleece-lined slippers. I made my way to the kitchen where I set the teakettle on the stove. As I waited for the water to boil, I took a deep breath, intending to rid myself of my pesky imagination. Instead, I inhaled the unmistakable odor of wood burning.

Puzzled, I walked to the fireplace and stared at it. I

held out my hand but no draft reached it proving the damper had remained closed, and the tinder and log were still arranged as they had been since my arrival. With proper heat installed in the cottage, I'd had no cause to use the fireplace and Fergal's words came rushing back at me: "You're the first to stay there, you know."

With the kettle still on the stove, I wrapped myself more securely and opened the door of the cottage. I stood on the threshold for a moment and breathed deeply, expecting a further assault of burning wood to reach my nostrils. But there was nothing.

Barefoot, I stepped onto the cold ground and made my way around to the opposite side of the cottage where, if I narrowed my eyes and concentrated, I could just barely make out a corner of Danny's cottage. It appeared dark, asleep as I should have been, and there was no telltale smoke coming from the tall stone chimney. As I surveyed my surroundings, I could see no other homes—asleep or otherwise—until I came back around to the opposite side.

There my eyes sought out the ruins. There was a chimney stack at either end, the stones still standing as if waiting for the inhabitants to start a fire. But between them stood only the front wall of the house, the branches of emaciated trees growing within, scraping across the stones in the cold night wind. In the darkness, it appeared hulking and forbidding, lonely and desolate.

When the teakettle whistled, it nearly threw me into a panic, the sound carrying across the open fields unhindered by woods or obstruction. I raced inside, removed the kettle and tried to calm my nerves. I'd left the door open in my haste and now I returned to it, closing it until I heard the reassuring click before setting the bolt back into place.

As I busied myself preparing my tea, I realized the

scent of burnt wood had dissipated completely. It was then that I turned on the lamps, purposefully setting the cottage awash with light. There was one thing I knew now; a conviction that grew in the center of my being and spread out to engulf me: that neither the voices nor the aroma had been my imagination.

6

The dew had dried on the grass and the mists had faded into the sunlight when I stepped outside and locked the cottage door behind me. It had turned into a beautiful day, the earlier cloud cover having traveled further to the east and I was in the mood for a stroll. I wasn't expected at the University of Galway until early afternoon; it would be a short trip and I had time to spare this morning.

The sunlight was misleading as a chilly wind whipped against my hooded jacket; it was April, after all, and even Ireland's mid-summer could prove to be colder than my thin blood was accustomed to. This was a transition month, where the winter chill and the summer sun competed.

Way off in the distance were the tell-tale specks of sheep on a lush green field but there was no sign of Danny and his cows. I turned in the opposite direction and made for the ruins. I'd grown accustomed to smooth terrain at my home in eastern Massachusetts, but here

I discovered a short walk could turn into a challenging one simply through the act of avoiding the multitude of rocks that jutted upward through moss and heather. Some were quite ominous-looking with sharp angles that could easily slice a bare foot, felt even through the thickness of my runners. I found myself focused more on the ground directly in front of me than on my destination.

I was surprised when I finally looked up and realized I'd reached the old gate. Winded, I held onto the stone post that held up one side of the gate. As I stood there with a stitch in my side and my breathing labored, my eyes fell upon the ground in front of me and instantly a chill sped up my spine.

The gate consisted of two equal halves that should have met in the middle to latch, but one half was pulled away from the stone post and was embedded deep into the ground. Hadn't I seen the two men open the gate? But that was impossible, I realized as I stared at it. It was quite obvious neither side had been moved in years.

What was also striking was the fact that on either side of the gate, the stone wall was missing. I could see a few stones here or there, so I knew where it once stood, but on a small island such as Ireland, it was customary for villagers to take the stone from abandoned or unused structures and reuse them. I had seen it time and time again with curtain walls and castle ruins.

As my eyes wandered down the pieces of wall that still existed—a stone here, a boulder there—I could not for the life of me understand why someone would drive a herd of cattle through a narrow gate when there was nothing stopping them from moving up the hill on either side of it.

I sat on one of the relatively flat boulders to catch my breath and take a few swigs from my water bottle. I faced uphill toward the ruins of the old manor house, which was not far from where I sat. It was completely silent here, as hushed as a cemetery and oddly, I rather felt like I was in one. Perhaps it was the ruins themselves, the skeletal remains of lives once lived.

My mother always remarked when she saw abandoned places, "Just imagine the memories there." While I might have been repulsed by derelict buildings and all the spiders and snakes and cobwebs that inhabited them, she managed to see their past—usually happy times, pleasant memories, children raised amidst laughter and peace.

I tried to imagine who might have lived in these ruins at one time and I marveled that they could have existed uninhabited for the past hundred years. It must have been a fine home when it was first built; it was two stories tall and judging by the chimneys at either end, there was ample room for a finished attic as well. There were seven windows on the second floor—three in the middle behind Corinthian columns and two on either side like east and west wings. Below the center ones was a massive doorway, the door long gone, flanked by side lights and then two more windows on either side to match those on the second floor. There wasn't a shred of glass in any of the openings and gaunt trees that had grown on the other side of the wall were peeking through them as if to escape. Yet even these appeared odd; the branches cragged like so many fingers trying to grasp a hold on the outside world to pull themselves through to the other side. It occurred to me that as green as the fields and trees were in the distance, the land between the gate and the house was barren and the branches I studied had no leaves on them at all, the trees most likely dead.

It would have been a grand home even if it was wide in length but narrow in depth but as I was able to see through the windows quite clearly, I saw a crumpled stone wall some distance behind it, leading me to believe it was nearly as deep as it was wide.

I knew a bit about Irish architecture though I could recite nothing about American, a result of years of research into Ireland's history and very little into American. I recognized the columns from the Palladian era, which occurred between 1720 and 1770, inspired by 16th century Italian architecture—I suppose it took more than a hundred years for it to make its way into isolated western Ireland. Most likely, the British would have brought the style here, and I wondered if this had been a British landowner's manor home at one time, similar to the one my own ancestors lived in during the same period.

Having caught my breath, I picked my way through decayed brambles and obstinate stones as I made my way closer to the house and eventually inside—or what once was considered the interior, as the roof was completely gone. It was here that I found blackened stone and recalled Fergal telling me the house had burned to the ground a hundred years before, but whether the blackened walls were from the fire or from Father Time, my untrained eye couldn't tell. Rusted rods clung stubbornly above the window openings, the draperies lost to the decades, and with the interior walls gone, I was left to imagine where the rooms might once have been. I discovered smaller fireplaces scattered throughout, perhaps in bedrooms, their chimneys collapsed. There were few stones here where there should have been enough for three more walls, but again it wasn't surprising as once again the Irish had a way of picking through ruins such as this one and recycling the stones into their own homes. For all I knew, parts of this house and the curtain wall might have been used to build several in the neighboring village.

There were several trees around the house, haphazardly set so they appeared not to be part of some grand landscaping plan. Like those I'd observed earlier, none were still living, their branches easily broken by a gentle snap.

I stood at the front door and tried to imagine what the yard would have been like in happier years. Beyond the immediate barren ground, the view from the hill was spectacular; it afforded views of the surrounding countryside that were so mesmerizing, I took out my mobile and began to snap pictures. The fields were divided by stone fences that made them appear like pieces of a patchwork quilt, with the narrow country road winding its way around them like an enormous serpent. In the distance I spotted the roundabout, one turn of which led to the village, and I could even make out the rooflines of the main buildings along the lane. I could only imagine the beautiful view that was once beheld from the upper floors of the house.

I realized as I stood there that a boulder was positioned almost directly in front of the door. I surmised it was most likely used as a stepping stone for getting in and out of coaches. My eyes traveled either side of the stone, identifying what might have been a circle in front of the house, each side meeting at the gate where I had recently rested. Stepping away from the house a bit, I could see my cottage below—the carriage house, Fergal had called it. I found that odd, as a carriage house was typically used to house a horse-drawn carriage but I had seen no evidence of a wider door that would have been necessary for the width of a carriage. It had quite obviously been converted into living quarters that occurred long before Fergal decided on his own renovations.

The style of the carriage house clearly marked it as much older than the ruins, predating even the Queen

Anne architectural period. Instead, it looked more like the stone cottages of the poor during the Elizabethan Age, which would have been a good hundred years before the main house was designed. I wondered then if it had been living quarters initially then turned into a carriage house, and then back to living quarters, but the transformations didn't make sense to me.

Realizing I was wasting the morning away, I took a few more photographs before strolling back through the house to the other side, where I snapped even more. The view here was even more impressive. It was clear where the hill abruptly stopped and turned to cliffs and as I approached, I could see the lough perhaps two hundred feet below. In the distance, I wondered if the wider expanse of water was the Atlantic. I imagined the cows that had grown spooked on the hills and running for these cliffs, and I shuddered against the thought. I was about to turn back when I saw another set of ruins which must have been the old British barracks.

If I'd thought the house ruins were large, the barracks were a monstrosity. I used my camera's zoom to study it, snapping all the while. The main building stood at least three stories tall in places and the flat roof was stone or slate, so it had withstood the centuries. At opposite ends on the north and south were rounded turrets that rose another two stories above the central building. I counted 12 windows on each floor of that structure except for the ground level, in front of which an entryway jutted away like a corridor. A stone fence in varying degrees of disrepair surrounded the building like an ancient castle curtain.

Both the building and the ruins would provide inspiration for scenes in my new series, so I took additional photographs from different directions, trying to capture as much as I could. I began to realize the barracks were hidden from view by the surrounding hills and it was only from the tops of these cliffs that it could be seen. As far below as it was, I wondered if they hadn't been like sitting ducks.

It was only then that I noticed a single oak tree and the bent fencing beneath it. It was only a few yards from where I stood and I marveled that I hadn't observed it before now. As I approached, I realized someone else had been there long before me; they had trampled down the fencing in such a way as to make it quite clear it had not been the result of an accidental storm. And inside that small enclosure were two slabs of stone—or what had been two slabs, but which were now broken into multiple pieces. Someone had gone to considerable effort to defile two gravestones.

I picked my way between them, brushing the moss and dirt from the faces while I tried to read the inscriptions but they were so faint that as I ran my fingers over them, I could barely recognize that an engraving had been there. I took additional photographs of each stone, my heart heavy with the spirits of those interred beneath who had been shown such disrespect even in death. Yet despite their condition, the oak tree was flourishing, made even more remarkable by the fact that nothing else appeared alive atop this hill.

As I finished up, I found the only sound was that of my own breathing. There were no birds singing, no sheep bleating, no sounds of modern life. As I returned to the ruins, the silence became eerily oppressive like a weight was descending upon me. Then across the hills I spotted a flock of birds heading straight for me. I stopped to watch them, relieved for the life they were bringing to this forlorn corner, but as they reached the hill below the one I stood upon—presumably, the one this landowner would have used for sheep and cattle—they abruptly turned at nearly ninety degrees, flying well to the south before turning once more to the west.

I could see no explanation for their detour and I found myself scrambling down the hill toward the cottage as quickly as I could muster.

I was so intent on avoiding the jagged rocks on the ground that I ran directly into Danny. I was brought up short and I began to beg forgiveness when his expression stopped me cold. His face had appeared to balloon in size much like someone suffering an allergic reaction, the pores wide and his skin as red as beets. Despite the early hour, he reeked of alcohol; his eyes were bloodshot with deep bags underneath and his clothes appeared to have been slept in.

"What are y' doin' here?" he bellowed, though I was only inches away from him.

My fingers tightened around the phone in my pocket. "Taking a stroll. What are you doing here?"

"You've no right to be here." The spittle flew out the corners of his mouth.

"On the contrary, I have rented this spot for the remainder of the month." I straightened my spine. "This is not your property. It is Fergal's."

"He had no business turning that place into a rental," he growled. "He should have left it in ruins!"

"That's between you and Fergal. Now if you'll excuse me, I have an appointment." I brushed past him, my eyes now riveted on the cottage at the base of the hill.

"Don't you dare come up here again!" he shouted after me.

I pulled my collar closer around my neck, as much to stop my shaking hands as to ward off the chill, but the trembling only subsided once I was in my car and I was putting miles between myself and Danny.

7

I arrived at the university with time to spare so I popped into the cafeteria for a bite. I had just paid for my meal and gathered up my tray when I heard someone call my name. Looking up, I spotted the historian Seamus MacGregor, better known as Shay to those that knew him, heading toward me. I would have recognized him anywhere; not only was he a renowned author of nonfiction but I had also visited his website before contacting him, ensuring he was the right person to approach about my research.

He was a tall man, head and shoulders above most of the others and if his height hadn't cut a striking figure by itself, his broad shoulders made him appear a leader. In fact, it was as if the waves parted as he approached and I had to remind myself the cafeteria was filled with students while he was quite obviously faculty, warranting the respect. Still, my heart skipped a beat as I watched him approach. He greeted me with a ready smile through a neatly trimmed beard that was a bit darker than his chestnut hair. "I would have recognized you anywhere," he said as he reached me.

I laughed. "I was just thinking the same about you."

"Well, it's grand to meet you in person finally, after all these months. Won't you join me? I'm just over there," he pointed vaguely behind him.

"I'd love to."

"Allow me to carry that." Without waiting for a reply, he picked the tray from my fingers and started back across the room, the throngs of students and faculty parting yet again. He arranged the tray across from his own, held the chair out for me and when he was satisfied that I was comfortable, took his own seat.

We chatted for a moment as he asked about my flight from America, where I was staying, and how my research was coming along.

"I've been dying to ask you," I said, "if your family came to Ireland around the same time of the Plantations?"

"A bit before," he said. "I participated in a genealogy project a few years back and my DNA confirmed what my family had passed down through the generations. I am Gallowglass—my ancestors were Vikings that mixed with Scottish Highlanders in the 13th century. We arrived in Ireland in the early 15th century and settled in the far western parts."

"So you're familiar with where my book takes place," I said.

"Intimately familiar. The Inishowen Peninsula is a world unto itself. I grew up in County Donegal, only a wee piece from where your ancestor would have first lived."

"So," I said hesitantly, "your family…"

He laughed as I faltered. "I can tell you've spent a good bit of time researching Ulster. Religion and political party are still major identifiers there and, I'm afraid, responsible for most of the divisions. But you won't find that so much in the Republic. We have comparatively little segregation here."

"That's a relief."

"But to answer the questions I'm sure you have, my family was well integrated with the Irish by the time the Spanish Armada sank off Ireland's coast and Queen Elizabeth I became alarmed at the possibility that another country would colonize us—so she sent British troops in to conquer Ireland."

"And that set off the Plantation Era."

"Precisely." He took a bite of his stew.

"So if your family was already here, you weren't part of the conquerors?"

"Highlanders were forbidden from taking part in colonizing Ireland for Britain." He laughed. "Britain had its own problems with us. No, the offer went out to those in the Lowlands that had converted to Protestantism as well as those in Britain and some in Wales. They were concerned because Spain was a Catholic nation while Britain had become Protestant, and they did not want the Pope at their back door."

"My ancestors were Calvinists from Wigtownshire."

"Ah, the Calvinists—better known as the Reformers. My family was staunchly Catholic and in the context of your book, they would have been on the opposite side. While your ancestor would have fought on behalf of King James, mine fought for Ireland. In fact, there's evidence to support that mine took part in O'Doherty's Rebellion of which you're writing."

I chewed a bite of food for a moment, deep in thought. "You know," I said finally, "At the time my ancestor came here, he was promised land in return for his service to the king."

"That occurred quite frequently during that time."

"But the land had belonged to someone else at the time," I pressed. "It wasn't just sitting there with no ownership at all."

"Ah, that was an interesting situation. The Ulster lands belonged to Gaelic chieftains or earls. There was a war that ended a few years prior to O'Doherty's Rebellion called the Nine Years War, which England won. The earls lost a great deal of their landholdings in their defeat, which King James then granted to subjects loyal to the crown."

"So what happened to the earls? Did they continue to live on smaller land parcels?"

"They tried and found it rather difficult. You must realize that some of the holdings—such as Hugh O'Neill's—comprised enough land to form a small country; in fact, his holdings were roughly five times the size of Monaco. They continued to hope that Spain would come to their aid and indeed, there was evidence that Spain intended to do so. But they had their hands full in a war with the Dutch, which ended in the Battle of Gibraltar."

"I've heard of the battle, but have to admit I know little about it."

He tore off a piece of his roll. "Ah, that would be a fine discussion over a pint sometime," Shay said, smiling. "Perhaps we can arrange it before you leave for the States."

"I'd like that. Who knows, it could lead to another book."

He laughed. "And it did. I wrote it myself."

Now it was my turn to laugh. "Then there's no one finer to have the discussion with, is there?"

He chuckled for a moment and then continued more somberly, "Suffice it to say the battle ended in a complete defeat for Spain, an utter disaster. Their navy was decimated and I'm afraid, so were the earls' hopes. The earls became increasingly concerned that England would learn of their attempted alliance with Spain and so, on September 4, 1607, they fled to Spain. Some say they fled for permanent asylum; others that they intended to raise an Army with their allies' help and return to Ulster."

"What happened to them?"

"The earls? Their plan was a blunder of monumental proportions. Spain was completely unable to assist them; they'd been brought to their knees. Hugh O'Neill went on to Italy, where he died in Rome in 1616, having never returned to his native land. Rory O'Donnell also died in Rome, most likely of malaria. Some of the Maguires of Fermanagh also defected, but some remained behind and pledged loyalty to King James—though their loyalty varied, depending upon the circumstances."

I'd finished my meal sometime prior but the conversation had been so fascinating to me and Shay's voice so soothing that I hadn't noticed the room had cleared out until he said, "Shall we go to my office then? I've some documents for you."

I felt as though I had stepped back in time as I wandered the National University of Ireland's halls at Galway. I learned from Shay as we strolled that the institution had been established some 170 years prior and was originally known as Queen's College, built out of limestone that was plentiful in these parts and in the Tudor architectural style that was so popular at the time.

Over the centuries, additional wings had been added as well as several buildings across its campus, seen through the windows as Shay pointed them out without slowing his pace.

His own office might have been used by another professor a century earlier. It had a musty odor of spent pipes and old paper and the ancient walls were in stark contrast with the computer and equipment that were arranged across his desk and credenza. He gathered up a thick folder and handed it to me as he urged me to sit in one of the chairs opposite his desk.

"You'll find information there on your ancestors." He pointed to a map of Ireland. "That is one of the places where he lived; it was across the lough from Cahir O'Doherty."

"That was exactly where I'd imagined him to be." I snapped a picture of the map.

Shay smiled, revealing deep dimples underneath the neatly trimmed beard. "Ah then, you've been on the right track." When I was finished, he pulled another map from under the first. "He must have distinguished himself during O'Doherty's Rebellion because King James granted him a thousand acres at the base of the Inishowen Peninsula."

"What has happened to the land?"

"I'm still in the process of running that down… It's changed hands several times, and there's evidence that his son was given additional land further east. He might have relocated there."

"I see."

"You might also be interested in knowing that your ancestor was called up again for service; this time to defend Londonderry from attack in 1641."

"Londonderry?"

"The slash city." He was leaning over the map pointing at the city on the lough, but at his words he glanced up with a twinkle in his eye.

I chuckled. "Some call it Derry and some Londonderry so it's shown on the maps as both—with a slash in between. Do I have that right?"

"Aye, and you do. You can tell a native Irishman and a Catholic from an Ulster Scot and a Protestant by which name they use. It was known as Derry for centuries before the Plantation Era, originally a monastery, I believe. But after O'Doherty's Rebellion, London had the city rebuilt with a defensive wall around it and renamed it Londonderry. The native Irish have never accepted the name change." He took the folder from me and rifled through it. "Ah, here it is. A roster of defenders dated 1641, and there is your ancestor." He pointed at the name. "He brought his sword with him."

"So that's why my genealogy charts refer to him as 'William with Sword'." I snapped a photograph of the list.

"Funny how those monikers occur, isn't it?" Then he abruptly changed the subject. "Have you ever read the *Outlander* series by Diana Gabaldon?"

"I'm a huge fan of both the books and the television series. But I'm surprised you know of it."

"Oh? Why is that?" He raised one brow.

"Well, it's kind of romantic… You know, Jamie and Claire…"

"And a man can't be romantic?" he teased. "Ah, but there's action as well. And if you're familiar with the series, then you're aware of the Jacobites."

"Yes. They were loyal to King James II and used his Latin name, Jacobus, which is how they came to be called the Jacobites."

"Well then, did you know your ancestors fought them?"

I leaned back. "Are you serious?"

"I am indeed." His eyes sparkled when he spoke as if he was relishing the conversation. "So you know James II was Catholic and had been king of what was known as the Three Kingdoms — England, Scotland and Ireland. He was overthrown and the Jacobites formed in order to pick up his cause and restore him to the throne. Another of your ancestors pledged allegiance to William of Orange, a Dutch Protestant — who, coincidentally, was William and Mary's son. I believe you've a university in America named after them?"

"Yes, in Virginia."

"Ah, well, in 1688 and 1689, your ancestor defended Derry from the Jacobites and King James II himself. They laid siege to the city but the Williamites prevailed. And your ancestor even helped to lead a group of men that escaped through enemy lines to seize some cattle to keep some of the Derry inhabitants from starving. They were spotted and fired upon, which led to the Battle of the Cows."

"The Battle of the Cows," I repeated. "You've just given me the backdrop for the third book in the series!"

"Well, it's all right there," he said, patting the folder.

We continued chatting well into the afternoon. The Irish have a way of spinning stories that can be utterly entertaining, and I felt the past beginning to visualize in my mind's eye. I knew where my dreams would take me tonight. Finally, as dusk began to fall, I knew reluctantly it was time for me to go. Shay walked me all the way to my rental car. The campus was quiet now, classes having ended, and a crisp wind was growing, rattling the spring leaves.

As I started up the car, I thanked him again for his time and the wealth of information he'd compiled for me.

"Oh, tis no bother at all," he said. "I love history

and I love research so when the two meet, I'm in my element for sure." He hesitated as though debating whether to say more. "May I ask you something?" he said finally.

"Of course."

"I… did not expect you to come to Ireland alone."

I chuckled. "That's not a question; it's a statement. Anyway, single ladies do a great deal these days… alone."

"Of course. Of course. I didn't mean to imply—"

"Of course you didn't. The fact is," I blurted, "I don't have a significant other in my life just now." Before he could respond, I changed the subject. "Tell me, would you be able to look up the ownership of a property for me?"

"Oh, for sure, that should be in the public records."

"Would you mind?"

"I wouldn't mind at all. What have you in mind?"

I gave him the address where I was staying. "I'd like to know the history of ownership," I added. I called up one of the pictures of the gravesite. "I haven't been able to see the names on the headstones, but I'm especially interested in this family and what happened to them."

"Send it to me," he said but I'd already hit the Send button and his phone beeped as he spoke. "Ah," he said, enlarging it, "I see what you mean. The inscription is nearly weathered out. I'll see what I can do, and I'll email you when I have the information."

I thanked him again and he closed the door and patted the side. "Off you go."

As I drove through the parking lot, I glanced in the rearview mirror. He was looking at his phone, perhaps still trying to make out the inscription.

8

When the clock struck eleven, it startled me out of my imagination. Once again, the present time had slipped past on silent wings while I had become completely immersed in my writing. Gone was the Ireland of the present as Ulster of 1608 loomed large in my consciousness, and I'd found myself shifting from the mind of my ancestor to the motives of the last Gaelic King of Ireland, Cahir O'Doherty. Once known as the Queen's O'Doherty for his loyalty to Elizabeth I in the Nine Years' War, he had touched off O'Doherty's Rebellion with the burning of Derry and become a wanted man even as he united clans across the island to fight against their English oppressors.

I leaned back in my chair and stretched. My tea was cold now, my meager dinner of scones—what the Irish referred to as biscuits—were nothing more than crumbs on a china plate. I rose slowly, continuing to stretch out back muscles that had become taut in my frenzied writing of a battle scene, and contemplated whether to brew another cuppa or call it a night. My eyes dropped to my phone, the screen dark as if it had already slipped into slumber, and then I abruptly changed course and sat back down.

My phone was automatically synced with my laptop and I retrieved the photographs I'd taken earlier in the day atop the hill. Viewing them on the larger screen, I was disappointed with my amateur photography. In virtually every picture except one, the sun managed to place streaks in the oddest of places—usually two and sometimes three. I could still see through the muted buttery splashes but if I'd paid more attention, I should have avoided them.

I focused on the single image that had not been ruined—a zoomed picture of the two gravestones—or of their fragments. I used my photo editing software to increase the contrast until the inscription, once faded by time and weather, began to take form. Then I moved pieces of the stones together, once more uniting them into what they might have been years ago. It was far from perfect, but as the letters became more legible I felt a strange mingling of excitement and trepidation, as if I was somehow disturbing the residents within the graves.

"Elliot Crutchley," I read aloud, my voice sounding odd in the silence of the carriage house. "October 19, 1904 to April 3, 1919." I pictured a young man—a boy, really—of only fifteen years old when death had claimed him. Then I scrolled to the second one, which took a bit longer. "Spencer Crutchley. November 22, 1902 to April 3, 1919." Only seventeen, and he'd died on the same day as his brother. Those unfortunate boys—and their poor mother.

When my phone beeped, I nearly jumped out of my chair. It was a text from Shay: *Can you chat?*

I texted back that I could and a moment later my phone rang.

"I'm not calling too late, am I?" he asked.

"Not at all. I was just working."

"I sent you an email, but I was rather excited about the information I discovered."

"Oh?"

"Aye. It's about the family that owned the property you're renting."

"Great! I was just—"

"The name is Crutchley," he said, his enthusiasm barely contained. "Sir Gregory Crutchley." As I repeated the name in my mind, Shay continued, "He fought for Queen Elizabeth I in the Nine Years' War and shortly after, was granted two thousand acres in the very spot you're standing."

"That was shortly before my ancestor arrived here," I mused.

"Aye. 1603 it ended and by 1604, Crutchley had been knighted and granted the land. I also discovered a census of 1910. The land was still owned by the family and had passed sometime between 1900 and 1910 to Ignacius Crutchley, whom I suspect is in direct line but I will need to verify that."

"I see."

"In the 1910 census, Ignacius was married to a former April Butler, who lists her prior standing at her parents' home in County Wicklow, an Irish family... Anyway, at the time of the census, they both list their ages as 28 years, and they had four children—am I going too fast for you?"

"Not at all. I'm keeping up." My eyes dropped back to my laptop where the gravestones were still displayed.

"Olivia, aged 9. Spencer, aged 8. Elliot, aged 6. Jayne, aged 9 months. And there are records of their possessions as well, including the head of cattle and other livestock—"

"Have you had a chance to look at the picture of the gravestones yet?"

"Only a glance. I've been concentrating on the ownership of the land there."

"I was able to make out the inscriptions—they're the graves of Spencer and Elliot, both died on the same date—April 3, 1919."

"Oh, now that is interesting. In the 1920 census—"

My mind was riveted on the photograph and a moment later, I realized I'd missed what Shay had been saying. "I'm sorry; could you repeat that?"

"I did a double-take as well. In 1920, the census shows the land holdings belonging to Peter Cassidy."

"Cassidy. That's—"

"The grandfather of the man you're renting the cottage from."

"So," I said, turning my back on the laptop in an attempt to better focus on our conversation, "You're telling me that the Queen of England gave two thousand acres to the Crutchley family in 1604—so the land was owned outright, correct?"

"That's correct."

"And it remained in the Crutchley family for over three hundred years, and then within a year of the boys' deaths it was sold?"

"That's precisely what I'm saying. That's not all, either. According to the census of 1920, Peter Cassidy lists exactly the same possessions as Ignacius Crutchley had ten years prior—though he lists the house in ruins so it would presumably be unassessed."

"So he not only bought the land, he bought everything on it as well?"

"I couldn't believe it myself. Usually, livestock would have sold off separately—you get more for them than

trying to sell everything in one parcel. Instead of the
house, though, it lists ruins as I mentioned, which would
have dropped the taxes, and by the 1930 census there
were no animals listed on the property at all. Once upon
a time, you see, a house was taxed by the number of
windows it contained..."

"Back to the boys," I said, "what would have killed
both boys on the same day?"

There was a moment of silence on the other end of
the phone. "The Great Famine was between 1845 and
1849, so it couldn't have been that," he mused. "And I
know of no epidemic in 1919. Say, what are you doing
tomorrow?"

"I'd planned to go to Burt Castle."

"Burt Castle, outside of Derry?"

"That's right."

"You're not going into Derry, are you?"

"I'd thought about it," I admitted.

"'Tis not safe. They're rioting."

"Why?"

"It's Derry. They're still fighting the War for
Independence there."

"Are you serious?" I asked, a half-smile on my lips.

"Aye. They get stirred up every few years, you
know."

"I didn't know."

"Say, would you care for some company? I happen
to be off tomorrow..."

I hesitated as I rolled through the stops I'd planned
to make.

"I can bring a chaperone, if you'd like," he added.

I laughed. "A chaperone won't be necessary. I'd enjoy
your company. I have to warn you, though, I'll be
stopping at sites where my book takes place—"

"You're warning a professor of Irish history that
you'll be researching history?"

"Sure you won't be bored?"

"Far from it. I can even drive us and take us off the beaten path—Inishowen, perhaps? Would you care to see the O'Doherty castles—or what's left of them?"

"I'd love that!"

"Eight o'clock too early?"

"Eight o'clock is perfect."

"Alright then, I'll see you then. Oh—and check your email."

"I will. Thank you. See you tomorrow."

We both clicked off and I sat for a moment staring at the gravestones, my mind rehashing all that Shay had found. I scribbled down what I remembered of the four children and their parents, along with their ages in 1910.Then I carried the dishes to the kitchen sink, rinsing them but leaving them for a proper washing until the morning, before taking my laptop into the bedroom.

I awakened at the stroke of midnight. I felt as though I'd barely climbed into bed and pulled the covers over me before I was reawakened and as I tried to snuggle deeper under the bedcovers, my fingers found the unyielding hard case of my laptop. Opening my eyes more fully, I closed the case and set it on the nightstand beside the bed. Then I groaned as I tried once more to protect myself from the chill, which pervaded despite a presumably new heater.

I'd taken my computer to bed with me, which I rarely did, but I'd been rather curious about the documents Shay had alluded to. As I closed my eyes, I could see them in my mind's eye: decade after decade of census declarations, centuries of amassing and maintaining landholdings, livestock and a myriad of possessions, only to have sold them for a tiny fraction of their worth.

The twelve chimes ended and I made a mental note to ask Fergal how to disable the sound at night. I didn't much mind them during the day; in fact, I'd grown to like them as they reminded me how long I might have remained bent over a computer, prompting me to stand and stretch. But there was really no call to be awakened every hour on the hour, now was it?

With the silence upon me, I tried to picture Ireland in 1919. The Crutchley family had weathered the Great Famine as well as other, more minor ones. Typhus was found in many of the rural counties of the day, especially on the west coast, but there had been no real epidemic— but then, I realized there wouldn't need to be a formal declaration of one to claim two boys' lives.

It occurred to me that they passed away the very same month as I was there now. I imagined the same weather, the same promise of spring, the hills dotted with lambkin and calves, winter snow giving way to lush green fields. Spring, with its awakening and renewal, would be a terrible time to die, with promises left unrealized.

My thoughts turned once more to their mother April, who would have been 37 at the time that both of her boys had died. To bury a child, even in those days before modern medicine, would have surely been unbearable. To lose two in one day, unconscionable.

I was drifting back into slumber, my thoughts still trying to conjure the image of a woman forced to bury her sons, choosing a hilltop overlooking the west for their gravesites, investing in beautiful head stones that would someday be toppled and split, when I heard the sobs again. I thought they had become part of my imagination as I hung there between sleep and wakefulness; perhaps I was even sobbing in my mind for a mother's broken heart.

It was the man's voice that caused my eyes to pop open.

"Now, now," he was saying, "they won't be coming back, love. Everything will be alright. We will be gone from here directly and we will never look back..."

I bolted upright, scrambling to turn on the lamp. The voice and the sobbing stopped abruptly as the room flooded with light.

Danny. It had to be Danny. But even as the thought crossed my mind, I knew it had not been his voice that I'd heard. This voice was cultured, the accent not as thick, the words more precise.

I don't remember when I finally dozed off but I slept fitfully, my dreams filled with the burning house, two boys dead before their time, and a mother bereft.

9

Shay arrived precisely at 8:00, and I was ready for him. I'd packed a picnic basket and was dressed appropriately for Ireland in a blouse, a sweater and a slicker with a hood and was wearing my most comfortable walking shoes and loose jeans.

If there was such a thing as reincarnation, he must have been a sea captain in another century, his bulk filling the door as I opened it. I could easily envision him commanding a fleet on the open seas. Of course, when the carriage house was originally built, men were much smaller, especially in Ireland, but he still cut an impressive figure. He wore a red and black plaid flannel shirt, the sleeves rolled above his elbows despite the chill, jeans and hiking shoes.

"Come in," I said, stepping quickly toward the kitchen counter.

He looked a bit nervous as he glanced behind him before entering.

"Anything wrong?" I asked.

He shook his head but his expression contradicted him as he peered through the open door again. "I did bring our chaperone," he said.

"Oh." I must admit, I felt a bit deflated; I was always sensitive to the energy around people and I hoped she wouldn't put a damper on the day. "Well, please invite her in."

"I'd better not," he said sheepishly.

Despite my initial reservations, I forced a chuckle. "Well, what good is a chaperone if she remains in the car?"

"None I'm afraid and I'm thinking I'll have to drive her home before we can start our day."

"Why?" I grabbed the picnic basket.

His eyes darted from my face to the basket and he gallantly took it from me. "Allow me."

"Thank you." I snatched my bag from the hook by the door. As he made his way to the car, I turned to lock up the carriage house. When I turned back around, I burst out laughing. "She's our chaperone?"

"Allow me to introduce Sadie," he said over the howls of a gorgeous mahogany Irish setter. She was pacing back and forth on the folded-down back seat of a Honda CRV, quite possibly one of the larger passenger vehicles one finds in Ireland—after all, the roads can be narrow and quite tricky. Yet despite the size, she took up the entire breadth and her constant strides were rocking the car. "I don't know what's got into her," he was saying as I strained to hear him over her wailing. "She's an old girl and even as a pup, she didn't excite like this. She's usually quite settled."

"Maybe she needs out of the car?"

"Tried it when I pulled up. She backed into a corner and wouldn't come near the open door." He opened the passenger door and I slipped inside. I adore dogs and I tried to turn around to pet her, but her eyes stopped me in my tracks. They were wide, the white showing all around, a clear sign she was frightened. Shay tucked the basket behind my seat and walked around to the driver's door, never taking his eyes off the dog. I could tell in his expression that he was a dog lover and he was very worried.

I tried murmuring to her, hoping the softness in my voice would soothe her but to no avail.

Once the engine had roared to life, he said, "I apologize. I thought she'd be a good idea; she hasn't been out so much lately… But I live not twenty minutes from here, and I'll drop her off and we'll be on our way."

"You think she'll be okay by herself all day?"

He glanced back at her. "I'll ask a neighbor to look in on her."

He turned the vehicle around and started down the drive to the road, but once we passed around the hill separating the carriage house from Danny's cottage, the howling abruptly stopped. I looked back at her to find her sitting like an old schoolmarm behind Shay, calmly looking out the window.

"I think she got spooked," I said, reaching back to stroke her silky fur. "She seems alright now. Perhaps we could just go on to Inishowen with her?"

He glimpsed into the rearview mirror. "I've never seen her act like that."

"It's the carriage house," I said quietly.

"You think there's a fox there?"

"A fox? Oh no. I haven't seen any wild creatures at all there… In fact, I haven't seen any animals on the property." I told him Fergal's story about the cattle running for the cliffs. "There's something there, some sort of energy…" I stopped short of saying more. I didn't need Shay, like the rest of them, to think I had an

APRIL IN THE BACK OF BEYOND   75

overactive imagination. But his next words surprised me.

"I was raised believing in taidhbhse—ghosts," he said thoughtfully. "All Irish are."

"Do you think those two boys—?"

He gazed at me before returning his attention to the road. "Spirits that remain on an earthly level are those suspended between this life and the next—if you believe in that sort of thing," he added hastily.

"I do believe," I said quietly. "In the States, I encounter more people that discourage the belief… but I believe."

We turned onto the motorway and for the next few minutes we were silent. I debated whether to tell him of the woman's sobs or the man's futile efforts at comforting her but thought better of the idea. It was turning into a beautiful day, the morning mists clearing out to reveal the promise of sunshine. True to Ireland's reputation as the Emerald Isle, the landscape that rushed past us as we gained speed was lush and green, the fields dotted with sheep.

"Usually," he said, "ghosts are the souls of people that feel tethered to their old lives. Perhaps they felt they had unfinished business, particularly family members that needed looking after…"

"Their mother?" I asked. "I would imagine a mother would feel inconsolably bereaved after the deaths of her two sons, especially on the same day."

"I've been thinking about their deaths."

"Oh?"

"I believe they might have died in the fire."

"Oh." I leaned back against my seat. "I must admit, that occurred to me as well. It would make perfect sense, wouldn't it?"

"We know when the Cassidy family purchased the property, the house was already in ruins."

"Then you're thinking the house burned to the ground with the two boys inside."

"It's possible, 'ey? What other explanation could there be?"

"The parents got out; the sisters, too," I mused. "But the brothers were trapped. Then," I said suddenly, "where would the family have stayed if their house was gone?"

"If they had relatives, they would have stayed with them perhaps."

"Or if that wasn't possible—for whatever reasons—could they have stayed in the carriage house?"

"The carriage house?" He frowned. "Oh no. Not at all."

"Why not?"

"Why, it was a carriage house," he said as if that explained everything.

"You're saying it would have had a coach inside it."

"Aye, and the living quarters of the coachman."

"They'd have had a coachman?"

"Quite possibly, given the size of their land holdings. It's likely they employed several servants; a cook or housemaid would have lived in the attic of the main house. A coachman would have tended to the carriage and performed the duties of a groom and farrier—perhaps even tending to the health of the livestock, though often they employed others for that..."

My mind had raced ahead. "So the coachman might have lived in the bedroom I'm renting now, and the coach would have been in the living area?"

"It would not have been the same size, but more likely a straw mattress. It could have been in the back of the carriage house, I suppose, but more likely than not in the loft."

"The loft." I pictured the tiny cottage with its high ceilings and skylights. The loft, I deduced, had been removed during the renovations.

"Is it possible that after the house burned down, the rest of the family remained in the carriage house?"

"Amongst the horses and the hay? Not at their stature, surely."

"But—playing devil's advocate—it was 1919. There were cars back then."

He stroked his beard thoughtfully. "Aye, there were some. But western Ireland would not have seen much of them. But I suppose it was possible—given the stature of the family—they might have had one."

Sadie stretched out on the folded-down rear seat and stuck her head in between us, providing me with ample opportunity to stroke her and murmur to her. Her fur was long and silky, so shiny it reminded me of a mirror. I'd had a collie once long ago and I knew just how time and labor intensive long fur could be for an owner. Her beautiful coat was a clear sign that Shay had taken excellent care of her. It was the measure of a person, I thought, how they treated their animals. She looked at me now with moist brown eyes, her previous agitation and fear completely gone.

Another wave of mists rolled in, settling across the motorway. Shay leaned a bit forward to focus on the road. I fell silent as I watched the weather close in around us, my thoughts returning to the Crutchley family. It might have been improbable for most well-to-do to live in their carriage house, I thought, but I felt a quiet confirmation in the depths of my soul telling me I was on the right track. After all, wouldn't a mother grieving her sons wish to remain close to them?

10

The mists rolling in from the sea had long cleared by the time we pulled down the picturesque road to Burt Castle, now beneath a clear azure sky. We climbed out of the vehicle, none more enthusiastic than Sadie, who had slept peacefully through most of the drive. We tended to her needs first, setting out a water bowl which Shay filled with bottled water. The castle beckoned us from an emerald hill and as we approached, I felt as though I was standing on hallowed ground. I had written about Burt Castle already, having researched it through endless hours and yet now that I was here, it appeared far smaller than I had imagined.

As if reading my mind, Shay said, "It's not what it once was, you know. It was originally built in the mid-16th century, most likely by Cahir O'Doherty's grandfather. It was strategically placed here because we're near the base of the Inishowen Peninsula and it was used to guard the O'Doherty's southern land holdings."

I didn't stop Shay though I already knew its history; fact was I simply enjoyed listening to him talk. His speech pattern had a melodious quality to it, quiet yet strong, a passionate thread weaving through his baritone voice whenever he spoke of historical events.

"It was an advanced design for its time," he went on as we strolled up the hill with Sadie running circles around us, her muzzle low to the ground as she picked up scents. "Scottish, actually. The Irish were still erecting castles with square corners, which could be collapsed through tunneling or torched by their enemies. That round tower on the side was considered innovative; adopted quite widely in the 17th century."

"I wonder why it didn't have round towers at every end?" I mused.

"It might have helped them when the British finally did attack it."

"As I recall," I said, "the British didn't originally attack this castle—during the Nine Years War, that is— because Cahir O'Doherty, at the age of fifteen, became the Gaelic Chieftain of the Inishowen Peninsula and he fought on the side of Elizabeth I."

He looked surprised for a moment and then chuckled. "Of course. I'd forgotten you're an avid researcher, too."

"And," I went on, eager to show a bit more of my knowledge, "Cahir was knighted by Elizabeth for his loyalty and became known as the Queen's O'Doherty. He was good friends with the first Governor of Derry, Henry Docwra, and also with Captain Henry Hart, who commanded Culmore Fort."

"Right up the way there," he said, pointing toward the northeast.

We reached the castle and I reverently placed my hands on the ancient stone. It was frigid. Life inside must have been drafty and cold. "Then Docwra was replaced by George Paulet," I continued, "and only God knows why he accepted the job because he hated the Irish and by all accounts, he despised Ireland."

"Most people fall in love with the isle as you have," he said. "With the Vikings, it was said they became more Irish than the Irish."

I shook my head. "History would have been so much different had Paulet never come here."

"Watch out," he chided. "You're beginning to sound like an Irish native for sure now."

"It's true, isn't it? Derry is just to our east over there and Paulet governed all of it. Yet that didn't satisfy him. He wanted Cahir's castles, even though London had expressly forbidden Paulet to take them."

"Aye, and that's true enough. Cahir even went to King James' court to make certain he held onto them after Elizabeth's death."

"Can we go inside?"

"There's not much to see, but sure. The door is over there."

We rounded the tower and entered through an open doorway, the proper door long gone, eventually finding ourselves inside of a courtyard that was bordered on all four sides by thick stone walls.

"The castle would have been surrounded by a stone wall called a curtain," Shay said, "but most of the rock has been carted away over the centuries. There was also a moat here at the time, if I'm not mistaken."

I made my way to one of the windows, a gaping hole that was no longer squared but weathered and battered through the years. "Amazing view from here."

"Aye, and it would be. It was the view that decided the site. The O'Doherty clan would have had a clear, unobstructed view of their surroundings so they would be fully prepared if an enemy was headed for their doorstep."

"It just occurred to me," I said suddenly, stopping in my tracks.

"Aye?"

"My ancestor was just outside this castle in 1608—in fact, he might even have been inside as I am now, a guest of Cahir's before he touched off his rebellion. After the burning of Derry, he came to the castle with troops sent by King James I and they laid siege to it. They bombed it—rudimentary bombs compared to what we have today—in order to free British citizens captured at Derry." I looked back at the gaping windows and wondered which of the damage had perhaps been caused by my own ancestor firing upon it.

Shay had crossed to the other side and was looking at a different view. "That's right. Only Cahir was not here—he had escaped to one of his other castles, further into the Inishowen Peninsula. But his wife was here; she was captured and sent to her family in Dublin."

"She was British, wasn't she?"

"She was indeed. It is part and parcel of what spared her life. She had to have known what Cahir was planning to do, and she remained in charge of Burt Castle and the prisoners while he fled."

"Whatever happened to her?"

He stroked his beard. "Her name was Mary Preston. She was a daughter of the 4th Viscount Gormanston. She had one daughter by Cahir; Eleanor was her name. Mary faded into obscurity after she was reunited with her family, who was most likely appalled beyond reason at her betrayal."

"Do you think she might have been a prisoner in her own home?"

"She was, actually, for a time. It was her father's position and her British blood that were the factors saving her from the same fate as awaited her husband; or she might have been sentenced to the Tower of

London. Instead, she was remanded into her father's custody."

I looked upward where once there had been several floors—living quarters, guard posts, perhaps even where little Eleanor had been conceived and certainly one of the homes where she spent her first years. Now there was only open sky, the floors long since caved in and the wood and any salvageable possessions carted off or lost to nature.

"Look here," Shay was saying as he turned back to the window. "That appears to be a grand place for a picnic, 'eh?"

It was cool on the side of the hill despite the warm sun, as if the seasons were competing for dominance. The view from our vantage point gave us a stunning vista of the lough on one side and Burt Castle on the other. I snapped several pictures, wanting to remember this scene for the rest of my life. I would have the photographs enlarged and framed, I decided, and placed in my office at home where I could lose myself in them every day.

The blanket beneath us contained the meager leftovers from our picnic; I'd raided the refrigerator and stocked up on cheeses, a sliced ham and a variety of breads, all laid in by Fergal prior to my arrival. Sadie shared equally in our stash, despite the fact that Shay had brought kibble for her as well.

Shay picked up the now half-empty bottle of wine and started to pour more into my glass, but I waved him off. "I'd sleep the afternoon away," I explained wistfully.

"Is that such a bad thing?" he joked. Then he grew somber. "I wanted to apologize for my brashness the other day."

"I hadn't noticed."

"When I referenced you being in Ireland alone..."

"Ah. Yes."

"I didn't mean to imply..."

"I know." An awkward silence ensued. "The truth is," I said, my voice growing quiet, "I was engaged to be married. In fact, I was left standing at the altar." I downed the final drops of my wine. "Quite literally."

His brows furrowed. "No."

"Yes. I'm afraid so." I stared into the distance. "We were moving to Dublin, he and I."

"He's Irish?"

"American. He was going to work at the Embassy."

"But he isn't there now?"

I shook my head. "I don't believe there is any feeling quite like being left at the altar." I turned back to face him. His eyes were filled with empathy, which gave me the courage to continue. "The church was overflowing with guests, the fellowship hall filled with gifts. We'd moved out of our shared apartment in preparation for the move to Dublin. We'd sold almost everything we had and had rented a furnished home in Ireland..."

"Could something have happened to him? An accident or—?"

I shook my head. "No. He'd simply changed his mind."

"And didn't tell you?"

I smiled wanly, the pit of my stomach feeling the same pain as the day it happened.

"That's inexcusable. Ghastly, even."

I took a deep breath. "There can be only one reason, don't you think? Minus an illness or an accident, one person leaves another simply because they believe that somehow, in some way, their life will be better if they move in a different direction and leave the other behind... The thing is it wasn't even the humiliation of being left at the altar that was the worst. The worst set in days and weeks later. It was the realization that the life I had planned was gone in an instant... The little things of waking up next to the person I loved, of exploring Ireland together, starting a new chapter in an exciting place, all our plans for a life together... just the knowing that I would have him by my side. It has been that overwhelming sense of loss that has been the worst."

"Did he ever explain himself to you?"

"No," I said. "He never did."

"Is he here now, in Dublin?"

"No." I wiped a small tear from the corner of my eye. Considering the time that had elapsed, I was surprised to find my emotions were still so close to the surface. "He helped plan everything, but in the end, he didn't want any of it... or so it seems." I managed a smile. "Anyway, enough of that. There's so much I want to see today," I added, taking care to change my voice from sorrow to optimism, even if I didn't completely feel the latter.

"You know," he said, topping off his own glass, "to see the Peninsula the way you should, you need several days." His voice had thankfully changed too, a signal that our painful conversation had come to an end.

"I was afraid of that. But I hadn't been in contact with anyone on the Peninsula, so I thought I would try a driving tour. I've a map with me." I dug deep into my jacket pocket and pulled out the carefully folded map I'd printed off the Internet.

He laughed. "I won't be needing the map, darlin'. I know it like the back of my hand."

"Then what do you suggest we see?" I stuffed the map back into my pocket as quickly as I'd pulled it out.

He peered upward at the skies. "Well, the clouds are moving in from the west and it's already early afternoon. Ever hear of Carrickabraghy Castle?"

"Another of Cahir's castles," I said, my heart skipping a beat at the mere thought of seeing it.

"We can be there in less than an hour, provided we don't make any stops in between. It's only a fraction of what it once was, of course, similar to Burt Castle here."

"So it's only an hour to the far northwestern point of the Inishowen Peninsula?"

"Closer to fifty minutes, I'd say. We've good roads there now, where in Cahir's time it was considered quite wild."

"I suppose that's why I thought it would take much longer."

"It did once. Modern times are grand though, are they not?"

Though I knew the time was slipping away, I was hesitant to leave our idyllic spot. We'd had the hill all to ourselves, and once more I was thankful I'd had the foresight to come in April before the tourists descended on the island. Soon visitors would threaten to outnumber the residents, driving on the wrong side and turning quiet, peaceful spots into a beehive of activity. "Have you always enjoyed history?" I asked.

"Oh, aye. The Irish—and the Scots, too—are born storytellers. Whether it is myth or fable, true history or embellished, the stories have been passed down through the generations, first from people who could neither read nor write and then into the capable hands of those that could. We appreciate history here and recognize it as part and parcel of the threads that make us who we are."

"I sometimes worry that the younger generations in America don't appreciate history. They often think what happened just fifty years prior is obsolete and irrelevant."

"I noticed something about the way history is taught in my travels between the two countries. In America, it appears to be a series of dates, names and facts that one must memorize in order to pass an exam. There is no personality to it at all. In Ireland, each fact is a story unto itself, a tale often spun with as much enthusiasm as a fairytale. By the time a wee one begins school, they already know their history—the beginnings of it, anyway."

"The history here dates back so far."

"And it does for sure. Thousands of years. When we reach Carrickabraghy, you'll be able to view ancient Celtic symbols, for example; they were hewn into the rock thousands of years ago and there they are still."

I smiled in appreciation. "In America, we think two hundred years is ancient history."

"Don't I know it. I went to an American antique shop once and had to laugh at what was called antiques. To us, it was just a bit of old stuff."

I wondered who he'd been referring to when he used the word 'us'. I began placing whatever was left from our lunch into the basket. "Have you been to America much?"

"Many times. Mostly conferences. I've spoken in Boston and New York... Went all the way to California once. Now that was a journey, I'll tell you true."

A drop of rain fell on the top of my head and I quickly pulled my jacket hood over my hair while we scrambled up.

"It's just a soft rain," Shay said as he gathered the blanket. "It's fast moving, and then the sun will come out again." He whistled for Sadie, who came bounding back to us from further down the hill toward the lough.

"Off to the back of beyond," he said. As we made our way back up the hill to Burt Castle where we'd have to descend to the other side, the sky opened up in a torrent that felt anything but soft.

11

The car smelled like wet dog and water was rolling off me as I settled into the front seat. "Soft, huh?" I said as I wondered what I would do to dry off.

I needn't have been concerned, however, as Shay reached behind the front seat to an oversized towel. He chuckled as though enjoying a silent joke as he handed it to me. I rolled my hair into it, squeezing the excess water out as he took a corner and gently swabbed the drops off my face. His tender movements caused me to hesitate, my attention riveted on his expression. His eyes did not meet mine but were concentrating on my cheeks and chin as he wiped away the raindrops. His eyes were vivid green, nearly the color of Ireland's plush fields and I marveled that I hadn't noticed their vibrancy before. The outer corners were punctuated with laugh lines so that even in repose, he appeared to be in a jolly mood. My eyes swept upward to his brows, strong and darker than his chestnut hair, before sweeping downward to the raindrops that clung to his beard. He smiled and my eyes darted upward to find him gazing at me.

For a moment, I wondered if he might kiss me. "Are you alright then?" he asked, his voice barely above a whisper.

With my eyes locked onto his, I found myself uncharacteristically tongue-tied.

The gaze was broken by a furry wet paw on his shoulder. He laughed. "Aye, Sadie," he said as he grabbed another towel and turned toward the back to dry her off.

"Do you always keep towels in the car?" I asked.

"Always. Between the Irish weather and an Irish Setter…"

The rain pelted the windshield, and when we were dry enough to continue on our journey, the wipers were challenged to keep up with the downpour. By the time we'd reached Cahir O'Doherty's westernmost castle, however, the clouds had moved further inland, leaving behind the scent of fresh clean air and an ocean breeze. As Shay parked the car, a flock of seagulls rose high from a thin strip of beach.

"So there you have the Atlantic," Shay said as Sadie bounded out of the car with the energy of a pup and began to explore, her tail wagging as though she'd encountered an old friend. "And there is Carrickabraghy."

It was a bit of a climb as the castle had been erected on a rocky promontory. To the northwest we had an unobstructed view of the rugged Irish coastline while in the opposite direction was a stunning view of uninhabited green hills. Despite the obvious state of decline, my romantic imagination could easily envision what life must have been like for the young chieftain and his British wife when the castle was in its full glory. They were bittersweet thoughts as I visualized a time of uneasy peace, a pact between the O'Doherty clan and the monarchs of England, a truce soon to be broken leading to devastation.

As if reading my thoughts, Shay said quietly, almost reverently, "The castle originally contained seven towers, but as you can see, only the one remains."

Indeed, as we approached there were a number of stones that could be identified as towers by their curving walls, but were now sadly reduced to only the lowest edges of the enclosures that had once stood there. The builders had taken full advantage of the rocky, uneven terrain, constructing sections on lower ground that then led to others on the higher points. At the height of the promontory was a rectangular tower perhaps three stories in height beside a much smaller circular one.

I was winded by the time we reached the top but Shay continued chatting as if we'd only been on an easy stroll. "The servants that tended to the castle would have lived in the immediate area here," he was saying. "They had homes scattered throughout and when the castle came under attack, they would have come inside the curtain wall—most of which has been dismantled."

"Why didn't someone keep it up? It must have been an incredible sight—one to rival any castle in all of Europe."

"And who would that have fallen to, to maintain it?" he asked with a pensive smile. "During and after O'Doherty's Rebellion, the British torched most of the peninsula in retaliation, driving out as many Irish as they could manage." He waved his hand toward the hills behind us. "They set fire to all that you see here, until it was nothing but ash. Most were serfs on the run for their lives."

"How horrible." I tried to imagine the beauty of the emerald hills reduced to gray, smoldering ash, the horror of which made me shudder.

"Aye, and Irish history is filled with such conflicts." He sighed and turned back to the castle ruins. "In any event, the serfs would not have dared laid claim to an O'Doherty castle; to do so was to establish oneself as Cahir's successor, putting a mark on one's own head." He held out his hand to me and helped me scramble up for a better view. His grip was strong and sure and it lingered for a moment after I'd regained solid footing. "I suppose the British would have claimed it directly after the rebellion—Chichester, most likely, as he claimed all of Inishowen—but it was eventually abandoned as it held no strategic importance for them— the English considered it too wild and remote. Then sometime in the 20th century, the Royal Navy used it for target practice."

"Tell me it isn't so!" My hand moved instinctively to my heart, my mouth open and my eyes wide.

His green eyes turned dark and brooding as he turned his attention to the ocean. "Aye. Their ship was just off shore there—where you can see the color of the sea change, the waters run deep. A Royal Navy battleship fired on Carrickabraghy with 42-calibre, 15-inch guns— very modern for the time—until all but these last two towers were obliterated. And you can see from the round one, it's nearly gone so it's truly just the one standing…"

We poked around the castle for a bit and then climbed down toward the shoreline. Shay was a step or two in front of me, his hand joined in mine as he led me safely across the ancient rock. Sadie was already in front of us, seeming to anticipate our movements. As we reached the thin strip of beachline, the vista was even more enthralling than that at Burt Castle, and my heartstrings tugged for those that were forced to leave it so long ago. Perhaps because of my writing and my obvious kinship to the feminine, I felt a connection to

Cahir's young wife. "Do we know which castle Mary Preston would have preferred?"

"Cahir O'Doherty's wife?" He threw a fetch toy he'd brought with him and watched Sadie tear down the beach after it. The sand was packed so hard that her paws barely made an imprint. "I suppose it might have been Burt Castle."

"Not this one? With this incredible view?" I waved my hand in a sweeping gesture.

"I doubt it. Oh, she would have been here some, sure she would. But this was a secluded place in their day. It's even remote in our day," he added, chuckling. "Travel was considerably harder back then, mostly on foot and I doubt if they had any decent roads out this way. I believe the O'Doherty rather liked it that way; less likely to smooth the way for an invasion and all."

I sighed. "I suppose. But I can see myself living here—in a modern house, of course."

"Of course," he said as we both laughed. Then he grew thoughtful. "It's wonderful for a holiday, of course. But it takes a special kind of person to appreciate the slower pace of life here. Going to a city like Belfast or Dublin is a big deal to those out this way."

"Donegal can't be far."

"A couple of hours—if we vary our route back to Galway, it's about halfway."

"What about the rest of the Inishowen Peninsula?"

"I've an idea. What do you say I pick you up early Saturday and we spend the weekend here? There's so much to see that if we try to do it all this afternoon, we'll be rushed. I can even arrange for horseback riding on Sunday morn, if you're up for a ride along the beach?"

"I would love that!"

"Alright then. I'll make all the arrangements."

"You sure that's not too much trouble?"

"Oh, no bother at all. I know people here."

"I bet you do."

He whistled for Sadie. "Then if it's all the same to you, we can take a drive toward Donegal. We'll have dinner there and I'll drive you home afterward."

12

We arrived at the cottage long after dark, having stopped in Donegal for a stroll in the park with Sadie before supper and then another afterward, past rows of quaint Irish shops that no doubt would be crowded with tourists in a few short weeks. It had been the perfect evening. The restaurant was quiet and sparse, yet another reminder the tourists were still weeks away. The food was served in a leisurely fashion the way Irish prefer, affording us ample time to discuss our favorite subject—Irish history—with Sadie curled up beside the table with her food and water dishes. Later, the stroll took us away from the square and along a ridgeline where we could view the clear night skies. I'd never seen so many stars as I had in Ireland and we remained for a long time sitting on a stone wall just picking out those constellations we recognized and enjoying the fresh night air.

By the time we pulled down the drive to the cottage, the lights at Danny's house were dark and other than a few stray twinkles in the village, it was as if the countryside inhabitants had all tucked in for the night. The few lights must be the pub and I wondered how busy they might be. I was just about to ask Shay if he had time for a nightcap when Sadie, who had been sleeping peacefully behind us, began to howl, startling us both.

"What the devil?" Shay exclaimed, stopping the car in its tracks to turn and stare at her.

"She sounds as if she's in pain," I said. I tried to reach her fur to stroke her but she was just out of reach.

"Doesn't she though? It came on suddenly, yeah?"

"When we get to the cottage, can you bring her inside? We can have a look in bright light."

"Grand idea." He reluctantly turned back to the wheel, his brow furrowed in worry. Despite the slow movement over the dirt and gravel road littered with potholes we pulled up just a few minutes later. By that point, she was pacing like a caged animal as she had when they had first arrived.

We both scrambled out of the car. I watched as Shay opened the back door. Sadie dashed past him like a streak of lightning and into the darkness of night. He whistled for her, quickly moving away from the car and peering into the shadows in the direction she'd headed. I could feel the anxiety dripping off him, despite the fact that he was clearly attempting to remain calm.

I opened the opposite door and retrieved the picnic basket.

"I'll see you in," he said a bit absentmindedly.

"Nonsense," I responded. "Go get Sadie. Do you need my help?"

It took him a moment to respond. The night had grown completely silent once again, her howls subsiding shortly after she'd jumped from the car. "I think she ran back down the way we came."

"I think so, too. I'll just put this basket by the door and help you find her."

"No," he said, surprising me. He turned back toward me. "You must be exhausted."

He was right; I was exhausted. Beyond it, really. Despite the fun I'd had, we'd traveled a long way and it had been a marathon day, especially for a writer more accustomed to sitting behind a computer. "But—"

"She's never run off like this before, and she's an old gal. I'll drive back down the drive and whistle for her. She'll come. Surely, she'll come." The last he said with a slight tinge of doubt.

"Then go."

"I'll see you in."

"No. You're wasting time."

He hesitated between me and the car, his eyes still on the drive. Then he turned to me. "You're sure you'll be fine?"

"Of course. Go." As he climbed back into the car, I added, "And thank you for a great day," but I don't think he heard me. He was too focused on turning the car around and heading after Sadie. I watched him roll along the drive, his window down so his whistles sounded like they were reverberating across the hills. Surely, Sadie would hear him.

I returned to the cottage and unlocked the door. Stepping inside, I flipped on the lamp by the door, bathing the front room in creamy light before I stopped cold.

Every cabinet door in the kitchen had been opened and every drawer pulled out.

On impulse, I closed and locked the door behind me. Despite what I was walking into, I felt safer inside the tiny structure than standing outside with no one besides Shay, who had his hands full already, or my curmudgeonly, alcohol-sodden neighbor Danny. My heart was pounding so thickly that I was concerned for a moment I would have a heart attack and I spent the first few seconds or minutes—time seemed otherworldly at that point—trying to calm my heart and my breathing. When I could finally focus without the ragged sound of my breath in my ears, I realized I hadn't moved from barely a foot inside the door.

My cell phone beeped and I jumped, my heart going into overdrive once more. I dug the phone out of my bag, setting the picnic basket I had still been holding onto the nearest counter. It was from Shay: "Sadie was waiting for me at the foot of the drive. She seems fine now. Go figure. Thank you for allowing me to be your tour guide."

I held the phone for a moment and then texted, "The pleasure is all mine. I had a wonderful time. Glad Sadie is okay."

I remained standing just inside the door as my eyes roamed the room. My laptop remained on the table in front of the window, the drapes still open. I stepped toward them on wobbly legs and closed them tightly. From there, I could peer into the bedroom where everything still appeared as it had that morning. I turned back to the kitchen and then I dialed Fergal's number.

He answered on the first ring.

"Someone has ransacked the cottage," I said without introducing myself.

He didn't hesitate. "I'll be there straight away."

I opened the cottage door when I spotted the headlights coming up the drive, the dramatic dips a sure sign Fergal was encountering the potholes at a quick clip. His car door opened almost before the engine was cut off, and true to his word it had taken less than five minutes for him to arrive.

When he entered the cottage and spotted the kitchen, all the color faded from his face. The distinct odor of alcohol permeated his clothing but he hadn't seemed to have been drinking so I chalked it off to his work at the pub.

"Is anything missing?" he asked.

"Nothing."

"You're quite sure about that?"

"I arrived with only one piece of luggage and my computer gear, and none of it appears to have been touched. The flat-screen TV is still there," I pointed out, "but feel free to have a good look around. I'm not familiar with everything you had here."

"I will at that." He left the kitchen for last and began in the bedroom, as if he wanted to start at the furthest corner from those open cabinets. I followed a few feet behind as he opened the closets, checked the windows and even under the bed. "You didn't lock any of the windows before I got here?"

"I didn't touch them. Were they unlocked?"

"On the contrary. Everything's tight, it is." He stepped into the bathroom momentarily and then headed into the living area, where he stopped for a moment to look at the television. "Have you had it on yet?" he asked.

I thought it an odd question given the circumstances but answered, "No. I've been too busy."

He half-nodded before moving to the living area windows to check the locks. "All's tight." He looked at my laptop as if expecting it to speak to him.

"Only the kitchen was... touched," I said.

When he turned to look at it, his face appeared to grow paler still, and it was quite obvious from his nervousness that he did not wish to go near the open cabinets. After a moment, I waltzed toward them. When I reached the first cabinet, all its contents had been strewn over the countertop below it. "Nothing appears to have been opened that I didn't open myself," I said, returning the boxes and cans to the shelves. "Do you have any homeless in these parts?"

"Homeless?" He looked at me as though I was daft. "No," he said. "No homeless. None at all."

"Well, even a family of mice would have been unlikely to push everything out of the cabinets like this. Will you give me a hand here?"

Though he appeared reluctant, he slowly came to my side and gingerly began to return the foodstuff to the other shelves.

"Fox, perhaps?" I asked. "Though I can't imagine how an animal could have gotten in here."

"The door was locked, yes?"

"Yes."

"You were out, I take it?"

"Yes. I—was researching today. I arrived home only a moment before I phoned you."

He nodded. We worked in silence for a few minutes; even the refrigerator and freezer doors were standing open, the contents scattered over the floor. As I picked them up, I noticed the items from the freezer were still frozen, the milk still cold. In fact, the entire cottage had taken on a massive chill. I made my way to the thermostat; it was exactly where I'd left it.

"Heater not working?" he asked anxiously.

"It's on and it's set," I said.

He joined me and poked around it for a moment.

"I can hear it running."

"Do you want a fire?"

I glanced at the fireplace. "I don't think that will be necessary. I'll be going to bed shortly. I'll be fine under the covers."

He stared at me as though I'd lost my mind.

I crossed my arms.

"You can't stay here," he said at last.

"And why not?"

"It's —" He swallowed and looked back at the kitchen, which was still only half organized. "You'd be safer, you would, in the bed and breakfast above the pub. I should have placed you there originally, a woman by yourself—"

"Nonsense. I didn't want a room above a pub. I wanted a cottage in the country, and that's precisely what I rented."

His jaw dropped. "You're not—this doesn't—?"

"Frighten me? No. I'm not easily frightened. Especially when it's Danny trying to run me out."

"Danny!" He placed his hand over his heart. "No, it can't be Danny. You're quite mistaken."

I told him then of our encounter on the hill and his opinion that the cottage should never have been restored.

"What were you doing on the hill?" Fergal asked when I'd finished.

I let out an exasperated sigh. Despite what I'd just told him, it hadn't seemed to register that Danny was the problem. "Taking a stroll," I answered without any attempt to conceal my impatience. "Is the hill off limits to me then? I rented a cottage in the countryside but I'm not allowed to stroll?"

He opened his mouth as if to speak and then closed it. I waited, my arms still crossed. My toe began to tap against the hardware floor.

"It's just that," he started finally, picking his words with care, "the ruins, you know, may not be safe. I would not wish for you to trip and fall up there; I'd feel responsible, I would."

"They were perfectly fine. The ground is level at the ruins."

He worked his mouth silently.

"You'd best tell Danny that his tricks are not scaring me."

"What tricks?"

"The woman crying outside my bedroom window, waking me in the middle of the night."

"What are you saying?" His hand moved from his heart to the table, where he appeared to be trying to steady himself.

"The woman crying. His wife, I suppose? Or a sister perhaps? Sent to spook me in the middle of the night?"

He swallowed hard. "There are no women at Danny's house." His words sounded disconnected and far away. "He's never had a sister and he's never been married. His mam passed on some twenty years ago."

It was my turn to reach for something as the room began to swim. My hands found the back of the sofa. "Then he's put someone else up to it."

"I know everyone Danny knows," he said quietly. "There isn't a woman around that would come around here at night—or in the broad light of day, for that matter."

13

I was not as brave as I hoped Fergal thought me.
I was accustomed to handling conflict, but only
within the pages of my manuscripts. I knew conflict
propelled book plots forward so I was always searching
for them, whether they were between two romantic
partners or political foes. But that's where I preferred
them to remain, where I could mold them into whatever
I needed them to be. I could be both killer and victim,
in control every step of the way. I did not deal particularly
well with drama in my own life, especially when it shows
up uninvited.

I sipped my tea, allowing the warmth to spread
down my throat and banish the chill I felt inside as I
gazed through the window beyond my laptop. It was a
pastoral scene laid out before me, one in welcome
contrast to the night before. On a neighboring hill, cattle
grazed contentedly; Danny's cattle, I realized. Finding
myself searching for him, I discovered him teetering
up from the far side of the hill, his walking stick
steadying him somewhat as he went.

Further into the distance were smaller, rounder pale dots, that of sheep at the end of winter, their thick coats in the final weeks before they were shorn. I picked out an occasional car meandering along isolated roads and when I used a phone app as a monocular, I could make out a parking lot at the edge of the village where rural residents left their vehicles to take the bus transport into more populated towns and cities where employment was more plentiful.

Reluctantly, I rose and made my way into the kitchen where I poured another cup of hot water and steeped my tea before placing a thick slice of sweet Irish breakfast bread onto a china plate. None of the dishes had been broken, which I thought a minor miracle, and none of the food ruined. And yet I had remained awake the remainder of the night, long after Fergal and I had finished tidying the place and he'd left for the pub to help his daughter close its doors for the night.

My thoughts had been so much of a jumble that I'd never crawled into bed. Wrapped within a thick plaid throw, I'd been physically comfortable despite the fact that I felt as if a wrecking ball had taken up residence inside me. I was over three thousand miles from my home in the States, alone in a rural cottage in the middle of a foreign country and someone wanted me to leave.

Oh sure, I could have rented a hotel room. There were high-rise hotels in all the major cities here that rivaled anything in the States with all the modern conveniences and 24-hour security. For that matter, I could have just as easily booked a room at Fergal's bed and breakfast and been only a minute away from the restaurant, the pub and plenty of company. But I hadn't wanted that. I'd wanted to soak up the rural environment as my ancestors had so many centuries before; I wanted to feel the countryside, to smell the unique aroma of budding plants—and yes, even of the livestock. I wanted to witness the sun rising over the hills as it had for millennia, turning fields into glowing green and melting the morning dew. I wanted to stroll the countryside and envision myself in the 17th century, an experience that would be reflected in the pages I wrote.

I was where I wanted to be.

I took a bite of bread as I returned to my seat. The smooth taste of citrus and banana helped to soothe my soul. I really must ask Fergal for the recipe.

I stared at my screen for a moment, the words of the last chapter I'd worked on just a jumble of characters now though in the hours that have since passed, they had taken on the shape and feel and emotion of a war between Britain and Ireland—a conflict still in evidence in the counties of Ulster today. My ancestor had left everything he had known to journey to a land he had never even visited, and I realized just how foreign it all must have felt to him; for if I felt off-center in this age of mobile phones and Wifi, I could only imagine what a tremendous step that had been for him in 1608.

On an impulse, I pivoted away from the window and turned my attention to the cottage. It was perfect for my needs and Fergal had really gone above and beyond to make sure of my comfort. I found myself replaying our conversation of the night before. So Danny lived alone. His mother had passed away two decades prior, and he'd never been married. There were no women in his household, no female relative he could cajole into helping to scare a lone woman out of the cottage. But I wasn't so sure he couldn't have pulled it off with a woman from the village, despite Fergal's insistence otherwise.

But what then? I wondered. What if he'd managed to scare me off the property? What if I'd taken Fergal up on his suggestion to move into the village where I'd be in a proper bed and breakfast with walls shared between myself and other guests? What then? Surely Danny would not have imagined he could frighten away every guest that rented the cottage. I'd leased the place for an entire month but most visitors would stay perhaps a few days or a week. At the end of the year, there would be dozens… Ah, but maybe that was it. Danny didn't want this rural existence to be disrupted by the comings and goings of a bunch of ill-mannered tourists.

Hhmm.

And so there I had it: Danny's motive.

My mobile rang, startling me out of my thoughts. Caller ID identified Michelle, and I eagerly answered it.

"I haven't rung you up too early?" she said.

"Not at all," I answered, checking the time. "I've been up for hours."

"Ah, wish I'd known. I've been waiting till a decent hour."

"What's up?"

"Well," she said conspiratorially, "are you sitting down?"

"I am."

"I was asked yesterday to perform some research on more recent Irish history. You know the Republic's Centennial is coming up, yeah?"

"I hadn't thought about it. I guess I've been too focused on the 17th century." My eyes wandered back to my laptop where O'Doherty's Rebellion had begun to come alive again.

"Okay well, I suppose it really started with the Easter Rising of 1916. You know about that though, yeah?"

"I do. It touched off Ireland's quest for independence."

"Well, only the latest round of it but you're partially right. Ireland's War of Independence—also known as the Anglo-Irish War, took place from 1919 to 1921. Not

that there was peace between 1916 and 1919, mind you;
it was all a period of unrest, to be quite mild about it."

In my mind's eye, I pictured the British barracks
beneath the Crutchley land, where the family would
have had a birds-eye view of the comings and goings of
the British soldiers. "Go on."

"Well, wouldn't you know it, your ancestors were
in the thick of it."

"Seriously?"

"Aye, and not only that but the family was divided—
part fighting for the War of Independence and a free
Ireland, while others fought on the side of the British."

"Are you sure of that?"

"Quite sure. I've some of the records, though I still
have some digging to do, so I'm certain I'll discover
more. So I was wondering, I was, if this was something
that interests you? If you might want to turn this into
another book, perhaps more of your historical series?"

"I hadn't thought about it," I answered hesitantly.
"The book I'm writing now covers only 1608 and
O'Doherty's Rebellion. Then I have the Eleven Years War
of 1641 to 1652, which I somehow need to condense…
Not to mention a third book covering the siege of Derry
in 1688. All of those involved my ancestors and led to
land grants in Ulster."

"Would you consider it if I managed to find out more
details?"

"Yes. Yes, I would."

"Particularly if the family was split in their political
allegiances, I think it would make for an interesting tale.
Brother against brother and all that, you know. Not only
would they have been involved in the War of
Independence but most likely in the Irish Civil War as
well. That started just one year after the War of
Independence ended, you know. Both were quite the

APRIL IN THE BACK OF BEYOND   107

guerrilla wars, particularly the Civil War. One never could be quite sure of the spies among them..."

"Yes," I answered. "You've made a good case for another book."

"Ah, good. That's what I was hoping you'd say. I'll send along the information I've discovered thus far, yeah?"

"Can you email it?"

"Most definitely. Oh," she continued, "I almost forgot. The area where you're staying was a hotbed of activity."

"How so?"

"There were British garrisons and patrols all through the area, participating in the Sinn Fein roundup and of course the Fenians—"

"I've heard of Sinn Fein but not the Fenians."

"Ah, that's a book in itself, it is. The Fenian Brotherhood was a fraternal organization dedicated to a free Ireland. They were quite the force throughout the island and often worked alongside the Irish Republican Brotherhood—or the IRB. It was a time of terror, it was. Anyway, somewhere close to where you're staying are the Crutchley Ruins—"

I sat up straighter at the sound of the name, a chill passing stealthily up my spine despite the warmth of the heater behind me.

"The house was burned to the ground on the order of the IRB," she was saying. "And two brothers—"

"—died in the fire—"

"—were shot—"

"What?"

"What?"

"Did you say the brothers were shot?"

"Aye. They were shot."

"And the house was deliberately burned?"

"On orders of the IRB."

I felt as though I was no longer alone and I pivoted in my chair to peer behind me. The room was just as it had been moments earlier, but I had the sense that someone was listening. I could hear Michelle's voice continuing but I moved the phone away from my ear as I strained to identify the other presence.

"—so if it interests you, I'll see what more I can turn up about it," she was saying.

"Yes, that would be great," I said, turning my attention back to the conversation. "Can you send along what you have on the Crutchley Ruins as well?"

"Consider it done."

We clicked off the conversation and as I laid the phone on the table, I felt as if I was being watched. I stood to look out the window. Danny was walking along the road, leading his cattle to another pasture as his dog bounded around the herd to keep them close. I grabbed for my jacket. It was time I paid the Crutchley graves another visit.

14

The skies had been cloudless and blue when I left the cottage but in the short time it took to ascend the hill to the ruins, in true Irish form, the clouds had rolled in from the ocean and I could hear thunder in the distance. I was curious about the thunder, associating it more with warmer weather than cold. The temperature on the hill had dropped, plummeted really, and despite the layers of clothing I snuggled around me I was shivering so much my teeth were chattering.

The ruins were as I'd remembered them from the first stroll up the hill, but then they wouldn't have changed, would they? I wondered what I'd expected to find here now that I was one step closer to knowing the truth. As my eyes surveyed the remnants of the home, they fell upon stones that had remained blackened despite a hundred years that had transpired between the tragedy and my tentative footsteps across the threshold.

So the sons hadn't perished in the fire. I considered phoning Shay with the news and then realized I'd left in such a hurry that I'd neglected to bring my phone. I peered downhill at the cottage, pondering whether to return and retrieve it, but decided against it because I didn't plan on staying here that long, especially with the chill winds buffeting me. In any event, I would see Shay tomorrow and I could tell him while on the drive to Inishowen.

I found myself striding through the house and back to the gravesites with an air of familiarity. This time around, I knew their names; I could hear them playing through my mind like a mother calling to her sons. April, how tragic, I whispered, my voice barely audible, to have lost your beautiful home to a fire and have both your sons shot on the very same day. As if in response, the bitter wind swept downward, shaking the branches of the tree that stood watch over the remains of the headstones.

As I remained there, the conversation with Michelle replayed in my mind. The fire had been intentionally set. Had the boys been shot as they ran from the flames? Or had the perpetrators waited until the house was empty before they set it afire? I didn't know which was worse, thinking they'd perished in a fire or knowing they had been shot. Either one was a horrific tragedy especially now that I knew it was murder.

Despite the ominous clouds that were blackening the sky, I wandered toward the cliffs. I made a mental note that while I could not see the abandoned British barracks when I was standing at the house, I could once I'd come within sight of the graves. Anyone venturing to the cliffs would also need to pass the gravesite in order to peer downward at the barracks. What side had they been on? I wondered. The logical part of my brain dissected the facts. The land had been granted to the

Crutchley family precisely because of their loyalty to the British monarchy. They must have remained loyal to Britain, I reasoned, or the land ownership could have been revoked at any time and by any monarch. My own ancestors had lost their lands when a Catholic King James had seized their possessions, only to have them restored when a Protestant William ascended to the throne. But nowhere in the census records did it show the Crutchleys had been without this land and all that had been built upon it—until this tragedy.

That would mean, I deduced, that they either remained faithful to Britain during the Easter Rising of 1916 and the subsequent War of Independence... or they were spies. And what would be a better place from which to spy than their own land overlooking those barracks?

I took off at a brisk pace walking parallel to the cliffs. It was perhaps a two hundred foot sheer drop and not even a footpath existed upon which a sure-footed mountain goat could descend, much less me in my city slicker boots. I walked perhaps a full mile on a narrow, overgrown trail, losing sight of the barracks at one point as the path entered a copse. As I followed the trace around the hills, I realized it must have once been a dirt road—perhaps even graveled, as I dislodged stones that had remained covered by encroaching grass and brambles. I lost track of time as I meandered ever closer, holding my hood beneath my chin to keep the stiff winds from blowing it backward. I was nearly to the first shell of a building when the first drops fell upon me and I dashed inside.

I found myself at the far end of a cavernous space that at one time had been divided into as many as a dozen separate rooms, as evidenced by the tracks left in the ceiling and floor tiles. The interior walls had been made of some type of plaster and now several layers of paint were peeling away from them. One long wall was half-covered by thick ivy that also crept across the ceiling, though there was no indication of its source and I marveled at its monstrous growth despite the apparent lack of soil or water. A sudden noise broke the silence and I jumped, laughing nervously when I discovered it was only the rain hammering against the panes.

I stepped to a window of old, imperfect glass and peered out. It was coming down in torrents now so thick I could not view anything that was more than a few inches away.

Birds rustled in a far corner, their nest having been built on a cornice that had pulled away from the ceiling. I stepped further inside, allowing my hood to fall away as I stuffed my hands in my pockets for warmth.

All of the windows remained intact, though some were broken. That in itself was remarkable as I might have thought a nearby resident would have chipped them out and used them in a newer structure despite their imperfections. There was also no graffiti, no telltale signs of teenagers smoking or homeless residents.

I reached the end of the room and stopped at a long narrow hallway. There were signs that a door had once hung there, the screw holes still visible despite the peeling paint. I hesitated and turned for a moment to look behind me at the room I'd just ventured through. Even the ceiling paint was peeling away and in some places, the wood and plaster had dropped onto the floor below, littering the surface with debris. It was still bucketing outside yet now that I had wandered away from the windows, it was eerily silent.

I started down the hall. It was narrower than those I'd grown accustomed to in the States; I could not imagine two men walking side-by-side. I pictured British soldiers moving through this same corridor and wondered as I stopped at each open doorway whether they had once housed offices or sleeping quarters. I must have moved further into the interior because the walls here had not crumbled as they had in the first cavernous room. Each room I passed contained two and sometimes three windows; they were tall, not at all like the narrow windows of centuries past that were built to allow firing but still afforded protection from assault. That meant, I thought, that the British were relatively confident it would not be attacked. I made a mental note to check for a barrier outside the building—the remnants of a wall, perhaps, and a guard gate. I wish I'd thought to bring my phone but perhaps I could return some other time to take photographs.

I reached the end of the corridor where an exterior door had been removed. As I stepped closer, I realized an overhang prevented the rain from entering and I stood for a moment and watched the water run off the eaves and down an embankment. From here I could see the cliffs and perhaps the thinnest slice of greenery atop them but that, I realized, might have been my imagination. In any event, the soldiers stationed here would not have been able to see the Crutchley land. Had they seen the house though? Had the house risen high enough for those on the second floor or in the attic rooms to look down upon the soldiers here?

I thought of the servants in those attic spaces, perhaps with tiny windows that nonetheless would have allowed spies to collect their data—but of what? Guard changes, I thought. Routines. Over time, they might have recorded all their movements. Could that have led to the executions of the two boys?

But here I was, deciding they'd been executed and all I knew was they'd been shot. During the fight for independence, weapons might have been plentiful and either side could have targeted the Crutchleys for a myriad of reasons. Still, I reasoned, the presence of the barracks bordering their land was too much to ignore.

Beside the door was a set of concrete steps with an iron railing. I hesitated for a moment but decided the steps looked sturdy enough; they were concrete, after all. And though there was plenty of rust on the railing, it was intact. A large window on the landing presumably allowed the sunshine or moonlight to illuminate the stairs but now they cast the reflection of the raindrops onto the concrete as if the storm had managed to come inside.

I decided halfway up the flight of stairs that a window provided a false sense of security as if I could leap to safety should someone suddenly appear before me. As soon as the thought crossed my mind, I realized that I was quite certain there would be no living persons here. Instead, I felt surrounded by the dead. It was an odd feeling; one of thick, stifling air that rustled and moved on its own accord amidst sounds I could not identify.

Upstairs was more of the same, though the rooms were larger leading me to believe they might have been sleeping quarters with several soldiers assigned to each room. I discovered holes in the walls that might have been bunks permanently affixed, one atop the other, and wondered when it all had been dismantled. They rather reminded me of cell blocks in a way. But I found the bulk of my curiosity was fixed to the windows and specifically those that were directed toward the Crutchley estate. The second story certainly provided more of a view of the surrounding area but it was still oddly positioned well below the cliffs on a jut of level land, which made me curious about the strategic importance of the barracks. Certainly the land atop the cliff where the Crutchley home had been would have been a far more desirable location; for weren't armies forever searching for the high ground?

But when I turned my attention to the opposite side, I came to the conclusion that they were focused as much on the sea as the land, and I wondered whether it had been built during World War I to protect the island— and thus, western Europe—from a sea assault, a bit like protecting the back door. Yet when I compared it to Carrickabraghy, set high above the cliffs with a commanding view of the ocean, the barracks simply and flatly came up short.

Another set of stairs beckoned me upward and I found myself on the roof of the building. It was still bucketing but an overhang had been erected at each of the four corners as well as the stairwell which might have protected soldiers from the elements while they were on guard duty. From this vantage point, I could clearly see the hill where I'd stood above the cliffs. Perhaps, being down in the bucket as they were, the guards could not have seen the Crutchley house at all. And I couldn't be certain that even from the attic, the Crutchleys or their servants could have viewed the goings-on at the barracks. That would make it less probable that the house was burned to prevent spying from its heights, but I hadn't yet ruled out the possibility.

As my eyes scanned the horizon, I spotted a vehicle making its way down the pockmarked road I'd traveled on foot. I almost missed it; the dark gray color blended almost seamlessly with the sheets of rain and had it remained still, I almost surely would not have seen it. But as I watched, it drew nearer, finally coming to a complete stop outside the barracks and the far door I had entered.

Danny, I thought in a panic. He was there and perhaps intoxicated despite the early hour. He'd warn me away from the barracks and it would be his second such warning to me. I felt the absence of my phone acutely now, admonishing myself with sufficient ire that I should never have left the cottage without it. It might have been my lifeline if things got ugly, had I not left the cottage in such haste.

The car door swung open and I breathed a sigh of relief when I spotted Fergal's shock of silver hair peeking from beneath his Irish cap. He placed his forearm against his forehead as if to channel the rain away from the brim of his cap and peered upward where I was standing. Spotting me, he gestured with a quick wave before disappearing in the direction of the building.

I made my way down the two flights of stairs, an echo returning each step but whether it was from my shoe soles or my heartbeat, I couldn't tell. I was relieved that Danny had not come to threaten me but I didn't know how Fergal could have found me or why he was there.

I was soon to find out.

I discovered him on the first floor, nearly ready to ascend the stairs when I popped down in front of him.

"Ah, and there you'd be," he said. He removed his cap and shook off the rainwater, drenching the debris-laden concrete beneath us. "You have no idea how concerned I've been for you, no idea at all."

"Concern for me?"

"Aye, and for sure. I was worried about you all the night long, didn't get hardly a wink, having second and third thoughts about leaving you out there in the cottage by your lonesome. So this morning as quick as I could after deliveries had been made to the pub, I headed over to the cottage to see how you were getting along."

"I'm fine," I said in an uncomfortably feeble attempt to reassure him.

He continued as if I hadn't spoken. "And there was your car, big as you please, right where it had been last night, but no answer when I knocked. I waited and knocked again, thinking, well, you know, you might have been in the bath or sleeping late... but I could not sweep away my anxiety."

"I'm sorry I worried you."

"So when I discovered the door unlocked, I made my way inside, calling for you. No answer frightened me more than I can say, especially when I spotted your phone sitting on the table there, and you nowhere in sight."

"How did you find me here?" The air had grown colder and I wrapped my arms around myself in a vain attempt to protect me from the chill.

"I made my way to the ruins and the rain had started, and I knew if you were out in the elements I simply had to find you... And I walked to the cliffs, first time I'd been to the cliffs since I was a wee one and I received quite the licks when my parents discovered I'd gone there... And I saw you from the cliffs standing on the roof here."

I placed a hand on his shoulder. "I'm so sorry I worried you. I took another stroll and the sun was shining when I left. I didn't expect to be gone so long but when I spotted these barracks, I decided to check them out."

His face appeared strained. "Are you accustomed to wandering into places where you don't know the history?"

"Well, yes. Actually I am. It's what I do."

He shook his head in disbelief. "Do you know the harm that could have come to you?"

I wrapped my arms more tightly against my torso as the shivering intensified. "No, I don't. Why don't you tell me?"

He opened his mouth as if to speak and then closed it again. I waited and hoped I appeared patient though

I felt anything but. "It's an abandoned building," he said finally. "It's unsafe." He waved his arm in the direction of the debris.

"It's made of concrete and stone."

"Yeah and still, it's been abandoned for nearly a hundred years. And apart from the condition of the building itself, what about wild animals that might have made this their den?"

"Wild animals. And what kind of wild animals do you have here, Fergal? Snakes? Spiders? Wolves?"

He swallowed. "I'm simply relieved you're fine and no harm has come to you."

"Thank you," I said, my voice softer. "I'm glad you came. I wasn't looking forward to walking back to the cottage in this rain."

He turned his attention to a window. "And for sure, I can see why you wouldn't be."

"Can I get a lift from you?"

"Oh, aye. I wouldn't be much of a gentleman to make you walk back when I drove, 'eh?"

I began to make my way through the long hallway. I could feel him behind me and I stopped at the end to look back. He was wandering more slowly, stopping to peer curiously into each room. "Have you never been here before?" I asked.

"No," he said. He didn't look at me when he spoke but continued to stare into one of the rooms for so long that I made my way back to him. Peeking inside, I could only see walls and a ceiling with paint peeling off in strips and a hundred years' worth of dust and dirt on the floor. Blinds had been placed on the windows and now one was lopsided, one end touching the sill while the other end tilted higher. I wondered if the former occupants had left it thus when they vacated and it had remained frozen in time through the decades.

"What do you see?" I asked when he did not move.

"History," he answered simply.

After a long moment, I asked, "Care to share it with me?"

He seemed to come out of his daze then and a mask settled over his features. "Oh, nothing I'm sure." He brushed past me and continued down the hall.

I followed after him. When we reached the cavernous room in which we'd both entered, I said, "But I love history."

He hesitated as though carefully picking his words. "Surely you know that England once occupied this country."

"Yes."

"These barracks were built as World War I was commencing to protect against invasion from the sea."

I waited for him to continue but he removed his cap once more and shook it, his attention riveted to his hands. "And?" I asked.

"And that's the story. Not much of one, is it?" He replaced his cap on his head. "Anyhows, I need to discuss something with you and to ask you for a wee favor."

We made our way to the open doorway where I watched the rain. "A favor of me?"

"Aye, and I do hope you'll accept. You see, I'd like to invite you to give a wee talk to the village folk."

"Oh?" I looked back at him but he had turned his attention to the floor.

"You see, when I returned to the pub after—well, after I assisted you at the cottage—Danny was there and deep into his cups. He'd been spinning tales, he was, and they weren't too kind."

"What kind of tales?"

"Oh, about you."

"What about me?"

He clearly did not wish to elaborate but I continued to press him until he said, "He thinks you're here to write a book about our village. The ruins, the graves, the… British."

"Oh. I see."

"And I stopped his foolishness and I told everyone there in no uncertain terms that you were not writing about us. That is true, isn't it?" He said this last as if he was uncertain himself.

"Yes," I said. "It's true. I am not writing about your village. I'm writing about my ancestor who immigrated to Ulster four hundred years ago, and about O'Doherty's Rebellion."

"And which side would you be taking?"

"Neither side. Or both sides. I'm writing what I hope will be perceived as a balanced telling of the Scots that came to Ulster—my ancestor came from Wigtownshire—and the O'Doherty's, who had laid claim to that same land for a thousand years prior."

"Ah."

"And I take it that you want me to talk to the villagers about my book?"

"Precisely." He looked at me then and forced a smile. "It would allay their… concerns."

"I see. Well, normally I don't give a talk about a book I'm currently writing. I wait until the book has been released, and then I give a talk and sell and sign my books."

"But you've written other books, 'eh?"

"Yes, but I don't have any with me."

"Not a problem; I'll get it sorted. You see, the bookstore in the village can order the books. I just ask that your talk be about why you're here now and what you're researching—outside our village." He waved his hand. "Outside all of this."

"Well, yes. I'd be honored. How long will it take for the store to get the books in?"

"Oh, perhaps a week or two. I'll inquire. But I need for you to give your talk this weekend."

"This weekend? Why so soon?"

He sighed. The rain was subsiding a bit but he didn't make a move to exit the building. "I need to stop the gossip. *You* need to stop the gossip."

"Oh." I fell silent. Then, "I'm leaving tomorrow morning for the Inishowen Peninsula—more research."

"Then you'll be leaving us?"

"Only for the weekend. I'll be back on Sunday. Maybe Sunday evening?"

"Oh, no, it cannot wait for Sunday. Tonight will be fine."

"Tonight?"

"Eight o'clock. Come early and I will have your supper waiting for you—on the house, of course."

"Tonight."

"Eight o'clock." He adjusted his cap and his neck scarf and before I could answer, he'd darted for the car. I stood for a moment, my mind not quite registering that he was standing in the rain while he held the car door open for me. Then with a deep breath, I made a mad dash through the storm for the warmth and safety of his car.

15

The supper dishes had been cleared away long ago and I sat nursing a hot tea while keeping an eye on the front door of the restaurant. I was seated in a quiet corner but then, any place in the room would have been deathly still as I was the only patron. It was nearing the time for me to enter the pub through the hall but no one had come through the restaurant en route to the pub. I suspected Fergal's good intentions had either been met with skepticism, the villagers hadn't received ample notice or they simply had no interest in me.

Fergal's daughter Nora swept into the room from the kitchen and paused at my table. "So how was everything? Good, 'eh?" she asked in her melodious, uplifting voice.

"Excellent," I said. "And more than enough. I can't eat another bite."

"Ah, that's what we like to hear, it is," she said. She brushed long locks of her auburn hair behind her shoulder. "Though we've some cobbler I bet you'd fancy."

"It sounds delightful but no," I said. I patted my stomach. "There's simply no more room."

Her eyes twinkled. "Just making sure, I was."

"I was supposed to talk this evening," I began uncertainly.

"Aye, and so I've heard. Danny was running his yap last evening, and Da said he'd got it all wrong."

"Do people usually listen to what Danny has to say?"

"Oh, here and there," she said in a noncommittal voice as she shrugged her shoulders.

With no one else in the room and Nora's friendly blue eyes twinkling, I asked, "Did I commit a faux pas by visiting the ruins by the cottage?"

Her pleasant smile waned. "It's just that no one goes to the ruins, you see."

"Why is that?" I diverted my attention to my tea.

"Why," she breathed, "because it's haunted."

"Haunted? Have you ever seen anything?"

"Oh, no. Since I was a wee one, my parents would not allow me to go near."

"Why do they keep the property if it's haunted?"

Her silence prompted me to look up to find her chewing on her lip. "You'll have to ask my da," she said. "In any event, it's time for your talk, so it is."

"Yes," I sighed. "But it doesn't appear that anyone is here."

"What are you talking about? The pub's full!"

"It is?"

"It is. They've all been waiting for you to join them!"

"Why didn't you tell me?"

"Because you were enjoying your meal."

I nearly turned the table over as I jumped up. Nora said something as I passed her on the way down the hall, but her words were lost on me. It wasn't until I'd opened the doorway into the pub that the cacophony of voices reached my ears. She had not exaggerated; all the seats were taken and several more were standing near the bar. I recognized Danny at the end of the bar nursing a drink, his back turned to me.

Fergal spotted me and came around from behind the bar, escorting me past everyone and onto the stage where he'd placed a microphone. I pictured live music on this stage, as large as it was in relation to the room, and I suddenly felt lacking. I usually spoke to groups when a new book had been released but never before about my ongoing research because frankly, I never knew where my explorations would lead. As the room came to a hush with a scattered Irish accent here and there, I also became conscious of the fact that I was an American writing about their history and presumably history they'd learned in school.

Fergal did a fine job of introducing me. He'd quite obviously visited my website where nearly every accomplishment was listed and as he spoke, my eyes roamed the audience. Danny had turned around on his barstool. Still nursing his drink, I noticed several men whispering something to him. I wondered if they were out for blood.

With Fergal's introduction coming to a close, the audience politely applauded as I took the microphone. I began by telling them of my father's interest in our ancestry and how it had led me to research several ancestors in the 18th century. The family's information had ended, however, around 1720 when they arrived in America. I had been curious about my heritage and I spoke of how one thing led to another, one person to the next, until I had traced back my ancestry to 1608 Scotland.

When I mentioned my family name, I felt many in the room relax a tad and I surmised it was because it wasn't Crutchley. More seemed to loosen when I mentioned the exact locations of the land that had belonged in the family, reaching from County Donegal to County Tyrone, places well north of here. I then began to pivot the talk to Cahir O'Doherty and O'Doherty's Rebellion, focusing on the research I was doing versus the story itself.

I suppose an hour had passed and perhaps a bit more. The faces were unreadable though one handsome woman nodded with a slight smile. Most of them appeared to be in the shadows as pub lighting tended to be lean and I found myself wishing I'd asked Fergal to turn up the lights a notch. One or two left as I was nearing the end, both men that appeared to have had their fill—of drink or my voice, I wasn't certain.

I finished my talk as I usually did, commenting on how wonderful the group had been and thanking them for their attention and then I opened the floor up to questions, which came fast and furious.

"Why are you here?" a woman asked bluntly. She appeared to be in her 80s, small and stooped with white hair. I must have gaped at her because she continued, "If you're writing about Ulster, why did you come here? We're nowhere near your research."

I glanced at Fergal, who was standing behind the bar now, his palms spread out across the counter as he watched me. "I'm here because I have had historians assisting me from the National University at Galway, and I've been taking advantage of the wealth of information in their library there."

"So you're doing all your research at the library?" a man asked. He said something else but it must have been under his breath. He set his empty glass on the counter and left before he heard my answer.

"I have also been to the Ulster American Folk Park, meeting with a historian there as well and I will be visiting the Inishowen Peninsula during this visit. I'll also be going back and forth to Dublin." I mentioned some key spots I'd already visited such as Burt Castle and Carrickabraghy.

"Are you writing about us?" A man's voice rose above the rest. Before I could manage to respond, the room erupted in a myriad of voices all demanding the same question. I glanced toward the bar where Fergal was attempting to quiet those closest to him, and I caught a glimpse of Nora as she made her way calmly through the raucous crowd, a tray of drinks held high.

When things settled a bit, I managed to say, "I'm focused for the foreseeable future on my own family history, and as far as I know none of them were ever close to this village; I've seen no evidence to suggest otherwise." I should have left it at that, God knows I should have but as the faces stared back at me, I added, "Why? Is there a story here I should write about?"

I don't know if I have ever seen a room filled with people so completely silent. It was as if time had frozen. Fergal stood with his hands planted on the counter once more, his mouth open. Nora stopped in mid-step with the tray balanced above her shoulder. Facial expressions were totally immobile and all eyes had widened. Not a single person moved.

After what seemed like an eternity during which my mind could not manage to process a coherent follow-up sentence, Fergal came to my rescue.

"And that's it for tonight, it is," he said as he swept across the room to pluck the microphone from my hand. "We've some of her books on order and I'll be announcing when they've arrived. I hear they're a grand read." In the back of my mind, I knew he had not a clue whether my books were even readable, and I felt a huge amount of gratitude for his hospitality. "In the meantime," he continued, "I've napkins here should you want an autograph." Nora shoved some bar napkins into his palm and he waved them as he forced a smile.

I did sign a few of the napkins, more than I would have imagined. There was a schoolteacher from the village middle school, several people that wanted to write books that asked how I managed to find a suitable publisher and several more that wanted to tell me stories of their own genealogy. But none of them mentioned the ruins, which had grown from an idle attraction to a mystery within my overactive imagination. By the time I finished listening to an older gentleman discussing his idea for a book on gardening and the secret to growing broccoli, I discovered the pub had largely cleared out and a musician was setting up on the stage behind me for those stalwart few that appeared ready to drink until the pub closed.

I love Irish music and it was a Friday night after all, but I made my way toward the door. I hastily voiced my appreciation to Fergal for the dinner and opportunity, to which he responded, "It's what they needed to hear, it was." I had no idea whether he was speaking of my work or my denial that I was writing about them, but I didn't stick around to find out.

16

I slept fitfully, my mind filled with a jumble of disconnected images and disembodied voices. Every drape in the cottage was pulled tight against the Irish countryside and every lamp was turned on in a futile attempt to shield me from the darkness that seemed so determined to encroach.

Fergal had insisted on following me back, escorting me inside and inspecting for intruders though I felt he was just as concerned about easing his own rising anxiety as my own. The kitchen—in fact, the entire cottage—was just as I'd left it. Even the cabinets that had been yanked over and the contents spilled felt now like just a bad dream.

And perhaps it was the recurring dream that I dreaded. It caused me to toss and turn this way and that throughout the long night, despite the fact that I had fallen into bed physically and emotionally exhausted, and I had but a few hours before Shay would arrive to whisk me off to Inishowen and hopefully to a place that was not haunted.

For I kept hearing Nora's words again and again, "It's haunted…" It became a refrain in my head, interjected with my own words, "Is there a story here I should write about?" when I knew perfectly well there was indeed a story and it was one they most certainly did not want exposed to the light of day. I saw the two boys brought out of the house and shot in my mind's eye and I felt the anguish of their mother until her torment became my own, and then the faces of those in the pub staring back at me at my dangerously naive question.

When I finally drifted into a restless sleep, I dreamt I was analyzing each of the faces in the pub in an attempt to identify the murderers for certainly they lived among the community as the discomfiting faces staring back at me told me they sheltered them still. When I awakened to the sharp light of the bedside lamp, I tried vainly to reassure myself that whatever happened one hundred years ago meant that no one staring back at me the previous evening could possibly have been the killer or killers; all the parties must be long dead.

And yet the events of that fateful day so long ago still plagued this village, and now I was becoming convinced that the victims haunted this very cottage.

When I heard the soft sobs, I realized I had drifted off once more and in my half-awakened state, I thought the cries were connected to my discordant dreams. I lay there with a groan on my lips not quite ready to spill out and wishing I could simply sleep peacefully before it was too late and I would be forced to arise for the long day ahead. I felt the bedcovers slip away from my bare shoulders and I fought to open my eyes.

When they finally did open, I discovered that I was completely uncovered. The bedcovers had been pulled to the foot of the bed and were shivering inches from my feet as they lay heaped into an unkempt triangle about three feet in height. I blinked once and then twice, my mind not grasping what my eyes were witnessing, for surely it must be a trick of the eyes to think the covers were still moving.

It was then that I realized the soft sobs had continued even after I had fully awakened and they were not part and parcel of my overactive dream state but they were real and they were coming from the direction of the blanket.

"You don't understand," came the sound of a woman's voice, wracked with anguished sobs. "They are still here."

"No, sweet darling," returned a weary man's voice that sounded so close I nearly jumped out of my skin. "They are with God now."

"I'm telling you they are not," the woman answered, her weeping growing more tormented. "They've never left. They're still here."

Within the space of a single heartbeat, I saw myself just a few nights ago, convinced the voices came from outside my window. Then I was pulled into the present to fight the horrifying realization that I was sharing my bed with two apparitions.

I slid my feet away from the covers in excruciatingly slow progress, afraid at any moment my movements would alert the phantoms of my presence. I tucked my feet and knees close to my torso as I came to an uneasy seated position, almost fetal in an attempt to occupy as little space as possible. The room was still fully illuminated and as I watched with wide, unblinking eyes, the covers appeared to become wet, the color darkened. I forced myself to glance at the ceiling, wishing the roof had sprung a leak during the night but it was completely dry, as my innermost soul knew it would be. Moreover, the heat came from radiators without blowers and the drapes remained perfectly still; there was no logical reason for the covers to be twitching as they were because there was no draft.

The room had become an icebox despite the radiators and I found myself shivering almost in tandem with the blanket. I had no idea how long I sat there, curled against the headboard and pillows, watching the foot of the bed and listening to the disembodied voices that filled the air. But then something seemed to snap inside me, fully awakening me to the present time and despite my fear, despite my trepidation, I grew impatient with myself. I reached a trembling hand toward the bedcovers, intent on pulling them over me to fight the chill as well as reassure me that they were not wet.

But at the precise moment I felt the dampness under my fingers, the sobbing stopped, replaced by a gasp that was not my own. I yanked the covers to the side, determined to discover what mechanical device lay beneath. The material jerked away from me as though I was engaged in a tug-of-war and the gasp was replaced with a woman's blood-curdling scream and a man's shouts.

I was waiting for Shay when he arrived, my luggage packed and stacked on the stoop outside the door. I was leaving nothing behind despite the fact that I wouldn't need half what I was taking on a mere overnight trip, and I would be expected to return here in less than 48 hours.

I'd spent the remaining wee hours of the morning packing even while my heartbeat raged within me like the drums of a hostile enemy. With the first vestiges of dawn, I threw open the drapes in both rooms, flooding the cottage with sunlight, thankful for a morning that wasn't arriving through a heavy gray mist. Now as the sun's warmth found its way through to me, I tried to convince myself that it had all been a dream even though I knew in my heart of hearts that it was not.

Sadie was not in the car when Shay put my luggage in the rear. "I left her at the base of the prior hill over," he said before I could ask, glancing at my expression. Having arranged the luggage without questioning the volume of it all, he closed the rear door and added, "She started her pacing as soon as we passed that cottage down below you, so I backed up and let her out."

I was silent as he accompanied me to the passenger door, opening it gallantly while I climbed inside. As I waited for him to round the car to the driver's side, I stared back at the carriage house, its recently painted pristine white stone at odds with the events that had begun to terrify me. I could not help but feel as if we were leaving others behind as Shay turned the car around, much as I did when I lived with my parents. It was ludicrous, I knew; and yet, I could have sworn the drapes rustled just so as we pulled away, as though someone was straining to watch us through the bedroom window.

Sadie was waiting where Shay had left her beside the lane, her ears alert and her eyes trained on the direction he'd driven away so we spotted one another as soon as we came round the bend. She hopped in eagerly, her tail wagging and eyes bright. I greeted her warmly as she lay down in her usual spot, her head between us where I could easily scratch behind her ear. But we hadn't driven more than thirty miles from the cottage when Shay pulled off the motorway and into a tiny village much like the one near my rental.

"What's happening?" I asked.

As he parked the car, he said, "We're going in for a cuppa. There's something wrong and I want to know what it is."

"There's nothing wrong," I said, but my voice was so tight that I couldn't even convince myself.

He came around to open my door and Sadie's as well. "Oh, there's something wrong alright. It's like a beacon attached to your head there." He tapped my forehead as I climbed out of the car. "And I aim to find out what's what about it, I do."

We passed a butcher shop and a hardware store before arriving at a quaint café. The businesses were joined together much as townhouses are and yet each sported an entirely separate ambiance. While the butcher shop was three stories tall and brownstone, the hardware store was two stories and painted a cream color. The café appeared to have been recently renovated with broad windows that stretched across the main floor, a modern front door and signage placed on the sidewalk that displayed the day's specials. Despite the early hour, my mouth was watering for Guinness Chocolate Mousse, Soda Bread Pudding and Irish Whiskey Truffles.

A bell jingled on the café door as we walked through and a willowy server behind the counter grabbed a couple of menus and headed toward us. I paused to admire the desserts behind the glass case.

"How are ya, Shay?" the server said as she seated us. "Tea for the two of yous then?"

"Aye, Bella. Thank you. And—"

"Milk for Sadie. I know. And I've a peanut butter cookie for her, too."

"Thank you, dear," Shay answered. I turned at the sound of the endearment, perhaps a bit too quickly. He caught my eye and added, "And I think my friend would like one of your pastries. The lemon curd sponge cake is especially good for breakfast."

"Sounds fabulous," I said, joining him at the table. The server wandered past the teapot and glass case to a room in the back. "You come here often?" I asked.

"Oh, a fair bit," he answered as she returned with a dog dish.

"Royalty always goes first," she said, setting it down in front of Sadie, who began lapping up the milk even while she crumbled the cookie into it. "Eh, girl?"

"Bella," Shay said, "I'd like for you to meet my author friend here."

"Oh, I know who you are," she interrupted. "I've read all your books, I have. I'm quite excited about my brother here showing you the sites. It gives us all a break from his history lessons." She slapped him light-heartedly against the side of his head.

"And meet my sister Bella," he said, trying and failing to dodge her hand.

"Glad to meet you," I said but Bella was already disappearing behind the counter.

She reappeared a moment later with tea and two dessert plates filled with lemon curd cake, which she set before us. "I'll leave you to it then," Bella said. "Call if you need me."

"You've been very silent this morning," Shay said, pouring the tea into our cups. "So tell me what's bothering you."

"I'm fine," I said. "Really I am."

"No. You are not. Did I do something to offend you?"

"No. It's just..." I hesitated. I added cream to my tea and stirred it for a moment.

"Well then?" he prodded. He cocked his head to the side and peered at me quizzically.

"No. You'd just think I'm crazy. I'll be fine once we get further down the road."

"Further from the carriage house, you mean."

"Yes." I avoided his eyes.

"Did something happen to you there? Has someone assaulted you?"

"No. Oh, no. Nothing like that. It's…" I hesitated again. I rather liked Shay and I did not want him to think I'd lost my mind.

"It's what?"

I took a deep breath. "Strange things happen there. You saw how Sadie has acted, almost like there is an invisible line that marks the property's boundary." Once I began talking, the words spilled out. I told him of the encounter with Danny, of the villagers' curiosity about me, and of the ransacked kitchen and the crying I heard every night.

"You should have phoned me," he said when I was finished. "I'd have turned round and come straight away."

"I know you would have, but Sadie needed you—and she didn't need to be brought back onto the property." At the sound of her name, her ears perked up. I reached beside the table to pet her.

"Do you want to move from there?" Shay asked. His voice had become quieter.

"I don't know." As I said the words, I realized how true they were. "It should be the perfect spot for me to write my book—"

"It should be," he said. "But it isn't."

"But it could be."

"But it isn't."

I hadn't realized that Bella had disappeared into the back room until the door jingled as it opened and she reappeared as if on cue. She swapped out our teapot for a fresh one and then focused on the rather large group that tumbled in. From their accents and conversation, they appeared to be Canadian tourists. She winked at us as if sharing a private moment and then quickly moved toward them, leaving Shay and I alone again. I felt Sadie's muzzle against my knee and reached down to stroke her silky fur again.

"The thing is," I said, "I can't get April Crutchley out of my mind. I feel like—well, like there's something I ought to be able to do."

"What can you do for a dead woman?"

"Is she dead?" I asked.

His eyes widened in surprise. "The information I passed on to you said she was born around 1882. So yah, I'd say she's dead."

"In body. But in spirit?"

He leaned back and studied me. "I see what you're getting at."

"It's probably crazy..."

"I don't think so." As I poured us both some fresh tea, he continued, "You know, when a person experiences something traumatic—especially if it's something horrific or violent—there's a belief that it creates what's known as a residual energy imprint."

"I've never heard that term before."

"Well, say you had a large row with somebody and both of you were shouting at one another and emotions ran high. So you leave the room only to come back to it later and the energy of that argument was still in the air. Has that ever happened to you?"

"More than once."

"It's the energy of our words and emotions. The closer the negative experience comes to our souls, the heavier the energy and the longer it takes to dissipate."

"So... you're a professor of psychic research as well as history?"

He chuckled. "Hardly. But the study of historical events also involves the study of the people that were there, does it not? And often knowing the history—a bloody battle, a tragedy, a great love... those emotions tend to remain in what is left behind."

"Which is why so many battlefields are rich with ghost sightings."

"Precisely. So if we kick this up a notch—several notches—imagine if you are a parent and your two cherished sons have been shot on the same day that your beloved home burns to the ground. Could the energy from those two traumas possibly remain for a hundred years?"

I sipped my tea. "I see your point... So it's an energy imprint and not necessarily a ghost? Then—what of the sobs, the voices, conversation? Surely that is more—"

"You're quite right. It would have to be, 'ey? The thing is," he said, his voice becoming more animated, "when I was a young one I knew of a house for sale." He leaned forward so our faces were only a few inches apart. "It stayed on the market for years. Now, that in itself is not unusual for a rural Irish farm and this particular house was out away from the nearest village... Anyway, I heard my parents talking about it and why it was on the market, seeing as how the owners were good friends of my family. And they'd put it on the market because it had quite suddenly become haunted."

"Just out of the blue?"

"Completely. And mind you, these were intelligent people, people of means. Not superstitious at all. But one night the man heard the front door opening and it being just him and his wife and he'd locked the door before he went to bed, why of course he went to see who it was. And as he reached the top step, he looks down below and he sees the front door is open and a woman is standing there in her nightie and she breezes inside and begins looking in each room."

"Who was she?"

"Here's the kicker. He could see straight through her. Oh, he described her to my parents, he did. I was outside the door, just a little tyke, hanging onto every word. Long blond hair cascading over her shoulders and down her back. A bit tan, which is completely out of step for an Irish woman. Willowy and with a presence as if she'd been a model. Dressed in her nightie and one so short he could nearly see her—well, that doesn't matter. What matters," he cleared his throat, "is she returned every night at the same time."

"Oh, my God. What did they do?"

"Well, they contacted the parish priest but no amount of blessings and sage and exorcisms could get rid of her."

"Did she hurt them?"

"No, not one hair on their heads. Oh, they'd find an item or two moved nearly every morning when they came downstairs and the poor missus became so anxious they had no other recourse than to put the house on the market and leave it to someone else to sort."

"Had they researched the home's history?"

"Oh, up and down and all around. There was nothing to suggest that the woman had ever been there. But there's more to the story."

I waited until I realized I'd been holding my breath. "Well, tell me!" I laughed anxiously.

"So they receive a call from the auctioneer—your equivalent to a realtor—and they're sending a couple out to see the house. So the knock on the door comes and my parents' friends are upstairs at the back of the house and I suppose they were taking too long to get to the door. So by the time the husband gets to the landing at the top of the stairs, the front door opens. And as he's looking down, in strolls the woman who'd been haunting the house."

"What?"

"You heard me right. Oh, she wasn't in her nightie. She wore a slicker and as she stepped inside, she closes an umbrella and out pops all that long blond hair they'd been seeing for years. It so unnerved the man that he fainted straight away, fell down the flight of steps."

"Was he killed?"

"Not even hurt. But when he opens his eyes, there's the woman standing over him and his wife is refusing to come off the floor above."

"What the hell?"

"So it turns out, this woman from America, she's been dreaming every night of a lovely home in Ireland. She sees it down to every last detail—the blueprint of each room, the furniture, the lough in the distance and the sheep in the field. She knows the house is made of brownstone and the location of each window and even that the front door is in dire need of paint. She knows the barn is in shambles, the roof is caving in, and she knows the cats have taken over it and even which ones are pregnant. She is the one haunting the house."

"But she's alive?"

"As real and alive as you and I sitting here. And yet every night when she fell asleep, she dreamt of this one place, this one house where she wanted to spend the remainder of her days. And she visualized it so completely, her spirit traveled halfway around the world every night to roam each room."

I wanted to laugh at the tall tale but I was halted by my own experiences at the cottage. I suddenly felt unqualified to determine the difference in an old wives' tale and what could actually have transpired.

"So, as it happens," Shay was continuing, "the woman still lives there to this day."

"The American?"

"Oh, aye. They had no other option than to sell her the house, for she was going to haunt it if they didn't. Her husband passed on maybe ten years ago, but she's still living there, living out her dream."

I leaned back in my chair. I felt my mouth gape open slightly but I couldn't manage to will myself to close it.

"So," he said, "would you like to meet her?"

We both rose at the same time, nearly bumping into one another.

"Bella, can we get—?" Shay began.

Bella shoved a box at him. "—the food to go?" she finished with a knowing smile.

I crammed the cakes into the box, realizing I hadn't taken a bite and every morsel looked scrumptious. Shay beckoned to Sadie and was nearly to the door when I said rather awkwardly, "Um, we haven't paid—?"

"Huh!" Bella said as she walked me to the door. "There's no call for payment." She nodded toward Shay. "He owns this dive in case you didn't know. I only work here." She squeezed my hand. "Take good care of him, will you?" Before I could answer, she had darted off to take the Canadians' orders, leaving me standing in the open doorway with the words still on my lips and a thought-provoking stop to make.

17

I was expecting a uniquely palatial home befitting of a woman's perfect fantasy so I was disappointed when Shay turned the car down a worn rock lane and brought it to a stop in front of a rather plain brownstone house. Oh, it was decent enough; two stories with an archway over the front door and vines climbing up the walls— snake vines is what my grandmother would have called it, since she found a snake in hers one time—but as there were purportedly no snakes in Ireland, I didn't recoil as we approached.

The small front yard was enclosed within a picket fence and was perhaps a dozen steps from the stoop. There was just one window on either side of the door and three on the upper floor. Shay knocked and we waited a respectable length of time before he knocked again.

Still receiving no answer, he tried the knob. It was unlocked and he gestured me inside. "It's fine," he said in response to my puzzled expression. "I've known

Anne since I was just a tyke. Auntie Anne is what I used to call her." As he joined me inside, he called out.

The first thing I was drawn to was the set of stairs that faced the foyer. My eyes followed the steps to the landing on the upper floor and I felt a shiver in my spine as I pictured the man that once lived there staring down at the very spot where I was now to watch the ghost of a woman enter his home.

Shay had disappeared down the hall and I followed after him, the rather ludicrous realization that I might be meeting an astral traveler causing me to purposefully keep him within sight. We entered the kitchen at the back of the house, a room with stone walls and an old-fashioned Stanley inset into what must have once been a substantial fireplace. A stainless steel refrigerator and a matching dishwasher appeared oddly out of place next to granite countertops that blended with the stone and an old country style porcelain sink in need of refinishing. We both peered out the window above the sink at the same time, and Shay said, "Ah. And there she is."

As he made his way from the kitchen through a tiny sitting room to the back door, I took a moment to gaze outside. A stone courtyard stretched from one corner of the house to the opposite end, changing levels with the uneven terrain. A very tall, svelte woman was tending to a raised flower bed filled with early blooming daffodils, the yellow and white colors brilliant against the stone. As Shay joined her, my eyes roamed to a nearby table where three places had been set beneath a centerpiece of crocus in a vivid blue vase.

A teakettle behind me began to whistle and I jumped. As I made my way to the stove to remove it, Shay popped his head inside. "Can you manage to bring that out here?" he called.

"Sure thing," I answered. I grabbed a tea towel to protect my hands against the heat and carried it out.

"Welcome," Anne said when she saw me.

I set the kettle on a table caddy. "I'm—"

"I know who you are," she answered. "I've been expecting you." She gestured toward the table. "Please. Sit."

"But how did you know we were coming?" I asked tentatively as my mind raced through the conversation with Shay and the drive to her home. He hadn't been out of my sight—or earshot—and I knew he hadn't phoned her.

She smiled indulgently and poured us each a cup of tea. If I had been expecting a witch, she seemed rather its opposite, her calm demeanor radiating outward like the love of a tolerant grandmother. "I dreamt of Shay last night," she was saying. Her accent was American with an odd inflection somewhere between Southern society and an Irish lilt. "He was paying me a visit and he'd brought someone for me to meet. Now that you're here, I recognize you from your book covers. It's nice to see someone from America, and an author is icing on the cake." She removed a dome-shaped lid from a plate. "Speaking of which, try this orange spice cake. It's a new recipe."

She set a slice on my plate while I tried to observe her without appearing too obvious. The long flowing hair was just as Shay had described it except for the color, which had turned solid white without a hint of blond or silver. Her eyes were an interesting shade of green that reminded me of sea green bottles, and despite the fact that her paper-thin skin was creased with wrinkles and laugh lines, she was a rare beauty. I could easily envision her with a modeling career.

"So Anne," Shay said, "I've divulged how you came to be here—"

"I see," she said. There was something in her voice that caused me to think she already knew that.

I took a bite of my cake, casting my eyes downward.

"Would you mind indulging us?" Shay pressed. "You tell the story so much more vividly than I."

She remained perfectly still beside me but I still kept my focus on the cake. "How do you like the cake, dear?" she asked.

"It's delicious," I said.

"Good. I made it just this morning. Popped it out of the oven only a short time ago. It should still be warm."

"It is."

She watched me take another bite and then began, "I don't remember when I first began to dream of Ireland." Her voice took on an ethereal tone. "I had never visited here; in fact, I'd never traveled outside of the United States. I'd never known anyone from Ireland, and I knew nothing of its history. Heresy to the two of you, I'm sure." She smiled warmly and then took a dainty sip of tea before piling another piece of cake onto Shay's plate as he finished his first. Instead of eating it though, he and I both had settled back in our chairs, our rapt attention focused on Anne.

"But the dreams persisted," she continued. "Each night I lay my head down on my pillow, I felt as though I was being transported to another place, another time. Initially, the dreams were hazy and I only remembered snatches of them here and there; they were gone by the light of day. In black and white, they were, like an old movie. But eventually they came into sharper focus and began to take on vivid color." She laughed softly, her laughter sounding like the ring of bells. "It was rather like going from Kansas to Oz."

"Was it this house you saw in your dreams?" I had set my fork down on the plate, pulled in by the sound of her hypnotic voice.

"Oh, yes. Without a doubt. But I didn't see it in the present time; I saw it as it used to be."

"Used to be?"

"Did you notice the lane you drove?" she asked, a sad smile forming though her eyes continued to remain perfectly serene.

"The gravel road?"

"Gravel." Her smile was patient. "No, dear; that's rock. During the famine, they put the people to work building roads—women, men and even children of all ages. They sometimes worked only for the meager meal they'd receive that day." Her eyes roamed over the cake and teapot. "But it kept them from starving; some of them, anyway. They dug up rock and boulders from the fields, transported them and broke them up by hand, first into medium-sized chunks and then into the smaller rocks you see there now. Painstaking work; backbreaking. The lane winds on past this house to the next village, a famine village they call it; it's been vacant for well over a hundred years."

She raised her cup of tea to her lips but set it back down without sipping. "This house was once a waystation of sorts, a place where travelers could spend the night and get a meal; whatever was to be had, you understand. Only one or two at a time, mind you; it's a small place, after all…"

"'Tell her how you walked through the rooms each night," Shay prompted, leaning forward.

"You love that part, don't you?" She smiled adoringly, her words revealing a history between them much like a mother and son. "Yes, it became a ritual. I suppose I'd been dreaming of this place for several years. Then I began to open the door and step inside. I moved from room to room, just admiring everything I saw, and I saw so much. It drove me crazy, wondering where this place must be. I explored—in my mind, of course, I wasn't a traveler—whether it might be in the United States or England or even France."

"How did you decide it was Ireland?"

"It was the road, you see. One night I dreamt of the road being built and I saw the lady of the house—this house—come outside with a pitcher of water to give to the poor people breaking their backs on those stones. They beat them together, the stones, you know, to break them up. The implements were rather crude and dull..." She took a deep breath. "So it came to me the next morning that the road had been built for the price of a meal. It took several more years of research before I came upon the Irish famine."

"You didn't know about the famine before you dreamed of this place?" I asked.

She shook her head. "It's not as if they taught Irish history in American schools, and I am not of Irish descent."

I nodded. For myself, I'd been led to explore Irish history through my ancestry but had that ancestry led me instead to France or Russia, I might have easily been writing my next book from the sands of Normandy or the square in St. Petersburg.

Shay's voice brought me back to the present. "Then she started searching homes for sale, didn't you, Anne?"

"I did. I researched county by county until I recognized the area; until I knew the roads and where they led. Don't ask me how I knew; I don't know myself. I applied for a passport for the first time in my life and I talked my husband into coming with me here to this county. Oh, that was back before the Celtic boom and the west of Ireland was wild, wasn't it, Shay?"

"Wild?" he laughed. "No. I was wild."

After a moment, she continued. "The residents here had listed their home for sale but for whatever reason, it hadn't shown up on the websites I searched. But we went into a town about an hour's drive from here and I described exactly what I was looking for. The auctioneer knew the precise house." She waved her hand. "And now I am here." She rose and began gathering up the items from the table. "Help me get everything inside," she said. "A shower is coming."

We'd no sooner settled into the sitting room than the skies opened up, a quick moving shower that would have drenched us had we remained outside. Anne chuckled as she observed my quizzical expression. "I'm not psychic," she laughed. "I broke my ankle a few years ago, and I can feel the barometric pressure change. And when you live in Ireland, you learn to keep one eye on the skies. If it isn't raining, it's going to."

She drew her legs under herself as she settled into her chair and studied me. "I was the most surprised of all when I arrived at this place; nothing like that has ever happened to me before or since. But you're not here to learn about my story. You're here for me to learn about yours."

I found myself repeating the experiences to Anne that I'd told Shay on the drive, ending with the wee hours of the morning when I tried to pull up the bedcovers.

"Has it ever occurred to you," Anne began, her eyes piercing mine, "that in that moment, you were haunting April Crutchley, same as she was haunting you?"

I felt my cheeks lose their color. "No. It hasn't."

"You know, there's a common misconception that our souls exist inside our body."

"I've heard that all my life."

"But that isn't accurate. You see, the body exists inside the soul." She waited for her words to sink in before continuing. "Our souls actually reach out well beyond the physical limitations of our bodies. It's how a mother knows when her child is hurt even when there is physical distance between them, or how a person can still feel the presence of a loved one long after they have

passed away. Physical bodies have finite lifespans, but
they are capable of regeneration in some instances. Did
you know if part of your liver is lost, for instance, it can
regenerate itself?"

"No. I didn't. But what does that have to do—"

"The point is," she continued patiently, "the liver is
part of you and yet there is so much more. If part of the
liver dies, you may not even realize it. The same is true
with the body in relation to the soul. The body is only a
tiny fraction of who you are. It will eventually die. But
the soul continues to live."

I formed my words carefully. "But once April crossed
over to the other side, wouldn't she have been reunited
with her two sons? Wouldn't whatever trauma that
existed for her cease to exist?"

"Yet didn't you say that she felt her boys as she was
crying? It's entirely possible that the woman was so
traumatized by the deaths of her two boys that their
souls remained with her, perhaps in a valiant but futile
attempt to comfort her. When she died, they—and she—
chose to remain with one another on this physical plane.
The trauma might have been so deep for each of them
that they feel bound to those lifetimes. It seems to me
the only recourse is to discover what actually happened
to her boys, the rest of her family, and April herself.
Perhaps then you can determine how to set her free."

"Set her free?"

"Dear, haven't you been listening? April Crutchley
never crossed over to the other side. She is still here,
living in the carriage house you are temporarily renting.
She may not have known of your presence until the
bedcovers she had gathered around herself were pulled
away from her. Whether her boys are still on this plane
as well is yet to be determined."

I sat silently, no longer hearing Anne's words, trying
to grasp the meaning of all that she was saying. I found

myself interrupting her, blurting, "How is all of this even possible?"

"I asked myself the same question once upon a time. I suggest you read works by Albert Einstein and Stephen Hawking. They can explain it far better than I ever could."

"But where do I even begin?"

"With time. Time warping, parallel universes, residual imprints." She hesitated. "Or you could simply begin by discovering what happened to April Crutchley and her two sons."

"And just how does she go about doing that?" Shay asked. He'd been silent through much of the conversation and now the sound of his voice brought me back from this other universe I'd felt myself pulled into.

"Records. It happened in 1919, you say? That was during the War for Independence. Many people on both sides were killed during that period; it was known as 'The Time of Terror'. There are lists, none of them considered complete, but I would begin there."

I told them of my friend Michelle and her discoveries. "She would be a good one to help us research," I concluded.

"She would indeed," Shay said. "Newspapers as well; many of them have been placed online."

"From 1919?"

"Oh yes. The Irish cherish their history—or some of us do."

"Do you know James Macpherson?" Anne asked Shay.

"The famous historian? I've traveled in the same circles as he—or I did at one time. He disappeared some time ago."

Anne chuckled. "No, he's still where he's always been but he doesn't receive many visitors. He's up in years now and suffering from ill health. But we've stayed in close touch, he and I; we met many years ago at a social not far from here. I can ring him if you'd like? See if he's up to chatting with you? I rather think he'd enjoy this challenge."

"You know," Shay said as we drove down the famine road away from Anne's home, "We don't have to do this. We can beg off and continue on to Inishowen."

"I feel like I'm being pulled in two directions," I admitted. "I'm here to continue my research of the O'Doherty Rebellion, and I know I need to do that. I'm on a deadline with the publisher, and…" I interrupted myself. "But I can't get April Crutchley out of my head. It's as if she's taken up residency there and…"

He reached for my hand and squeezed it. "Then we'll pop into Mr. Macpherson's place; he sounded like he was eager to see us."

"That was very nice of Anne to phone him."

"You'll find many people here that are willing to help an author with her writing — or with her mysteries."

"You sure this isn't putting us too far behind?"

He shook his head. "I'll phone the B&B and let them know we're running a tad later than expected. If need be, perhaps we can spend another night on the Peninsula, just to make sure you've seen all the sites you've needed to."

"You can do that? Don't you have work on Monday?"

"Don't you worry about that. I can make arrangements if it comes to it. This is historical research, after all." He smiled.

I relaxed into my seat but stole a look at Shay. His eyes were focused on the road, one stray lock of hair across his forehead. It was next to impossible to find someone willing to change plans on a dime like this, and yet it's often the way of life for a researcher and author. But as we settled into the short drive ahead, it occurred to me that we both were cut from the same cloth, albeit on separate continents. We were each avid historians, researchers and authors. I stole a peek at his hands on the steering wheel; there was no ring and no telltale sign there had ever been one. I was being silly, of course. I cleared my throat and looked out the window at the passing scenery.

James Macpherson's home was not far from Anne's and as it turned out it was on a northward route which placed us closer to the Inishowen Peninsula. An energetic, fleshy woman greeted us at the door who turned out to be his nurse. "Don't keep him long," she stated as she let us in.

"Don't listen to her," came a gravelly voice. As the nurse turned to glare behind her, Mr. Macpherson rolled his wheelchair into the foyer. "I haven't had a visitor in quite some time. Agnes, have Siobhan bring us some tea and biscuits."

"We've been stopping for tea all morning," I said, stepping forward to shake his hand. "We'll only be staying a few minutes at most."

"Then have Siobhan bring me some Jameson's," he directed.

"It's not yet noon—" Agnes began.

"What are you, a clock?" He retorted. He waved us into the front room as Agnes made a puffing sound and disappeared down the hallway. The room was dimly lit

and it took a moment for my eyes to adjust. The
wallpaper was dark, perhaps burgundy but I couldn't
quite tell in the muted light. The drapes were pulled
tight and the room had a chill to it. My eyes roamed to
the fireplace where the embers were cold and a bit of
draft emanated from it as if the damper had been left
open. "Hand me that throw," Mr. Macpherson said,
gesturing toward the overstuffed sofa.

As I handed him the heavy plaid throw, he arranged
it over his legs and tucked it neatly into the chair sides.
"Mr. Macpherson—"

"Mac," he corrected. "Everyone calls me Mac."

"Yes, sir." I felt as though I was in the presence of a
very important man and the nickname wasn't coming
readily to my lips. He didn't wait for me to continue
but settled with a wheeze in front of an ancient-looking
desktop, switching it on and bathing the room in its
blue glow. It was then that I noticed the wall-to-wall
bookshelves so overladen with books that volumes had
been placed horizontally atop the rows and stacks were
arranged haphazardly on the floor, leaving only narrow
passageways in which to move.

"Pull up a chair there," he said, nodding.

A young woman of perhaps twenty made her way
into the room, balancing a tray atop a pile of books on
the coffee table. She began to pour whiskey into a glass
but Shay held out his hand to stop her before she poured
two more glasses.

"Over here, Siobhan," Mac said. She stepped
forward and handed him the glass. "Don't leave just
yet." He downed the whiskey and handed her back the
glass. "More."

As she poured a second glass for Mac, Shay moved
stacks of books from the chairs to the tabletop, carefully
balancing them so they wouldn't topple. As I scooted in
close to the computer, Mac said, "So now, Anne tells

me you're interested in a specific set of names, young men that died in 1919? Just so happens, I've been compiling a list for years. It isn't completed—far from it, and chances are, it will never be—but we'll see what we can find."

He opened a spreadsheet listing names in alphabetical order. "You were looking for Crenley?"

"Crutchley," I corrected. I spelled it as I watched him scroll downward.

"Leave the whole damn bottle," he said as Siobhan began to remove the tray.

"How many names are on this list?" I asked as Siobhan set the bottle beside the computer.

"Oh, a thousand give or take a few." He scrounged around on the tabletop until he found a pair of lenses. "There, that's better," he said, perching them onto the end of a bulbous nose. "Not all are Irish, mind you," he continued, peering over the top of the lenses at me. "This column here indicates their group. Those in light orange represent the RIC—Royal Irish Constabulary—the Black and Tans and other troops loyal to the British. And these here in light green were IRB, Sinn Fein, the Dail—a variety of similar groups fighting for independence. The blue entries were Irish civilians. But it can't be completely accurate, you see, because some who were listed as civilians might very well have been operating underground, unaffiliated openly with any group. Ah, here we are."

He stopped scrolling. "Were these the two gents you were searching for? Crutchley, Elliot. Crutchley, Spencer. Both shot to death on the evening of April 3, 1919."

"How are they categorized?" Shay asked.

"Ah. They're red."

"What does that mean?" I asked.

"They were civilians but loyal to Britain."

"What does that mean exactly?"

"It means," Shay said, his voice taking on the excitement of the discovery, "in the War for Independence, the Crutchley family were Loyalists—loyal to Britain and the British monarchy. In contrast, the Republicans were those that wanted Ireland to become a Republic."

"You must understand," Mac added, "this was a guerrilla war. There were no front lines. There were no battles. It was sometimes brother against brother and often neighbor against neighbor. This county where the Crutchley men were killed was overwhelmingly Catholic. I'd wager the Crutchleys were Protestant—not that it guaranteed their loyalty to Britain, as some Protestants were as fiercely loyal to Irish independence as any Catholic. But they would have been most definitely in the minority."

"Their home overlooked British barracks that had been built during the First World War to fend off an attack from the sea."

"Ah. Then the barracks would have continued in use until Ireland was granted its independence." He poured himself a more generous amount of Jameson's than Siobhan had. "That should have provided them with some security."

"Obviously, it didn't," Shay interjected quietly.

"Does it say where they were killed? Maybe they were some distance away, even in another county—"

"Place of death is listed as Crutchley Manor. I'd venture that's their home."

"There's no sign there now," I said. "I'm renting a carriage house on the same property that now belongs to the Cassidy family."

Mac scrolled horizontally through several columns and came to rest on one. "Ah. They were shot on orders of the IRB."

"Why?" I breathed.

He shrugged. "I list the facts—names, dates, categorizations. I don't know the why of things at all." He studied my face for a moment and his expression softened. When he spoke, his voice took on a kinder tone. "But if I had it to guess, I'd say it was simply because they were British sympathizers surrounded by Irish Republicans. There is one more thing," he added as an afterthought, tapping his chin, "in that area, it's highly likely that Michael Collins himself ordered the killings. I hope you find this information helpful to your research."

Helpful, I thought. Helpful seemed like such a positive word, one that would be used to gather information for good. Instead, I felt a sinking in my soul as though I was heading down a dark tunnel, and the more I learned of the deaths of Spencer and Elliot Crutchley, the more disturbing it became.

18

Despite our prior detours, we arrived at the bed and breakfast shortly after noon. The earlier clouds had flown swiftly past, leaving a crystal blue sky behind and sunbeams that reached through the car's windows to warm us. On our previous excursion to Carrickabraghy Castle, we'd been driving from Burt Castle so we'd taken the northern route and on our departure the skies had been growing dark. This time round, we took the southern route, eventually turning onto a dirt road sprinkled with gravel.

"Is this another famine road?" I asked.

"Oh, not at all," Shay said. Sadie's head popped up from where she'd been sleeping peacefully to peer out the window. As though she recognized the area, she sat up and began wagging her tail. "In this part of Ireland," Shay continued, "they did not suffer the effects of the famine as they did elsewhere."

"Why was that?"

"Well, and I'm sure you know much about the famine with your writing, so stop me if you know this already?" I nodded my consent. "The famine did not occur due to lack of food. It occurred because the vast majority of the food that was grown here was shipped by the wealthy landowners to Britain."

"But the potato blight?" I asked.

"Oh, there was the blight and all, no doubt about it. But even so, there would have been enough potatoes not affected to have fed the entire Irish population. But when Ireland was a colony of Britain, they were regarded as their 'breadbasket' where crops and livestock were raised for the benefit of the Brits. The landowners were largely Brits or Scots with contracts to sell their crops outside the country. So in countless situations, the Irish who worked the fields were sent home hungry while the food they gathered was shipped elsewhere."

"That's inhumane!"

"Don't I know it, 'ey? There's rarely an old Irish family that exists today whose ancestors did not suffer. A good many families were entirely wiped out. It was the lucky ones that managed to leave the isle for America, Canada, Australia…" He turned off the road onto a narrower lane.

"And what about this area? You were saying they weren't affected?"

"Not so much, no. This area was not under the heavy thumb of the English. The terrain here is wilder and the people here tended to themselves, much as the Scots-Irish did that immigrated to the Appalachians in America. Though they suffered from the same potato blight here as in the rest of the isle, the decent crops were not exported and they had the livestock as well." He drove through a small forest, emerging into a clearing.

The Atlantic Ocean stretched out before us, her endless waves reflecting the clear blue sky. A distance from shore, a pod of whales breached the water, their spouts acting as geysers as they sprayed out the ocean water in unison. I rolled my window down and took a deep, cleansing breath of the salty air and listened to the seagulls and dolphins, their caws and cries carrying across the distance.

As we came to a stop, I reluctantly dragged my attention from the pastoral scene to lay eyes on another one: a group of tiny stone cottages clustered between a group of shade trees and the ocean cliffs. The first two were absent their roofs, the stone still arranged neatly up opposite sides to form an inverted 'v' where the roof would have begun, the interiors so barren that I could see the ocean straight through their windows. At least two more had been renovated with slate roofs and fresh flower gardens adorning their walks. Cascading pansies poured out of flower boxes set into deep window recesses and filmy curtains inside gave the appearance of cozy, well-kept homes.

As we stepped out of the car and stretched our legs, Sadie bounded off, barking excitedly.

"Ah, and there you'd be!" exclaimed an ample woman with a round face. She approached us with a quick step but stopped to pet Sadie as the dog excitedly descended upon her. "And there's my darlin' Sadie. I've some treats for you, I have!"

A door opened and closed just beyond the two finished homes and I realized several more cottages were dotted beneath the trees. A man soon joined us, the resemblance between him and Shay so remarkable I could not overlook it.

"My mam," he said as Shay met his mother and planted a kiss on her cheek. "And my da," he said, briefly hugging the older man.

"Call me Maurie," the woman said, giving me a solid hug.

"Eoghan," the man said. "Spelled in the Irish tradition, pronounced as the American 'Owen'." His eyes sparkled as if he was secretly laughing, and I immediately got the impression he was in a perpetual state of happiness. "Have you luggage then?" he asked, turning his attention to Shay.

"Aye, in the boot. I'll get it sorted later."

"You'll do no such thing. I'll get it in for you while you twos go with your mam. She's baked up enough for a navy, she has."

"I'll help you then."

"You will not. Enjoy being a guest for a change, or I'll put you to work and you'll have no time to enjoy…" he glanced my way "…your weekend."

Maurie wrapped her arm through mine. "This cottage will be for you and Shay," she said, quickly adding, "It's been made into two separate suites so I'm afraid you'll need to go outside to one another's door."

"And she'll be watching," Eoghan called over his shoulder.

"Da!" Shay exclaimed in mock indignation.

"It isn't much," Maurie was saying, "Just a bedroom and bath on either side. There's a teapot in each as well as a fireplace. And the water is clear enough to drink straight from the tap."

"They've been modernized," Shay said, stepping ahead of us to open the door to a separate, larger cottage.

I stepped inside to discover an open floor plan with smooth stone flooring and a combination living area, dining and kitchen. The windows appeared recently replaced with large plate glass that afforded gorgeous views of the water, nearly seamlessly marrying the inside with the outdoors. The aroma of herb-crusted chicken reached my nostrils, and until that moment I hadn't realized how hungry I'd become for something other than biscuits and cake.

"My parents have a year round home across the lough from here," Shay said as he pulled out a chair for me at the table. "My cousin married into the Doherty family and when she and her husband passed on, my parents bought the set of cottages here. They'd been used as fishing lodges for decades, but my da and mam are setting them up now as guest cottages."

"What a beautiful idea," I sighed. "I may never want to go back home!"

Maurie's eyes met Shay's over my head before he moved to a chair opposite me and she hurried into the kitchen.

"Can I help?" I asked, ready to pop back up.

"You can," she answered. "There's a kettle on the table there, if you wouldn't mind pouring the tea."

As I began to pour, she returned with a whole roasted chicken surrounded by potatoes, onions and carrots. "I normally don't have a big lunch like this," she said, "but I didn't know your plans and thought you might be out at suppertime."

Eoghan joined us. "Twas easy to see who owned what," he said, "and I've set the luggage just inside each door."

An hour later, we were still chatting. Eoghan was a born storyteller, and it was easy to see where Shay had inherited his love of history. His father made the Inishowen Peninsula come alive in my mind, and I was excited to learn that the cottage where I would be staying had been standing in that location during the time of the O'Doherty Rebellion, though it had been modernized many times over. Today with the present renovation, it sported solar panels. A wind farm just off the coast also helped to ensure that each cottage was completely self-sufficient.

I was also interested to learn that their cousin had married a Doherty—the same family as the O'Doherty's but through the generations at least one branch had dropped the 'O'. Some said it was to Anglicize it as they settled under British occupation. Others claimed it was a byproduct of the Irish custom of naming children after older relatives; after a time, there could be dozens of men with the same name. Modifying the last name made it easier for the postman to properly recognize to whom the mail was addressed.

Shay slapped his knee. "I'd love to sit and visit all afternoon, Mam, but we need to go if we're to see the sites."

Reluctantly, I rose. Despite the research that loomed ahead, I was thoroughly enjoying our visit. "Can I help you with the dishes?"

Maurie waved me away. "No. You're a guest, and Shay is right. I understand you're writing a book about these parts and will need to see many of the ruins and settings. You haven't much time before the sun sets, so go." She reached to the counter and grabbed a basket. "There's food aplenty so you're all set."

Shay accepted the basket and kissed his mother on the cheek. "Thanks, Mam."

His father had already moved to the open doorway where he was peering out. "You'll have the devil of a time finding Sadie. She's run off with the pack, so it seems."

"She always does, 'ey?"

Eoghan stepped aside to let us pass. "She knows her way home, and we'll be waiting for her. Oh, Shay, before you take your leave, will you help me carry that furniture into the barn there? I'm keen to refinish it."

I took the basket from Shay and watched as the two men hauled a dresser from the side yard into the barn. "Thank you so much for everything," I said as Maurie joined me.

"It's my pleasure, it is." She studied me for a moment with sharp blue eyes. "Be kind to my son, 'eh?"

"Of course I will. You know, you're the second person today that asked me to treat him well."

"Ah, you must've seen my Nora."

"Yes," I laughed. "As a matter of fact, I did." Then I grew serious. "But Shay doesn't appear fragile to me."

"Looks can be deceiving, dear. I don't suppose he's told you he was widowed last year?"

My breath sucked in involuntarily. "No, he didn't." I peered in the direction of the barn but the men had disappeared within.

"No, well, he wouldn't."

"Do you mind—?"

"Don't mind telling you at all. It was cancer. Ovarian cancer and by the time they found it, she had only months to live. Shay took leave from the university and cared for her himself every day until she was gone."

"I'm so sorry."

"We all are, dear. You know, he gave Sadie to her their first Christmas together. Ever since she passed, the dog's been inseparable from Shay. I believe she's gone through her own mourning, she has."

The men emerged from the barn laughing, and I joined Shay at the car as Eoghan rejoined Maurie. "Aren't you concerned about leaving Sadie to roam?" I asked as Shay placed the basket behind the front seat.

"Not here. Mam and Da have several dogs of their own, and she's always excited to find them."

"I didn't see any when we approached?"

"No, I suppose you wouldn't in midday. They'll be down at the water's edge. They play all the day and then come home for their supper."

"And you're not worried about anything happening to them?" I pressed, trying to imagine this happening in America and coming up short.

"Anywhere else, oh sure. But not here." He opened my door and waved me inside with a flourish. As we pulled away, I glanced into the side mirror. I caught a glimpse of Eoghan returning to the barn, and I could have sworn that Maurie was dabbing at her eyes as she watched us drive away.

19

Buncrana Castle was an imposing sight, the sort of structure I could envision in the first chapter of a horror novel in which an unwitting child is brought to live with distant relatives after the death of her parents, only to discover strange occurrences and family secrets. It was a stone structure with stark architectural lines, a rectangle filled with soulless windows that appeared to watch us as we crept past before crossing the Castle Bridge, a narrow stone structure with six commanding arches. The lane eventually led us to the original Buncrana, for it was the original that I was interested in.

"Ah, and there it is," Shay said as he came to a stop in front of a much smaller structure. "I see they've done some work on it."

"What kind of work?" I asked as we both got out of the car and made our way toward it.

"I'd read the O'Doherty descendants are restoring the keep." As we drew closer, he continued, "The original was built in the 14ᵗʰ century; two stories, I believe it was. An O'Doherty expanded it to three stories in 1602 — "

"—six years before my book takes place," I finished excitedly. I snapped some photographs. It was a narrow building with an insufficient number of windows for its advantageous position on the banks of the River Crana.

"In 1608, there would have been a stone wall around the keep for additional protection," Shay was saying, "but I understand when the Vaughn family built the second Buncrana Castle, the one we just passed, they used the stone from the wall here. Frankly, I'm surprised they didn't tear the whole lot of it down."

"We're all fortunate they didn't," I said. "Perhaps if the O'Doherty family is restoring it, they can bring the keep back to its original glory."

"It would have been a glory it hasn't seen in over four hundred years. After Cahir attacked and burned Derry, English forces burned the castle, all but what you see here. Arthur Chichester, the English Lord Deputy, inherited almost all of the Inishowen Peninsula after the Rebellion was put down. He already had a home in Dublin and thought this part of Ireland completely wild—which in an Englishman's eyes, I suppose it was. So he leased Buncrana to the Vaughns. It was Henry Vaughn that built the newer Buncrana Castle—oh, in 1718 or thereabouts."

We stepped inside the structure but with the roof gone, it was like standing in an open courtyard, very much like the Crutchley house had been. The similarities struck me; how both dwellings had been burned to the ground nearly three hundred years apart but during the same seemingly endless struggle between Great Britain and her smaller, more defenseless neighbor to her west. I wondered if people had been killed here as well, either from the burning or shot in retaliation for Derry. How such a magnificent emerald island could have such a sad and discordant history was enough to overwhelm me.

"We'll have to return once the restoration is complete," Shay said as he picked his way through brambles. "It's not much to see, but it would have been here that Cahir and his men planned their escape to the south across the Lough Swilly."

"I can picture it now," I said, strolling toward the water. "They left during the night, hoping to reach the Gallowglass MacSweeneys. From there, they rallied all of Ulster and parts well south of here in what they thought would be the final war for independence. Cahir was everything they needed; he was learned, he was charismatic, he was a leader. They had faith he would lead them to victory."

"As it turned out, he would become known as the last Gaelic king in all of Ireland." He sighed. "It's a battle still fought in Ulster—which is why," he turned toward me, "as I recall, you chose to stay in the Republic."

"Silly of me, wasn't it? I would have been so much closer had I stayed here. But being a woman traveling alone..."

"I understand. I might have been the same way. Be grateful you didn't book a hotel in Derry; they've had quite a bit of rioting there of late, and I understand at least one fatality."

"It's crazy, isn't it? Here it is the 21st century and a part of Ireland is still trying to gain its independence from England."

"Aye," Shay said with a wink and a smile. "And it's your ancestors that supported the British occupation."

"Like I said, it's crazy. Were my ancestors on the wrong side?"

"Ah. The answer depends upon who you ask."

We walked for a while along the river bank as I marveled at the Castle Bridge and its six arches. "How old is the bridge?"

"It was built in 1718, I believe. It most definitely was not in existence when Cahir was escaping."

"That's why he and his men rowed up the lough," I mused aloud. "Otherwise, they would have ridden his horses across that bridge and to safety."

"It wasn't far from the other side of the lough where your ancestor would have been staying with Captain Stewart."

"I must see it."

"Tomorrow, on our way back?"

I nodded. "What's next?"

"What's next…" He rubbed his beard thoughtfully. "I suppose it's a scenic drive around the peninsula. I can show you where and how the people lived during the time of the rebellion, and we can picnic along the shore if you'd like? I read this morning the Northern Lights are expected to make a display and if the skies are clear, we can see them from Carrickabraghy Castle."

If only I had the power to control time. I would have slowed down each moment to stretch it out forever. I would have frozen Shay's expressions at one time or another, just to study those green eyes and how they darkened at some times and lightened at others. I would record his voice as he explained so much of Ireland to me. The consummate historian, his voice was both soft and strong, rising with the telling of swordfights and passionate politics, the sadness of the years when Gaelic culture was outlawed by the British, and ultimately of the enduring optimism of the Irish soul.

I could listen to him forever as the rest of the world slipped away and there was only the two of us caught between parallel worlds where knights protected the castles and fair maidens awaited their return. I could feel Mary Preston's presence as though she was waiting still for her husband Cahir to return to her, pacing the floors in towers at each O'Doherty castle we visited, looking out upon the same vistas as I was doing now, some four hundred years later.

We had returned to the northwestern Carrickabraghy Castle just as the final vestiges of daylight struggled to remain, spreading out our picnic supper in the waning warmth of plush green grass. Maurie had provided enough food for several meals but with our conversation still as mesmerizing as it had been hours earlier, we barely ate. We did, however, make a serious dent in a bottle of viognier from a County Cork vineyard.

Now the basket was sitting idly on the grass, neatly repacked, our picnic blanket draped over it as we dangled our legs from the shortest of the castle walls and watched the sun set over the Atlantic Ocean and the westernmost outcroppings of ancient volcanic rock. It was a sunset like no other as if the skies were descending upon us, the clouds that swept in from the ocean growing ever closer as the entire sky appeared to turn red-orange before morphing into a brilliant shade of cherry and finally into the color of brick that grasped vainly at the horizon as if wishing to remain before being whisked away from us.

As the night descended, the warmth receded and I shivered involuntarily.

"Are you cold then?" Shay asked.

"I feel like a weenie with you sitting there in your short sleeves."

He laughed, the sound emanating from deep inside his chest. "Nonsense. I'm accustomed to it." He hopped down from the wall and I expected him to turn back to help me down but instead he was off like a shot to the picnic basket, returning with the blanket and the bottle of wine. He handed the bottle to me but set the blanket off to the side and scrambled back onto the wall, the toes of his shoes catching the minutest crag of each stone as his fingers fumbled for those that were higher.

As he settled into his seat beside me, I felt the blanket being draped about my shoulders before he pulled me toward his chest. "Is that better?" he asked, his arms tightening about me.

"Much better," I answered. I eased the bottle to my other side, finding a flat stone upon which to perch it. I wanted the warmth of the alcohol to heat my insides but I did not wish to break the spell that had descended over us.

Shay placed his chin gently atop my head. "Look there!" he whispered in awe, pointing toward the horizon. With the final vestiges of light, a whale breached the water, its entire body propelled out of the ocean as if the waves had expunged nothing more than a feather before it twisted and whistled.

"It sounds like a woman singing," I said in awe, my voice hushed as though the whale could hear me.

"That it does. In fact, many a whale's whistle has been mistaken for the song of the selkies and sirens." He sighed, his breath tickling my hair. "As a lad, we came here throughout the year to visit my cousins. I was always drawn to this castle as though I'd lived here before, centuries ago. I always managed to find a way to escape from the others and come here alone where I would spend hour after hour simply watching the waves and the skies. We're only a bit of a walk from the B&B, you know."

"I didn't know. I feel a bit directionally challenged."

"Ah, I won't allow you to get lost. Fact is, I can find my way back in the dark through that forest. Truth is I often did."

"What were you thinking when you were here?"

"Oh, I suppose it depended upon what was happening in my life at the time. It was always as though the waves could carry my troubles far out to sea or bring hope in the form of white-frothed caps landing at my feet."

With the sunset becoming only a distant memory, the darkness was soon replaced with countless stars twinkling down upon us. It might have been only a few minutes or an hour that passed before the skies changed from deep blue to ribbons of spectacular green and neon pink, for time no longer mattered as the rest of the world faded into oblivion. The ribbons danced and pulsed as though they were alive, a vibrant ballet of the skies that twirled and dipped, bowed and soared.

"I came here not too long ago," Shay said after a long moment of silence, "when I thought I could no longer..." he paused "...move forward."

I touched his knee as it rested beside me, trying to find the right words in which to respond.

"There is something soothing here," he continued, "that convinces a man that he can move on. He will find the courage to take that next step, no matter how small it may be and one step will lead to another and then another until the path that laid behind fades away." His voice was barely a whisper carried on the light breeze. "Then there is nothing left but the stairway to the stars."

Somewhere behind us an owl hooted followed by a long, forlorn howl.

"Wolves?" I asked, peering behind us into the dark.

"Not to worry. Wolves have been extinct on the island for more than two hundred years." He followed my concerned gaze, narrowing his eyes as if to see better as he peered at the forest and the rugged hills beyond. "It's a dog; perhaps a hybrid. In Cahir's time when this castle was at its finest, they would have heard both wolves and dog-wolves... I wish I lived then."

"Despite the wars and political upheavals?"

"Aye. Even despite all that. I wager I'd have been quite content living here when all of this—" he waved his hand as if attempting to find the right words "—wasn't in ruins."

A chill wind carried on the mounting waves and instinctively, I settled more firmly against Shay for warmth as he strengthened his arm around me. It felt so peculiar to be nestled against him like this, and yet strangely so familiar. I'd been attracted to him from the start, though I thought it had more to do with our shared fascination with Irish history than romantic stirrings. Though I knew from researching his professional credentials that we were about the same age, he having graduated from the university a year before me, I'd assumed he'd be married with a cluster of young children, two and a half cars in the garage, a cat and a dog. Well, he had the dog.

I felt his chin moving across my head, his beard tickling my scalp. I turned slightly toward him and his lips brushed against my forehead. "Warm enough?" he asked. His voice was a hoarse whisper, the voice of a man awakening next to me on a lazy summer morning.

"I must have very thin blood," I chuckled. I tilted my head upward to look into his eyes. "I don't know if I will ever be warm enough."

He was only an inch away, his face illuminated by the colors surging across the night skies. I wanted to reach up and run my fingers across his beard. As my eyes wandered across his face, I met his eyes. He was watching me curiously.

"The Northern Lights are reflected in your eyes," he whispered.

I remained silent, my hand finding its way from beneath the blanket, my fingers reaching out to touch his beard. It was soft. Silky. I watched my fingertips gently rolling over his face. His lips were slightly parted; my eyes lingered there for a moment before returning to his eyes. They were mesmerizing, made greener by the Northern Lights.

He leaned down and I instinctively tilted upward to meet him. His lips were soft, gentle. And yet as his arms encircled me, I knew this was a man who knew what he wanted. I closed my eyes and allowed myself to surrender to him. I felt wanted, desired, for the first time since before my wedding, the wedding that never happened.

I don't know how long we remained embraced in one another's arms. I only know that the chill evaporated, replaced by a warmth that surged through my body. Eventually, we pulled reluctantly apart, turning our attention to the ocean once more. We remained there with surges of passion and occasional intermissions, the roiling waves reflecting the northern lights until it was impossible to determine where the water ended and the skies began.

In the shadows of the castle ruins, I felt like Mary Preston herself, imagining her peering out her bedroom window onto this same vista, perhaps after making love to the man she adored. I wished Shay could take my hand and lead me indoors to a castle in its prime, lay me down and make passionate love to me while the Northern Lights illuminated our bed through the open windows. As we remained there in a weightless abandon, I felt the whitecaps whisking away my troubles until they vanished on the dark side of the horizon.

20

When Shay pulled the car to a stop in front of our cottage a few hours later, four Irish setters bounded around us, barking excitedly.

"Sadie's brother," Shay explained as I stroked a setter slightly darker than Sadie's mahogany. "Name's Paddy, for the saint." A more heavyset setter with a white face and more ginger color muscled in. "That's Teresa, their mam. And this here," he added, stroking another heavyset setter with dark coloring and a white face, "is the da, Frances."

"Paddy, Teresa and Frances?" I laughed. "All saints? What happened with Sadie?"

He chuckled but there was a tinge of sadness in his voice as he replied. "My parents didn't name her."

The door to his parents' cottage opened as Eoghan popped his head outside. Seeing that we had returned, he waved and then discreetly closed the door but not before all four dogs bounded inside.

"He didn't have to leave," I protested weakly.

"It's their telly time," Shay said. "Besides, he wouldn't be knowing if we want company, now would he?" He hauled the basket out of the car. "I need to return what's left from our picnic."

"Would you—?" I hesitated, glancing at the door of my room.

"I'll walk you to the door, of course," he said, apparently mistaking my question. Surprisingly, the door was unlocked and the room key lay atop the dresser visible from the door. The lamp was on and the fire lit, my luggage set neatly beside the dresser. Before I could speak, he said, "There's no crime here, virtually none at all. Your things are safe left in the room, locked door or no."

I stepped inside.

"See if everything is good for you, then?" he asked, remaining on the stoop.

"Everything looks great."

When I turned around, he'd taken a tentative step inside. "Ah then," he said, "I'll leave you to it. There's hot water in the facility for your bath; just turn on the water heater beside the sink and it'll be hot in an instant. I see Da started a fire; it'll keep you warm through the night. And if you should need anything, just text or phone me up. It doesn't matter what time of night it is."

"Thank you." I returned to the door. "Everything looks great; it really does."

"You know," he said, his voice growing quieter, "you don't have to return to the carriage house at all. You can stay right here for as long as you'd like, and write your book without the specter of the Crutchleys interrupting."

"It's very tempting."

"You'd be a stone's throw away from all the sites you're writing about."

"You make a compelling argument."

"Think about it, will you then?"

"I will. And thank you for a perfect day."

"No," he said. "Thank you." He held onto the basket a bit awkwardly and I found myself reaching for it. I closed my fingers around his for the briefest of moments before taking the basket from him and setting it just inside the door.

"It may require refrigeration," he said quietly.

"If it lasts that long," I said.

"Oh, it can last as long as you'd like it to."

"Are we still talking about the picnic basket?"

The most subtle of smiles crept across his lips.

"How did you say I should turn on the heater for hot water again?" I asked.

"I'll show you, if I may."

"Please do."

As he entered the cottage, I closed the door behind him. Despite his assurances, I quietly locked it. When I turned around, he'd already entered the bath and was reaching upward to point to the water heater. "It's this switch right here," he said as I joined him.

I moved up behind him and slipped my arms around him. He smelled of the fresh ocean air at Carrickabraghy. I closed my eyes and rested my head against his back. After a moment, I felt his hands upon mine, gently moving them away from him as he turned to face me before placing them back around his waist. I found myself now with my head resting against his chest. I could smell the salty air upon him and could feel the grains of ocean salt on my skin. My clothing felt oddly clammy now that we were inside with the warmth of the fire, and my hair weighted down from the Irish mists.

"Would you like me to show you how quickly the water heats?" he whispered.

I turned my face upward, my eyes meeting his. "I'd love that."

Without taking his eyes off me, he switched the heater on. "By the time you're undressed, the water will be hot," he said, his voice husky.

"Prove it."

He smiled again and his eyes took on a mischievous glint as he unbuttoned the top button on my blouse. I watched his face as he moved downward, my cheeks becoming warm as his grew flushed. Before the last one was unbuttoned, I'd begun to return the favor, revealing a strong chest lightly covered in light brown hair. As he unsnapped my bra and it fell away, I pressed against him, allowing the soft chest hair to tickle my skin.

His lips found mine as his fingers moved to my jeans and mine moved to his. Stepping out of our shoes and socks, we found the bathroom beginning to fog as he turned on the shower and beckoned me inside, leaving our clothing in a combined heap on the bathroom floor.

The warmth of the water cascaded around us as he joined me. We moved under the water and I closed my eyes, envisioning us beneath a pristine waterfall as our kisses grew more passionate and the seconds turned into minutes. When he eventually pulled away, it was to sit in a molded shower seat in the corner while he tore open a packet of soap.

I adjusted the showerhead so the water would spray directly on us and then I straddled him on the seat.

If anyone had told me only one week ago that a handsome man would lather every inch of me while I had my way with him, I would not have believed it. And yet it happened... again and again. There was something so incredibly sensual about the combination of a massage with soft, silky bubbles and the rough texture of his fingertips that drove me to complete ecstasy... And that was before we even made it to the bed.

Now the fire was dying down, the room encased in a soft glow as he lay on his back and I curled around him. I felt as though I was seeing the room for the first time, the energy in the air changed into something that caressed my soul. My eyes rolled lazily over my surroundings as I began to drift off to sleep, my lids heavy and my heart light. It was half the size of the carriage house; where the former consisted of a large living-dining-kitchen in addition to the bedroom and bath, this was only the bedroom and bath. Still, it was a large room with walls of freshly whitewashed stone, soft white bedding with the faintest pattern of periwinkles, an overstuffed chair in one corner and a straight-back in another, the small dresser and a miniscule wardrobe... And this one had an incredible man beside me, his arm wrapped around me, his fingers leisurely caressing my skin.

Staying here was tempting. My fatigued mind began to rally against me, thoughts better left for the light of day insisting on disturbing my rest. I found myself measuring the two cottages in my mind. This one was smaller than the carriage house yes, but perhaps I could make do. I would ask on Sunday whether there was a small table I might borrow, as the dresser would be completely inappropriate for my laptop and I would strain my back trying to write in bed. It didn't have a kitchen and I felt a pang of guilt considering the food Fergal had laid in, and wondered how I would manage here in that respect.

I was finally winning the battle over my mind, my body succumbing to the comfortable, warm bed and Shay's body next to mine when he spoke. He'd been quiet for a long time and I'd thought him asleep, but now he said in a voice rough with drowsiness, "I know what it feels like to have planned out your life only to have it all taken away."

I wanted to murmur a reply but I was halfway between wakefulness and slumber, and sleep was winning out.

I dreamed I was moving from my parents' home to an estate that resembled the newer, imposing Buncrana Castle but was situated above the cliffs overlooking the abandoned British barracks below, only the barracks were not deserted. They were bustling with activity as strange vehicles pulled up while others pulled away; Lancias, my subconscious whispered, from the year 1919, the Italian trucks outfitted in the back with open pens of a sort but instead of livestock, they carried British soldiers well protected behind the slats of wood and armor, their rifles at the ready.

Some of the soldiers were dressed in black jackets and tan pants, the colors more vibrant in my dream than reality probably permitted, as if the universe was telling me the Black and Tans were the most feared of the British forces because they were often no more than thugs and killers roaming the Irish countryside. In contrast, sharply dressed and disciplined Brits in proper uniform also arrived and departed in the same type of Italian vehicles, creating a constant stream of activity.

I found myself on the second floor of the manor house then, as if magically transported from the British barracks back to the house. I held a child in my arms; a tiny girl born prematurely, her copper locks curling about her pale cherub face. I was a young woman, appearing to be no more than 19 years of age, a tiny slip of a woman barely over five feet tall and perhaps weighing all of ninety pounds.

A young man entered the room with narrow shoulders and lanky physique and as he joined me to pull back the baby blanket and plant a kiss on his daughter's forehead I noticed he had a kind face with large, compassionate eyes and a ready smile. I knew instantly that he was a good man, a charitable man, even-tempered and loving.

Then I was standing at the window alone and the room had changed. I was watching two young men herd cattle home from the fields with the help of a couple of sharp border collies while a young woman, herself now 19, emerged from the house to call out to them. Her bright copper hair made her identity unmistakable: the prematurely born baby had grown into a woman.

I felt my heart swell with pride. This was my home; I wanted nothing more than for the fields of green to beckon me every day for the rest of my life. I wanted to plan more flower gardens around the house, adding to the elaborate ones I already had. It was spring and the butterflies were flitting, the birds were singing and the sun was shining.

Then clouds began to descend, blocking out the sun. A dark energy slipped over the fields, the gardens and the house. Candles in the room were snuffed out though no one was near. I felt as though I could not catch my breath as panic rose within my chest and thumped against my mind. Everything I loved was being destroyed, everything I lived for was going away, and my life would be changed forever…

I awoke with a start. It took me a moment to realize where I was. Sometime during the night, Shay had rolled onto his side, his broad back facing me, his measured breathing alerting me to his slumber.

The room had grown chilly and I rose on shaky legs and padded over to the fireplace where I stoked the peat. It was much warmer by the fire and I sat cross-legged in front of it, staring into the flames while I sought to fully awaken. Even here, April Crutchley was reaching out to me. Even here, she struggled to have her voice heard, her story told. I felt broken as though my soul had been ripped from me and I fought off tears that threatened to overwhelm me. And yet I knew they were not my tears but hers; it had been April as a young woman that journeyed to a manor house far from her childhood home. It had been April that had married the thin young man with the kind eyes. It had been her daughter she'd held in her arms and she'd watched from the window nearly two decades later.

The Crutchley home had been her home, and I had to find out why the shadows had descended upon it.

Eventually, even the fire was not enough to warm me and I found myself back in bed, pulling the layers of bedding around me to stave off the chill. As I curled against Shay's back, he stirred, rolling around to wrap his arms around me. I waited for his eyes to open, but they didn't; he was still asleep as I should be. My body wanted to sleep, needed to sleep, but I found myself opening my weighty lids time and again to assure myself of safe surroundings. Finally, as I drifted off to slumber once more, I saw myself on the roof of the British barracks, studying the terrain that surrounded me. As though I could see through the eyes of a bird, I simultaneously spotted Fergal standing atop the cliffs staring back at me. And yet I knew as sleep finally overcame me that when I'd been at the barracks I hadn't been able to see him at all.

21

I arrived at the breakfast table before Shay, which surprised me as I'd slept late and sometime in the wee hours of the morning, he had slipped out of my room. By the time I'd fully awakened, I thought I'd surely kept him waiting. I found Maurie at the Stanley, an impressively large stove and oven upon which she was busily cooking. If I hadn't been hungry before, I was ravished simply by smelling the rashers and sausages. Eoghan had been sitting at the table but he rose when I entered, setting his newspaper on the sideboard behind him and hurrying to fetch me a cup of hot tea.

"Shay's out back," he said, nodding his head toward the window as he poured my tea.

I glanced out the window as I settled into my seat, spotting Shay surrounded by the four dogs as he set bowls down in front of them.

"All of 'em love that lad dearly," Eoghan was saying as he watched Shay over my shoulder. "A dog can see through to a man's soul, you know."

"And how did you sleep last night?" Maurie asked, turning halfway around with a spatula in her hand. "Well, I hope?"

I hesitated for a moment; wondering if they knew Shay and I had been together, I suddenly felt like a teenager. "Oh, yes," I said finally. "Like a baby. The room is very comfortable."

"Ah, good, good," Maurie answered, turning back to the stove. "It's what we love to hear, it is."

"And how did the research go yesterday?" Eoghan asked, returning to his seat across from me. "Did you see everything you needed to?"

"Even more. I'm thrilled with everything; I had no idea that so many of these buildings still remained—"

"—more or less," he interjected with a broad smile.

"Yes. More or less," I agreed. I sipped my tea. "Still, it was surreal to stand in the very spots I've been writing about, especially Carrickabraghy Castle—"

"Carrickabraghy, you say?" Eoghan's brows shot up.

"Yes; it was Cahir O'Doherty's—"

"Oh, I'm quite well acquainted with it, I am."

"Of course. You grew up here."

"It's just that I'm surprised he brought you there."

"Eoghan." Maurie's voice was stern though she kept her back to us.

Puzzled, I said, "It was part of my research."

"Still, I don't believe he's ventured there since she passed—"

"Eoghan!" Maurie turned around, her eyes alit. "That's quite enough." Turning to me, she added, her voice softening, "Fetch me the platter on the sideboard there, please."

I retrieved the platter and held it as she loaded it with eggs, blood pudding, sausages, rashers and potatoes. "My goodness, this all looks delicious."

"It should keep the hunger away till late in the day."

I placed the platter in the center of the table and returned to my seat. I heard the front door softly open and close.

"Shay tells us you might be staying with us a wee bit longer," Maurie said as she shut off the stove dials.

"I would love to," I said, "but I'm not sure I've finished at the place I've been staying." I felt the heat rising in my cheeks as Shay entered the room.

"Good morning," Shay said. He met my eyes and smiled. He kissed his mother on the cheek on his way to the teapot and lingered beside me for a moment, his hand caressing my hair as he planted a soft kiss on my cheek.

"Well," Maurie said, her eyes sharp, "should you change your mind any cottage is free till the end of the month."

"We've a larger one for you," Eoghan said, watching Shay over his teacup as his son sat down beside him. "One with a desk for your writing."

"Oh."

Maurie joined us at the table. "It's just that we thought since it was only the one night, you'd like to be closer to Shay in case…"

As her voice faded, Eoghan finished, "in case the fairies overtook you during the night."

"Oh, stop it," Maurie said, batting at him as he ducked beyond her reach. "That's all superstition, it is."

"The fairies?" I watched as Maurie loaded my plate and Shay passed his. "Do tell."

"Woodland fairies. They usually do no harm but sometimes they get a wee mischievous—"

"Will you stop it now?" Maurie admonished. "You'll scare the poor girl and she'll never visit us again."

"Did you sleep well, fairies notwithstanding?" Shay asked with a playful grin.

"I did, thank you. Like a babe in the arms of an angel."

"Hopefully not a hairy, scary angel."

"Oh, hairy not scary," I murmured, hoping my words were audible only to him. "It's a lovely room," I said louder as I avoided Shay's eyes and glanced around the kitchen. "And a lovely place."

"Mam and Da have put a lot of work into it, they have. And how's the season looking for you?" he added, gazing at his parents.

"This will be our best yet," Eoghan said proudly as he puffed out his chest a bit. "Starting the first of May, we're booked solid through September, we are."

"Really?" I asked.

"Aye, it's true. We've hired on a couple 'o gals from the village, we have. Cleaning the rooms and running errands and such."

"Eoghan is turning one of the cottages into a dining hall," Maurie added. "We might need to carry the cooked food to it, as we haven't had a commercial kitchen installed there just yet."

"I've still to get it sorted," Eoghan said.

I watched him spread a hefty slice of soda bread with orange marmalade. "Do the Irish eat like this every day?"

"Oh, no," Shay chuckled.

"In the old days," Maurie said, "we were lucky to get a quarter o' this. Times were tough then."

"But not as bad as our ancestors had it," Eoghan said. "If they'd had rashers and sausages once a year, they'd be lucky and it would be on Christmas Day, it would."

"I heard that my whole life," Shay said. "I grew up hearing of the famines."

"You know Mary Margaret from down the way told me they hardly mention it in the schools these days?" Maurie said indignantly.

"If they attend my classes, they hear of it for sure," Shay said. Turning back to me, he said, "I heard you when I came in, you weren't certain you'd stay here where you'd be closer to your research?"

I kept my attention on my plate, wishing to avoid his eyes as I answered. "I haven't decided yet. There are still a few things I'd like to attend to at the other place. No offense."

"None taken," Eoghan said.

"Remember the offer stands, dear," Maurie added. "But only through the end of April, as we're booked solid May through—"

"—September," Eoghan finished. "I'm sure she heard us the first time."

I glanced at Shay, who had fallen silent. He was busy with his sausages, eating like a man that was ravished. I wanted to stay; I truly did. And I wanted him to remain as well, though I knew he surely had obligations back at the university. And yet I couldn't manage to get the words out that would make the commitment, even though I knew all it would take on the other end was a phone call to Fergal. I'd paid in advance for the entire month and I wouldn't expect any of it to be returned. I had a hefty advance from the publisher and I hadn't spent much of it at all. No; there was something else, something calling to me across the miles, beckoning me back there as if April herself was pleading with me to return.

22

There was an ever-present mist in the air, carried from the deep blue ocean set before us and deposited upon us like the softest of hands. I breathed in deeply, realizing that here in Ireland where the air is still unspoiled I could breathe the air I was meant to breathe. The temperature was perfect; perhaps it might have been a tad chilly but I'd remedied that by burying my head against Shay's back to feel his warmth spreading through to me. There was also warmth from the horse beneath us as we made a leisurely sprint across the wet sands at the ocean's edge.

It had been years since I'd ridden a horse, too many to remember so Shay had suggested we ride together. He was confident atop the tall mare as if he belonged there, blending into it as one and I blending into them both. The horse was dappled brown against a stark white canvass, a stout horse I could easily envision pulling a wagon in days gone by. She had a wide back that we settled into easily and as the minutes ticked by, I became more relaxed and confident atop her.

"Carrickabraghy," Shay said, pointing up ahead. I peered over his shoulder at the castle in the distance, magnificent even in ruins as the morning sun glinted off its ancient stone walls. He pulled the horse to a stop and half-turned so I could hear him better. "Your ancestor would have visited the castle from the settlement of William Stewart by coming up that lough there—the Lough Swilly. The coastline is too jagged for a large ship to pull to shore so he would have anchored off shore there and taken a rowboat the rest of the way."

I peered to the west and tried to envision the ship anchored off the shore. The sun was gaining in strength, its rays glinting off the ocean waves. A pod of dolphins broke the surface, laughing like a group of children. Seagulls soared above them, occasionally diving into the water to snare a fish. I watched as one brought a fish nearly as large as itself to a group of rocks just off shore. The black rock appeared to come alive and I gasped.

Shay followed my gaze. "Seals," he said, smiling.

"You grew up here?" I asked in awe.

He nodded. "Beautiful, isn't it?"

"It's stunning. I never want to leave."

"You don't have to."

I remained silent, my eyes riveted to the ocean wildlife but my thoughts wandering to a continent hundreds of miles away. Could I truly stay? I had an apartment in Massachusetts, but truth be told I'd sold or donated most of my possessions when I was planning a life in Dublin with my husband… a husband that never materialized. We'd decided moving furniture and belongings would be costlier than renting a furnished place and starting over. Since he'd stood me up at the altar, I'd been forced to start over on my own—but could

I do it now—leave it all behind, move to Ireland and truly begin again?

The horse began to move again, this time at a relaxing walk and I realized Shay was still pointing out things my ancestor would have seen or done on his journey to visit Cahir O'Doherty at Carrickabraghy Castle. I raised my face upward to feel the sun upon it and took a deep breath, settling in to listen to Shay's distinctive brogue and wishing this moment would last forever.

The day, like the one before, had flown past in the blink of an eye no matter how much I longed to hold onto it. I had to admit the best way to see Ireland, particularly for the type of research I required, was with an expert in history, and none could have been better than Shay. He not only knew where I should go and what I should see even when I didn't, but he also had the distinct advantage of having grown up a stone's throw from most of the places we visited. Ireland was, after all, only a bit larger than the state of West Virginia so I would imagine he'd had ample opportunity either in his personal or professional life to have visited every site on the island, and he clearly relished the opportunity to play tour guide.

By mid-afternoon, we arrived at Fort Stewart—or rather, the former site of it where my ancestor would have arrived some four hundred years earlier. The original fort was burned to the ground in the Irish uprising of 1641, a conflict that other ancestors had fought in, increasing their land holdings when the British emerged victorious once again. Though I didn't have the pleasure of seeing the castle where they would have stayed—and possibly help build—it was awe-inspiring nonetheless. I took countless photographs though I doubted I would need them, as the terrain and the vistas felt imprinted on my consciousness. Ireland has a way of seeping into one's bones so I felt as though I was part and parcel of her.

We finished our tour at Ramelton not far from the Lough Swilly and a bit further southwest from the original castle. Stewart had formed the village in the 1600s at a time when my ancestor would have been traveling back and forth from his own lands granted to him by King James I after helping to quash the rebellion of 1608. Frankly, it hadn't appeared to have changed much at all, which I loved. The stone bridge over the River Lennon had stood since the days of knights and horses and I felt transported back in time as if I had stepped through a time portal. We'd long since traded the horse for Shay's automobile but I wished now we were still on horseback.

"The village," Shay was saying as we parked the car and set off on foot to explore, "was the setting of the mini-series *The Hanging Gale*. Have you seen it?"

"No; what's it about?"

"The Great Famine. You might want to see it. Two brothers—Joe and Stephen McGann—were researching their Irish ancestry just as you are doing now, and they decided on the idea of *The Hanging Gale* based on information they uncovered."

"So it's a true story?"

"Inspired by one. Kindred spirits, you are."

"*The Hanging Gale*," I whispered the name, committing it to memory.

"Aye. You see, during the time of the famine, tenant farmers were allowed six months' delayed rent, which was due when the crops were harvested; the process was referred to as a 'hanging gale'. Of course during the famine, the crops were ruined and tenants were put out, their homes burned or razed so they could not come back." His voice faded for a moment before he continued, "Anyway, there's a lot of action in the series. I think you'd like it."

"It sounds very interesting. Yes, I'll see if I can find it. Tell me—were your ancestors put out?"

"Everyone in Ireland is related to ancestors that were either put out or did the putting out," he said. "All of this would have been O'Donnell land." As he changed the subject, he stopped us at a corner and nodded to our surroundings. "They, like Cahir O'Doherty, would have had numerous castles erected at strategic points to protect from invasion."

"If the O'Donnell's owned it, how did my ancestor come to live here with Captain Stewart?"

"Ah, the English. They don't much care if the land belongs to another when they colonize, now do they?"

"You mean they simply took it?"

"Not without a fight, I'll tell you that. Many a fight, come to think of it and those in Ulster are still fighting it to this day… Before breakfast, my Da told me about a Catholic church that was burned during the night."

"Last night?"

"Aye."

"Where?"

"Just over the border. You see, though it's been more than 400 years, the Irish are still trying to rid themselves of their English conquerors. Northern Ireland might just be England's last colony."

"Truly?"

"England currently has fourteen overseas territories—those outside of England, Scotland and Wales—but they are all remnants of territories that are self-governing, no longer considered part of the United

Kingdom. India, for example, or Canada, Australia, Hong Kong—even the United States. Only Northern Ireland is still governed by London. Only here does the war go on with the Brits believing anyone that isn't British is a class beneath them, often subhuman."

"Do you think Northern Ireland will ever be united with the Republic of Ireland?"

"In my lifetime?"

I nodded.

"That's anyone's guess, I'm afraid."

"What about you? What do you think is right?"

We reached the edge of a cemetery and wandered inside, finding a stone bench under an ancient shade tree. As I admired the Celtic crosses from this vantage point, Shay answered, "You consider yourself an American, aye?"

"Well, yes."

"And you said your ancestors arrived on American soil in—what, 1720?"

"Thereabouts."

"Mine came here 300 years prior to your ancestors arriving in America."

"The fifteenth century?"

He nodded. "Am I Irish? Most definitely. My birth certificate, my passport and 600 years of Irish-born ancestry says I'm Irish. But to the Irish? I'm Gallowglass, a heritage of Vikings and Scots and many an Irish maiden. So when you ask about Ireland reuniting, you'll find high passions on both sides of the aisle. The Irish want it back and the English out of their affairs. The Scots and the Brits want it to remain part of the United Kingdom. The Scots and the Brits of Northern Ireland say they've been here for 400 to 600 years or more and Ulster is their country, too—just as you, with your Scot-Irish heritage, claim the United States as your country."

"Why was Ulster broken away from the rest of Ireland?"

"There was a vote. Most of the counties—County Donegal included, which includes the Inishowen Peninsula and here, where your ancestor once lived—voted to form the Republic of Ireland. Six counties had more Protestant voters than Catholic, though I suspect a fair amount of voter suppression, and they were primarily of Scot and Brit descent. You see, only landowners could vote and Catholics were banned from land ownership until very recently. So the Scots and Brits, overwhelmingly Protestant, voted to remain part of the United Kingdom. They were afraid, you see, of the Pope ruling here. So those six counties—Ulster—were divided from the Republic."

"And this all took place in 1919, 1920?"

"It wouldn't be until 1922 when the Republic was officially established, though the vote occurred in 1918. It was nasty business and many an Irishman was furious at Michael Collins for signing away the rights of Ulster."

"Michael Collins—the same one we were told about yesterday, who likely knew about the Crutchley murders?"

"Likely knew about it, 'ey? He might have ordered it. In the War for Independence from 1919 to 1921, the Irish were fighting the English. After the signing and the war with Britain were over, another war began: a guerrilla war, our Irish Civil War. It lasted from 1922 to 1923. That war fell apart when Collins was killed—by Irishmen opposed to dividing the island into two separate countries."

"So Michael Collins agreed to let Ulster remain with Britain?"

"He did, and that's what caused his own death at the hands of Irishmen. He said it was a start just to stop the violence and be permitted to form the Republic of Ireland. But half the country—thereabouts—was furious. So it launched a war. In 'Camp A', shall we say, you had those that wanted a complete break with Britain to regain control of all of Ireland. In 'Camp B', you had those willing to sacrifice Ulster for the good of the rest of the country."

"But if Michael Collins was an Irishman and the Crutchleys had lived in Ireland for 300 years by the time of the Republic, what would have caused the order to murder the boys?"

"I suppose that's what we need to find out, 'ey? Their murders occurred in 1919 at the start of the War for Independence. The Crutchley family was originally British—"

"—and most likely loyal to Britain. Yes, I've been round and round with that."

"Possibly. But they could have been spies for either side. They could have been aiding and abetting the Brits, making them traitors to the Irish cause. Or if they supported the Irish, they would have been traitors to Britain."

"But if they were loyal to the Irish, Michael Collins would not have ordered their murders."

"No."

"I want to know what occurred, why it transpired, and what happened to April Crutchley afterward. No— I *need* to know."

Shay stood and pulled me to my feet. Our eyes locked; in his, I saw longing. "Are you truly determined to return to the carriage house?" His voice was unexpectedly sad, though he smiled gently.

"I would be lying if I said I was not conflicted," I answered. "Remaining on Inishowen is so tempting... for a variety of reasons."

His smile broadened.

"But first," I continued, "I feel this pressing need to return to the Crutchley estate. I don't know why; I wish I did. But something—someone—is pulling me back there."

"And afterward?"

"Afterward?" I repeated.

"After you take care of whatever it is you need to do there—what then?"

I rested my head against his chest. "I honestly don't know," I murmured.

We embraced until Shay reluctantly pulled away. "The day is getting on," he said. His voice had taken on a wistful quality, but when he cleared his throat and continued, he sounded more like the professor I'd met in the university cafeteria. "What say we take a stroll through town and find us a place to eat. I can't have you going back on an empty stomach, now can I?"

23

Though the hour was late, we took a detour to deliver Sadie to Shay's home. It was only a short drive from the carriage house, situated almost midway to the university. It was a large home, the kind of home one would expect to be filled with a lot of children, and I wondered if he had purchased it when he was married and if they'd had plans for a family. The depth of the tragedy he'd gone through sank deeper into my heart as I realized how his future had been snatched from him with his wife's illness. At least I could console myself with anger against my runaway fiancée; Shay would have been left with overwhelming grief.

When he opened the door, we were met by the largest white Persian I'd ever seen. She made a beeline for Shay's legs, rubbing against them and purring.

"I just need to check on their food," he said. "I'll only be a sec. Come on in, why don't you?"

I followed him down the hall to the kitchen where two more cats were waiting; a gorgeous Siamese and a stunning British Shorthair with a silver coat and amber eyes. The cats greeted Sadie as though she was one of them before meowing and weaving between our legs.

"I'd left them some dry food," Shay said, eying the dishes that were still half full. "Do you mind if I feed them some wet food? It'll only take a moment."

"Go right ahead," I answered. "Take your time."

"Make yourself at home then."

As he went to the pantry to retrieve some cans, I made my way from the kitchen into the den. Pictures on the fireplace mantle drew me in and I found myself studying one prominently set in the center. It had obviously been taken on his wedding day; his wife was still dressed in her gown, a flowing white number with countless crystal beads. Her hair was dark brunette, her eyes large and russet under long, curled lashes. Her smile was broad, revealing perfect white teeth. Shay appeared younger than today by perhaps ten years or so, his hair a tad darker and his face less lined. It made sense; I assumed his wife had not yet been diagnosed and perhaps when this picture was taken, she had been healthy and full of energy. The things life can throw at us, I thought. None of us know what the future could bring and how our lives will be disrupted. Life was rather like a meandering tunnel; one never knew where they'd be spit out.

I hadn't realized Shay had joined me until I felt that odd sensation that another's eyes were upon me. As I'd been studying the picture, I suppose Shay had been studying me. I turned toward him and smiled. "Are they fed?"

"Aye."

"You have quite a pack here."

"Four in all."

"I wondered if you had others," I chuckled.

"Four is quite enough. Shall we get you home then?"

Home. The word resonated in my mind as we turned onto the narrow lane leading to the carriage house, a lane that once would have led all the way to the Crutchley house. Somewhere under the grass and weeds one might still be able to find the parallel ruts from those days before the famines and before the starving were put to work breaking stone for a pittance of a meal.

It was nearing midnight and I was tired, my thoughts already on the warmth of the bed that awaited me when Shay stopped the car.

I glanced at him but he was staring straight ahead. "What's wrong?"

He nodded toward something in front of us. As I followed his gaze, the ethereal images of two boys herding their cattle from the pasture faded in and out as if the shadows were dancing across them. "Do you see that?" Shay's voice was hoarse.

"Yes." My throat had gone dry and my own voice sounded tense in the confines of the car.

"This is what you told me you saw before?"

"Yes."

We sat for a moment longer and then he switched off the headlamps and cut the engine.

"What are you doing?" We were still only halfway down the lane to the carriage house.

He reached above us and switched the interior light off. "I don't want the light to shine when I open the door."

"What?"

"I'm going up there."

"Why?" My voice was shrill and I fought to tamp down my anxiety.

"Stay here." He opened the door slowly and quietly stepped onto the lane, his eyes still riveted to the scene before us.

"The hell I'm staying here," I said, opening the passenger door.

He was already a few steps in front of me. He moved like a tiger that has spotted his prey; each step was measured and silent. I fell in behind him, my breathing ragged and loud in the quiet of the night. There were no owls hooting in the distance, no crickets or frogs breaking the stillness and as we inched ever upward on the lane I felt as though we were sliding into a separate dimension.

Somewhere in the back of my mind I knew we had left the doors open to the car, the keys still dangling in the ignition. Somehow I felt Danny's cottage a short distance around the hill, darkened and sleeping. I felt the presence of the carriage house as we passed it, the door lamp casting muted light across the lawn until it grazed the lane, my feet carefully stepping into the next shadow.

I could not hear the cattle though we continued to approach. I saw a head dodge this way or that, could envision their mouths opening in snorts or grunts. Two dogs came into the picture as though there were curtains on either side, appearing from behind the veils to join the cattle on center stage. They ducked and darted, their heads held low, ever on the watch for a strayed cow and yet the yips and barks I should have heard were lost in the winds that blew through here a hundred years ago.

The road stopped and yet Shay continued to press forward, the terrain becoming steeper and rockier as we drew ever closer. I was panting now and my forehead was covered in perspiration and yet I knew I could not turn back. I had to remain with Shay. I longed to ask why we were moving steadily toward the ruins, or what he hoped we could possibly accomplish there, but the words were frozen on my lips.

The air grew icy but there was no wind, as if time itself was suspended.

Then the herd parted to reveal two young men, boys really; and they were looking at us.

Shay stopped and I was so mesmerized that I started past him but he reached out to grab my arm. I have no idea what amount of force he might have used because in that instant, I barely registered his hand upon me. I only knew my feet had stopped and I was staring uphill at two boys that stared back at me.

Their baggy pants were dark, their shirts light, but I could see the giant tree that stood behind them. My brain slowly registered that I could see it because I was looking through them; the combination of their light and dark clothing was casting the tree into curious shadows. I knew they were looking at us though I could not see their facial features, but rather judged their stance from the position of their bodies. Their faces glowed eerily, the outlines blurry. They grew even hazier as I realized they were beginning to run.

In an instant the cattle dispersed in a panic, rushing down the hill toward the pasture from whence they'd come while the two boys raced upward in the opposite direction toward the house. They reached the open doorway almost at the same time, catapulting over the threshold. As they stepped inside the walls, everything vanished: the boys, the dogs and the cattle were gone. All that was left were the skeletal ruins, dark and forbidding against a sky filled with ominous clouds.

Then the sound of the car horn split the night.

I stumbled backward over the rocky terrain, barely catching myself from tumbling. Shay was already racing toward the car, his feet scarcely touching the ground. I could feel the lights in Danny's cottage flipping on, though I could not see around the hill. When Shay was almost halfway back to the car, the horn suddenly stopped as the car began to careen backwards down the lane.

⚜

"I know I shut off the engine," Shay was saying as my shaking hands unlocked the doors to the carriage house.

"I saw you do it."

We slipped inside quickly and he turned and bolted the door as if that would keep the phantoms out. I had news for him in that respect. At least the kitchen was exactly as I'd left it two days earlier and as far as I could tell, there was nothing out of place in any of the rooms. No cabinets left open, no food flung across the floor, and the bedcovers still gathered into a cone near the foot of the bed.

"You're not staying here," Shay was saying. He was standing at the window, peering out in the direction of the ruins.

"That reminds me, my luggage is in the boot."

"You didn't hear me. I said you're not staying."

"I heard you." With him just a few feet away, I mustered the courage to pull the covers over the bed before turning them down neatly. No more cones for me. "But there's no reason for me to leave."

He gaped at me for a moment in disbelief. "I would be remiss," he said, his voice strained but measured, "if I didn't point out to you that this land is a wee bit haunted and you've no business remaining here alone and unprotected."

"I'll be fine."

"Then I'm staying with you."

I stopped in the doorway between the bedroom and living area to stare at him. "What about Sadie and the cats?"

"They'll be grand. Grander than us. At least their house isn't haunted."

I crossed over to him and rested a hand on his shoulder. "I appreciate you wanting to protect me; I really do. But I'll be fine. You're due back at work in the morning, and you'll sleep better in your own bed, yes?"

"Pardon me," he said, "but did you happen to notice that a spirit started my car and placed it into reverse? I caught it just before it hit the ditch. What if you were driving down the lane and an angry poltergeist decided to send your car flying? There's an awful lot of negative energy here." As if to prove his point, he rubbed his bare forearm where hairs had begun to rise. "I can't in good conscience leave you here alone."

"Maybe Danny did it."

"The bloke next door?"

"Yes. He doesn't want Fergal to rent out this carriage house; he told me so himself."

"Oh, that sounds practical doesn't it, except for one thing? I was racing toward that car the moment the horn sounded and I would have seen a man jumping out and running down the lane."

I perched on the sofa arm. "They haven't hurt me," I said quietly. "I've seen the two boys twice now, and I've heard their mother almost every night. They've frightened me, but they haven't harmed me."

"But they're intensifying, don't you see? The kitchen torn to pieces. Then my car starting on its own and rolling off. I can't protect you from something I can't see."

"Maybe they're trying to tell me something."

He joined me at the sofa, sitting down heavily. "Say that they are. What could you possibly do to help them? Say the boys want you to know they were out in the field or herding the cows home or they saw their house in flames; what could you do about it? It took place a hundred years ago. Everyone associated with what happened is dead."

I sat for a moment in silence. "Are they?"

He shook his head. "Listen to yourself. It was a hundred years ago. If there'd been a babe in one of the sisters' arms, that child would have lived a life and surely would have passed on. Even if you did manage to find a centenarian, they most certainly would not remember what occurred when they were but an infant."

"No. But maybe they told someone. We don't know what happened to the boys' parents or their sisters. Maybe April Crutchley had another child—she was only 37 at the time, so it wouldn't have been out of the question. Or surely the two sisters—"

"So what if they did? And what if you learned precisely what happened? You can't change history."

"Maybe not." I took a deep breath. "But every night I listen to April Crutchley crying; her heart has to be breaking every single night, as if she is reliving what happened that day. Their bodies might have died but their souls are still here."

He ran his fingers through his hair. "I return to my original question. Even if everything you say is true, then what could you possibly do about it?"

I shook my head in silence. To be honest, I didn't know if I could do anything at all. I was a stranger in a strange land, an American that had never experienced life in Ireland. And Shay was right; the War for Independence and the ensuing Irish Civil War had ended nearly a century ago. Today Ireland was a different place; at least outside of Ulster. If this had happened there, I would have understood it more fully because the native Irish were still fighting for independence in Ulster. But here... here, it didn't make sense.

"And there's something else," Shay was saying. "Why is the mother crying for her boys every night? Wouldn't she have joined them when she passed over?"

I felt a chill creeping up my spine as if someone unseen was listening to our conversation; the odd sensation of someone watching me was back and I nervously peered around the room. "I don't know."

After a moment, he continued, "Well it seems to me there's more we don't know than what we do."

His words hung in the air. He was right, of course. But I had to keep trying.

24

The lamp dimmed briefly before returning to its original glow. Electrical surge, I told myself but I pulled the throw around my shoulders more snuggly as if it could morph into a protective cloak. Shay had left a few minutes earlier after quite the debate. Under normal circumstances, I would have jumped at the chance to have him sleep beside me again, repeating our passion from the prior night, but there was now the constant sense that I was being watched and I'd be damned if I put on a show for apparitions. Despite his insistence that I come with him to his home, an unseen force was keeping me here as firmly as if they'd encircled my body with weighted chains. Moreover, I'd been so tired when we'd arrived that I'd thought by now I'd be in bed sound asleep, but the events of the night had instead brought me fully awake.

I'd set up my laptop in its usual spot and brewed myself a cup of tea. I'd also discovered a slice of packaged orange cake in the cupboard, and while it couldn't compare with the fresh pastries I'd sampled over the weekend, it was enough to pump up my sugar level for a night of writing. Before diving back into my book, I logged into my email and was busy culling the necessary from the spam when I came across an email from Michelle. I opened it to discover an attached picture and a note:

> *Hope you're having a grand time with your research and travels. Found this on an Australian university website; scant information but I'm trying to sort out more details. This is the Crutchley family taken the summer of 1919—from left to right: Spencer, April, Elliot, Olivia, Ignacius and Jayne. I've reached out to a counterpart in Sydney and will let you know when I have more. Thought you'd want to see it.*

Australia. How strange. I downloaded the attachment and opened it. It had obviously been scanned and the photograph hadn't been positioned evenly because it was slightly askew. It was, I suppose, originally in black and white but had turned shades of sepia. I was thrilled at any rate to have a photograph; I hadn't even considered that there might have been one.

The family was standing in front of their house. I zoomed in to look at each face in turn. Spencer, I reminded myself, was the eldest son. He stood only a breath away from his mother and instead of looking at the camera, he was looking at April. He was also very blurred; a result of moving when the picture was taken, I suppose. That was a shame, because I would have liked to have seen his face.

April's image was sharper. She had light-colored hair; perhaps light brown or even auburn. It was pulled away from her face, revealing a round jawline with deep impressions around her mouth, the kind one sees on a person that is always smiling. I zoomed in further. There was something about her eyes, though; a droop at the outer corners, dark circles under her eyes and a deep crease between her brows all revealed an overwhelming sadness. She was staring into the camera lens seemingly unaware that her eldest was looking at her.

On her other side, it was almost a mirror image. This time it was Elliot; slightly shorter, lighter hair, but he was also turned toward his mother. The boys must have moved at the same time because they were both blurred to the same respect, impeding any ability for me to see their faces in any detail at all. They were, I thought, very much like the apparitions Shay and I had witnessed.

Olivia was next. She was standing too close to Elliot, nearly knocking elbows with him, but she like her mother was staring at the camera. She might have been a younger version of April; the smile was there as if instructed to do so, but the eyes betrayed an inner melancholy.

Next was Ignacius. He was the tallest among them. His shoulders were narrow and his physique was thin—almost too thin, I realized. His clothes hung on him and though his eyes appeared kind, his entire face drooped. Loose skin hung under his chin like one that had been much heftier but had lost weight quickly. He held Jayne's hand in his. She barely reached higher than his waist, and she appeared to be turned to stare at those at the opposite end. Her mouth was slightly ajar and her face abnormally pale.

I spent a good bit of time looking at each one again before moving to their surroundings. The house was behind them, covered in flowery bushes. Something bothered me about the photograph, something I couldn't quite put my finger on.

The clock chimed to mark the four o'clock hour. I thought I'd silenced that clock, I thought before returning to the picture. Then it struck me: the house had already been burnt to the ground. The bushes were flowering not only along the front of the house but through the house, through the windows that were only gaping holes now. The stones were still marked with streaks of soot where the fire would have raged upward and the roof was nearly gone save for one corner that appeared dangerously close to collapsing. Yet despite such devastation, the flowers had come back as if determined to survive.

But it couldn't be the summer of 1919; the boys were already dead. I returned to Michelle's email and read it again. She must be mistaken. Yet it certainly must be the Crutchley family, as they were standing in front of the clearly recognizable ruins. Their sizes matched what I knew of their birthdates, and the flowers would not have been so mature in the early spring. No; the picture must have been taken the year before and Michelle had typed it incorrectly. Unless…

I zoomed out just enough to center April in the picture flanked by her two boys. And there it was: the outline of the ruins emerging through her sons. I thought my eyes were playing tricks on me but the closer I studied it, the more convinced I was that the two young men standing on either side of April Crutchley had not moved just as the picture was taken. They were blurred and opaque because they were dead.

I leaned back in my chair. That meant after their murders their souls remained behind—and were haunting their mother.

25

Dawn was ushered in with the crack of thunder, snatching me out of the alternate universe I'd journeyed into as I worked on my manuscript. Now that I had been to Derry, Burt Castle, the Inishowen Peninsula and Ramelton, I could make the scenes come alive with the scents, the sounds and the images of Ireland that made this island so unique. It was not a surprise that *Game of Thrones*, perhaps the most watched television series of all time, had been filmed in Northern Ireland. Once out of the larger cities—of which there were few—time slipped away and it was so easy to imagine oneself living in centuries past.

There were still places I needed to visit, including Kilmacrennan where the climactic battle scene took place. It was a bloody encounter that altered Ireland's destiny and that of its people and I felt a strong urge to walk that hallowed ground myself. We had been surprisingly close to it when Shay and I had been at Ramelton but it had been late in the day and as the sun had set and darkness had crept in, we'd decided to postpone it for another time.

The more I considered his offer to stay at the B&B on the Inishowen Peninsula, the more sense it made. Any additional research I needed to do in Dublin or Galway paled in comparison with staying exactly where the action of 1608 had taken place. I'd come to think of the carriage house as my home but perhaps the truth was that I was only an interloper here. I belonged in Donegal.

So when Shay texted at half past six asking if I was okay, I responded immediately by phoning him.

"Everything okay?" he answered.

"Yes. Everything's fine."

"I worried about you most of the night," he confessed. In a lighter tone, he added, "No more ghosties?"

I laughed a bit nervously, my eyes instinctively wandering the cottage looking for signs that April had been there while I worked, which seemed ludicrous as the night shadows began to vanish. "No more ghosties. But I have been thinking about your offer."

"Oh?" His voice perked up.

"I think you're right. I didn't know about your parents' B&B when I booked this one, and it's so much closer to the sites."

"I'll give them a ring up and let them know. Do you think you'll be there today?"

Another crack of thunder shook the cottage, followed by a wicked bolt of lightning. "I'm not familiar with the roads once I exit the motorway. Maybe I should wait until this storm passes?"

There was a moment of hesitation on the other end. Then, "Aye. That would be the smart thing to do. I've the radar on my screen now and this is just the start of it. It looks like it'll be bucketing until early evening. Tomorrow's predicted to be sunny."

"That would make for a better drive," I said reluctantly. Now that I'd made the decision to leave, I wanted to make the move. I could continue to research the Crutchley family from the safety of his family's property. "You know what? I'm going to wait and see what it does today. If the rain stops at a decent hour, I'll go there tonight."

"I'll let them know." He gave me the phone number there as well. "So," he continued, "perhaps this weekend I can join you there, 'ey?"

"That would be lovely."

We chatted for a couple of minutes and then he begged off so he could get ready for a class he had to conduct first thing this morning, with an assurance to phone me later. "Promise me," he said, "If you need me, you'll text or call straight away."

"I will, and if you try to phone me and I don't answer, you'll know the ghosties have gotten me." I don't know what compelled me to say that and the moment the words left my mouth, I wished I could take them back. I laughed but it came out a bit forced. "Just a joke."

"Right." He sounded unconvinced. "So we'll chat later, 'eh?"

After clicking off, I cleaned off the table from my tea and snacks and made my way to the kitchen to make a bit of breakfast. It was a shame, really, for all this food to go to waste but I consoled myself with the knowledge that Fergal would probably move it to his restaurant and make use of it there. I figured out my plan of action as I cooked some rashers and sausages. I would not notify Fergal that I was leaving until after I'd already cleared out and was comfortably settled in the new room. I would not ask for a refund as I felt pangs of

guilt considering all he'd done to renovate the carriage
house and prepare it for my arrival. But for all I knew,
he already had a stream of guests booked through the
summer as Shay's parents did.

While the meat cooked, I poured another cup of tea
and opened the drapes near the table. It was most
definitely a dreary day and I was grateful that I was not
one of the scores of people having to walk to the bus to
take public transportation into the city, as so many from
the neighboring villages did. The skies were awash in
dark gray and black clouds, the kind that cause one to
dash for shelter. Shay's description of bucketing was
apt. It would be a grand day to remain inside where it
was dry and warm; it was the perfect day to work on
my book.

Through the drenching rain, I spotted a herd of
cattle making their way into the fields and I froze with
my teacup partway to my mouth. Then I spotted a
bright red jacket and heard the faint whistles as the dogs
rushed forward to shepherd them into a near field. It
was Danny, I thought with relief. No ghosts this
morning.

But as quickly as the relief settled over me, an
uneasiness grew. While the cattle were funneled by the
dogs through a break in the hedgerows, Danny stopped
and turned around. Sheets of water rushed over the
window glass so everything appeared like a French
impressionist painting, but I could have sworn he was
staring straight at the carriage house.

Perhaps it was Danny's presence that caused me to
switch gears and begin to research the Crutchley family

in far more depth than I'd previously attempted. Each time I glanced up, he appeared to be standing in such a way as to face directly toward the carriage house, despite the wicked weather. With my rental in the drive, the lights on and draperies open, he no doubt knew I was here and was attempting to intimidate me.

It was amazing when one searched on a name how many hits can be returned and how quickly down a rabbit hole one can slide. I could find nothing on the Crutchley family in Ireland's online records other than what I already knew. As a writer of historicals I knew how to research even if the process proved slow and tedious so I began to employ the same methods as though I was writing a book about the Crutchleys, typing in what I already knew to find out if any sites with that information could provide me with a tad more.

It wasn't until I began my research on Australian sites that I hit pay dirt. April and her husband Ignacius and their two daughters, Olivia and Jayne, had moved to New South Wales in early 2020, less than one year after the boys' murders. I discovered April's date of death in New South Wales in 1947. April 3 loomed large, a date I was certain I would always remember and I could not avoid being stopped cold in my tracks to make the mental note that she died on the 18th anniversary of her sons' murders and the loss of her beloved home. As I took a screenshot of the page and calculated her age to be 65 when she passed, it occurred to me to switch gears and enter several genealogy websites. Entering her name, dates of birth and death, I eventually discovered a family tree posted by Stella Crutchley Grafton Shaw.

Stella Shaw listed her date of birth in New South Wales in 1965; 22 years after April had died. She had also posted her email address and place of residence as Lismore for those Crutchley descendants that wished to contact her. Her mother was born Isabella Butler

Crutchley Singleton in 1937, also in Lismore and married a Grafton, and Isabella's mother—Stella's grandmother—was Jayne Crutchley Singleton.

Holding my breath, I clicked through to Jayne's page. She was born in 1911 in Ireland in the very county I was sitting, and I had no doubt she'd been born in the house atop the hill. Had she been birthed in a hospital, I reasoned, the name of the village would have been listed; but in 1911, all but the wealthiest most likely gave birth at home perhaps with the help of a midwife. Jayne's date of death was in 1983 in Lismore, New South Wales, Australia.

I leaned back in my chair and took a sip of tea that had long grown cold. That meant Stella would have known her grandmother for the first 18 years of her life.

So Jayne, the youngest daughter that witnessed the murders of her brothers—or at least witnessed the aftereffects—was dead. No other siblings were listed after Jayne, so I had to assume April and Ignacius had no other children. Not that I could blame them, I thought. I stood and stretched, noted that Danny was still standing in the field with his cows in the rain like a complete idiot, and took a break to brew more tea.

Returning to my laptop a few minutes later, it struck me to have a closer look at Stella. I began an email but thought better of it; I was a complete stranger, after all, and she could easily dismiss me as a kook. On a whim, I searched the online telephone directories for Shaws in Lismore and got a hit on her name. She was married to Raymond Shaw and they had two children.

Taking a deep breath, I phoned. A woman answered on the second ring. I introduced myself and added, "Would you happen to be Stella Shaw?"

"I am, and I can't imagine why you are phoning me." Before I could muster an appropriate response, feeling now like I should have rehearsed this whole phone call beforehand, she added, "I've read all your books. I'm a huge fan."

"You have? Oh, you have. Well, thank you."

She chatted for a moment about her favorite and then stopped herself midway. "Oh, I'm so sorry. I'm blathering on and you must have a reason for phoning. Are you after Ray then?"

"After—oh, no. I wasn't phoning for Ray. I was phoning for you, actually."

"Me?"

I could feel the wheels turning in her mind. "Actually, I'm in Ireland right now. I'm staying in a cottage next door to some ruins—"

"—the house my nana was born?"

"Your—pardon?"

"Nana Jayne. You're staying on her old property now?"

"Yes. I believe I am. And I've been doing a bit of research on Irish history and I came across a few bits and pieces about their home. I know you're too young to have known the period—I'm interested in 1919, during the Irish War for Independence—but I was hoping your grandmother Jayne or her mother April might have left some documents?"

"What kind of documents?"

"Anything really that might shed some light on that time period."

There was hesitancy in her voice when she responded. "If there were, I haven't the faintest where they'd be… I'm sorry I can't be of help to you."

I felt like a sinking woman. I'd found the ship and managed to catch the line but it was being pulled ever so quickly through my hands. I couldn't let this conversation end as quickly as it had begun. I just couldn't.

But before I managed a reply, Stella asked, "But would you like to speak to my mother?"

"Your mother?" I could hardly believe my ears. "Jayne's daughter." I glanced quickly at my notes. "Isabella?"

"She lives with us. But—and I hope you don't mind my asking—could we do this in a video call? I just want to make sure you're who you say you are."

"Absolutely." I could hear the syllables stumbling over themselves. We quickly swapped contact information before ending the audio call. I jumped up, rushing into the bathroom to peer into the mirror. I looked a mess. I hadn't changed clothes since the day before and I looked it. I ran a brush through my hair, grabbed a clean sweater to hide the wrinkles in my blouse, and was back at the laptop in three minutes flat. Trying to tamp down my growing excitement, I began the video call.

Stella answered quickly as though she'd been waiting. It must have been nighttime there because the room behind her was dimly lit. I held back a gasp when I saw her, as her cheekbones and deep indentations beside her mouth bore a striking resemblance to April Crutchley in the only photograph I had of her. Her hair was auburn and her eyes a startling bottle green. She recognized me immediately from my book covers and began apologizing profusely.

"No need to apologize," I said. "Crazy things happen these days. I don't blame you one bit for wanting to make sure of my identity. But—I'm sorry, I didn't check Australian time before I phoned. I hope I didn't call too late?"

"It's half past eight," she answered. "Not late at all."

I glanced at the clock on my screen. Ah, nine hours difference. Good to know, I suppose.

"Ray is bringing my mother in," she was saying. "She needs a bit of help, she does. She won't be able to speak with you for long, I'm afraid, as her energy isn't what it used to be. But her mind is sharp and she remembers far more of her childhood than she does what happened yesterday." At that, she rose from her chair and scooted it out of the way.

I watched as a wheelchair was placed in front of the camera. The woman appeared to be in her 80s, which fit with the scant information I had of Isabella. Her hair was snow white and pulled back from her face, revealing the same distinct jawline and indentation, as if she'd spent a lifetime laughing. I could see the resemblance immediately, as though I was looking at April Crutchley at various stages of her own life.

"So you're phoning from Ireland?" Isabella asked in a slightly reedy voice. Her head had a delicate tremble to it.

"I am," I answered, smiling to set her at ease. "I believe I'm staying right next door to the house where your mother might have been born."

"Are you in the carriage house then?"

I couldn't hold back a gasp. "You know about the carriage house?"

"I do. Did you tear it down and build a new one?"

"I—no. I'm only leasing it for the month. But they didn't tear it down; they renovated it." I quickly added, "Were you ever here?"

"I was and I remember it as though it was yesterday. It was 1968, the year after my grandfather died. His name was Ignacius Crutchley. His family built that house, you know, in the 17th century."

"That's why I'm calling. I wanted to know more about the house." I tried to find the right words. "And also why they left."

"Then you want to know about the murders."

Her forthrightness shocked me. Now that I had her in front of me, I wasn't sure how to proceed without offending her. I'd never had a poker face.

"Are you going to write a book about it?"

"Well, I don't know. I wouldn't do it unless I had your permission, of course."

She nodded. One brow rose as though she was silently assessing my intentions.

"I've fallen in love with the area," I said, stretching it a bit. "But I understand that no one wants to live on the property since the house burned, and I was curious why that was."

There was a moment of hesitation. "Fetch me a glass of water," she said to someone out of range of the camera. While she waited, she said, "My grandparents lived with my family when I was a child, until Nana April's death in 1947—I was ten years old at the time—and Papa Ignacius—or Papa Iggy, as we liked to call him—passed in 1967 when I was thirty."

"Did they ever speak of Ireland?"

"If you're referring to what happened there, Nana and Papa never did. But my mother did. She honored her brothers every April 3 until she passed over." She took a deep breath. Someone handed her a glass of water and she took a healthy gulp of it before handing it back. Her hand, like her head, had a tremor to it but her voice was strong and sure as she continued. "It was 1919. The Great War had ended just the previous year but fighting continued in Ireland against the Brits. Since the Easter Rising of 1916, the call for Ireland to become a nation independent of England had grown. There were numerous factions engaged in spying and guerrilla warfare—attacking the Brits, the RIC and the Black and Tans—and then fading quickly back into the shadows."

She spoke as if she was reciting the story and it occurred to me that perhaps every April 3, Jayne honored her brothers with the retelling of their story. I pressed the Record button on my screen, and silently berated myself for not doing it earlier.

"To be fair, the RIC and the Black and Tans were doing their share as well. They often burned entire villages, putting the whole of the population out of their homes, attempting to ferret out the spies and traitors. The Black and Tans were particularly vicious; they were not military personnel, you know. The Brits were short-handed in fighting the Irish so they hired thugs and killers, so many they didn't have enough uniforms for them all. So they put a mishmash of clothing on them; that's how they came to be referred to as the Black and Tans, for their tan pants and dark green — almost black — shirts." Her voice had taken on a vicious tone, despite her genial appearance. "Many people died on both sides, you see, during the Irish War for Independence. It made no difference if they were man, woman or child; they were all considered combatants, every one of them."

I heard a murmur off screen and she shooed them away. "Don't coddle me," she said before continuing. "My mother's brothers, Spence and Elly, and my grandfather Iggy raised cattle on that land you're leasing now. The Crutchley family had raised their beef and dairy cattle for three hundred years at least, perhaps more. They were loyal to the English crown to the day they died and mighty proud of it. They didn't condone violence and they disliked the Black and Tans, but when one is loyal to Britain, well... You don't have to agree with everything a country does in order to remain patriotic."

So many questions were racing through my mind but I was hesitant to stop her long-winded story, riveting as it was, to ask them. I hadn't realized until that moment that my breath had become shallow and I was hanging on every word.

"The boys caught some of the Volunteers—that's what they called themselves—crossing their land to spy on the British barracks at the cliffs there, where both RIC and Black and Tans were stationed. It was mighty easy to deduce what they were up to; they were passing information on their movements to the Irish fighting for their independence. Well, it simply wouldn't do to have the Crutchley land used as an outpost—it endangered the family, as the Brits could think them spies as well. So the boys and Papa Iggy confronted them, told them they were on private property and to bugger off."

My mouth had grown dry as I pictured the events unfolding just a short distance from where I sat.

"The story goes," she continued, her voice as animated as if she'd lived it herself, "that on April 3, 1919, the villagers marched down the lane toward the Crutchley home. It was dusk and they'd lit torches though they weren't to be used solely for finding their way. The Irish Republican Brotherhood—the IRB—had ordered the murders of Papa Iggy, Spence and Elly. I suppose they wanted to send a message to other loyalists not to stand in their way."

She paused while she signaled for more water and the glass was handed back to her. After she'd had her fill, she wiped her mouth with the back of her hand and continued, "Papa Iggy wasn't there; he'd gone two villages over to discuss the cattle auction so he didn't return until it was too late. Spence and Elly were driving in the herd from the fields and they saw the villagers coming. They knew. My mother said they all knew. They just didn't know how far they would take their vengeance."

She wiped her forehead with a tissue and dabbed at her eyes. "Well, Nana April, my Auntie Ollie and my mother were in the house at the time. The villagers arrived at the same time as the brothers, and while some of the men restrained the boys, the women were ordered out of the house. They were made to stand a few yards in front of the house, looking back at the house, while it was torched. And while it was burning, Spence and Elly were directed to stand right in front of the stone so they were facing their mother."

She dabbed at the outer corner of her eye again and retrieved another tissue before she continued. A low voice murmured to her just off screen. When she spoke again, her voice was strained. "Don't tell me again that I need my rest," she said to those in the room with her. Then she turned back to me. "Two of the men shot Spence and Elly. They aimed for the knees, my mother said, and when the boys crumpled to the ground, they shot them in the hips."

"Oh no," I heard myself breathe.

"They all left then, scattered like shooed flies. My Auntie Ollie was sent first to the barracks. They had medics there. But there had been an attack on the old road to Dublin and all the medics had been sent there. There was no one that could—or would—help her. Not a one of them came to my family's aid. She then took the dangerous trek to the village opposite our own, knowing all the while that the IRB and Volunteers were roaming the countryside as they always did after an attack on the RIC and at any moment they could do to her what they'd done to her brothers. Despite the dangers, she made it there, but the doctor refused to come, said if he aided the enemy he'd be shot, too. 'The enemy'." She spat the words. "They all knew my mother's family; they'd known them for generations. They'd never been 'the enemy' before."

I waited for her to continue and the moments passed with only the sound of her angry tears. I began to worry that Stella or Ray would stop the conversation and I would be left wanting the rest of the story. As my heart ached with the family's, I began to understand more fully the trauma that had been inflicted, a trauma that reached down through the generations.

Isabella took a raspy breath. "By the time Auntie Ollie returned to Crutchley Manor, hours had passed. The boys lay dying in the dirt outside the home. Nana April was frantic. She'd torn off her dress so she was nearly naked in the cold, ripped the dress to shreds to make tourniquets for the boys' legs. The house was burning down around them. They had nothing to drench the flames and they couldn't dare go back in for fear it would collapse around them, so they had nothing more than their clothes and their hands to try and save Spence and Elly."

She paused and took another labored breath. "My mother, who was eight at the time, was told to keep pressure on the hip wound to try to stop the bleeding. They could put tourniquets on the legs, you see, to try and stop the blood flow from the knees but they'd both been shot in the hip and…"

Stella's voice was louder now and male hands came into view, whisking the wheelchair out of range of the camera. A chair was pulled up and Stella's face appeared next on my screen.

"I'm sorry," I said. "I didn't mean to upset her." I dabbed at my own eyes, the tears as real as if I'd been there myself. I felt a draft breeze past me; startled, I looked behind me, expecting to find that the door had blown open. Though everything appeared as it had before, I had the distinct impression I was not alone.

"I grew up hearing the story," Stella was saying, as if oblivious to my abrupt inattentiveness. "But I thought she should tell you herself." I turned back around to face the laptop as she shook her head. "Nana Jayne, I'm told, was affected the rest of her life. Of course, I never knew her before—I came along decades later—but she had recurring nightmares about that day. She'd awaken screaming for someone to help, insisting her brothers were bleeding out and asking if any of us heard them crying out in pain. I was told Spence died ten hours later and Elly the next day. Papa Iggy came home two days later to find his wife and girls in the carriage house, the house burned down and the boys' bodies lying next to the smoldering ruins. He dug the graves and buried them himself."

"Did they catch the ones that did it?"

"Catch them? I doubt if they even tried. Everyone in the village—those that had been their friends for decades before the War for Independence—they all had been there. They all had witnessed what happened. But everyone refused to talk."

"But the RIC—"

"They had their hands full with attacks on their troops. They couldn't spare the manpower to hunt down killers of civilians. Ironically, as it turned out, the Crutchleys hadn't been spies for the British; they'd declared themselves neutral, so there was no incentive for the RIC to seek justice."

I knew my mind needed to process all that I'd been told, and I was grateful I'd recorded much of it. But there was more I had to know before the conversation ended. "What happened to April?" Again the breeze blew past me; this one so strong that strands of my hair wafted outward.

"April... that's a long story, I'm afraid. Have you the time?"

"Most definitely."

"Well," she continued, "immediately Papa Iggy tried to sell the cattle; he'd made arrangements to sell some of them—that's why he'd been gone at the time of the attack—but the buyers reneged on the deal once they learned what had happened. The cattle—or anything produced on their land—was boycotted so they were suddenly without income. They'd moved into the carriage house while Papa Iggy tried to sell the property, but the IRB blocked the sale. Finally, in return for their word that they'd leave Ireland, the property was purchased for fifteen pence an acre, only a pittance of what it was worth."

"So April moved to Australia soon after?"

Stella nodded. "Nana April, Papa Iggy, Auntie Ollie and Nana Jayne. The journey was five months from Galway to Sydney and I've been told that shortly after they lost sight of Ireland, Nana April became catatonic. They didn't have the full passage fees so when they arrived in Australia, they became indentured servants—even my Nana Jayne, at eight years old. Because Nana April was unresponsive and therefore incapable of working, their terms were doubled. They worked ten years apiece to pay off the debt, living in nothing more than a shack and working solely for the roof over their heads and one meal a day."

"I had no idea," I said. "Had I known the full story, I would never have called and upset you and your mother..."

Stella shrugged and managed a weak smile. "Nana April and Papa Iggy lived with Nana Jayne until their deaths, and Nana Jayne then lived with us until hers..."

"But your Nana Jayne married?"

"Papa Steven was killed in World War II. She was a widow for the last forty years of her life. My mother doesn't even remember her father; he'd left for the front lines when she was still a small child."

"I'm so sorry for your family's tragedy," I said. Even as the words left my lips, I knew them to be completely inadequate.

"Well, I need to sign off now," she said. "I hope you got what you called for."

We ended the chat then, and I sat in stunned silence for a long time, my eyes riveted to my keyboard but not seeing it at all. Instead, the events of that day played out in my mind's eye. Realizing the scenes lacked details I'd been given, they replayed again and again. I knew now why the land was haunted—haunted by the souls of the brothers and by the mother that would not leave them; even though her body was forced to abandon them, her soul would not.

26

The phone rang, startling me out of my thoughts. I answered to discover Michelle on the other end.

"You're not going to believe this," she said breathlessly. "I've discovered who killed the Crutchley boys."

"It was the villagers," I said. My voice sounded disembodied, as if I was still in a stupor, suspended between the present day and what had occurred here a hundred years prior.

"Two brothers were responsible," Michelle continued as though she hadn't heard me. "They were acting, so the story goes, on the orders of the IRB, possibly Michael Collins himself."

"Yes, I've heard that. I just—"

"So the brothers were Daniel and Luke O'Ceallaigh. Daniel was sixteen at the time; Luke was twenty." I wrote the names on a pad beside my laptop as she spelled the last name. "Pronounced like O'Kelly, yeah? Just in the Irish spelling," she ended.

"Any word on what happened to them?" I asked.

"Well, they were never arrested, never tried, if that's what you're asking. There was a guerrilla war going on, you know. Thousands of deaths never saw justice served."

"I see." The air in the cottage had grown uncharacteristically hot and humid. I checked the thermostat and as I walked past the fireplace, I held out my hand. No draft, which meant the damper was closed. I could open the damper or better yet, find a window that wouldn't let in the rain and get some fresh air in here. I could feel the beads of sweat popping out on my forehead.

"Daniel lived to the age of 90, can you believe that?" Michelle was saying. "He died of natural causes."

"So he passed in…"

"1993. His brother Luke passed four years earlier, also at the age of 90. It doesn't seem right, does it?"

"No," I said slowly. "It doesn't." I wanted to tell her all that I'd learned but the horror of the situation was taking hold in my psyche and I felt a pressing need to brush it off before I spoke about it. I still felt a presence in the cottage and despite my mind's logical arguments, I sensed that April was there listening. It was a disconcerting feeling, rather like gossiping about someone who was within earshot of the conversation.

"Listen," Michelle continued, "I don't feel right about you staying there."

"I know. Shay said the same thing."

"Shay MacGregor? The historian you were meeting up with at university?"

"Yes. Turns out his parents own a bed and breakfast on the Inishowen Peninsula."

"That's serendipitous." I could feel her smiling on the other end of the phone. "Why do I have the impression that you've hit it off with him, 'ey?"

I chuckled. "We're just friends. But I'm packing right now and clearing out today, headed up as soon as the weather clears."

"It's cloudless in Ulster."

"Oh?"

"I'm looking out the window right now. Blue skies."

"Good." I stopped trying to find the damper handle inside the fireplace and turned around to peer out the front window. The buckets of rain that had come down earlier had ceased, leaving in its place a fine mist. As I approached the window for a closer look, I noticed the fields were beginning to become obscured by a thick fog. "I've only the two bags to pack—my luggage and my laptop case—and then I'll be headed north."

"Give me a ring when you get there, 'k? Just want to make sure you get there safe and sound, you know."

I chuckled, but it sounded a bit forced as my throat had become dry. "I'll be fine. After all, I've traveled all the way from America, haven't I? I think I can make it a couple hours up the road."

"Yeah, but it's just the thought you're staying next to a killer's house—"

"What did you say?"

"Didn't I tell you? The murderers' names—Daniel and Luke O'Ceallaigh."

"Yes, but what does—?"

"Daniel O'Ceallaigh. The third, to be precise. He lived next door to the Crutchley estate until his death."

"Danny," I breathed.

"His grandson lives there now. Last of the line, from what I could find."

"I've got to go."

"But—"

"I'll call you later. I've got to go."

I don't remember clicking off the phone. I barely remember rushing into the bedroom to retrieve my luggage, tossing it onto the bed and packing it so haphazardly that I barely managed to get it closed. I vaguely recall the shampoo and toiletries in the bath, but I made the instantaneous decision to buy them at Inishowen rather than unpack and repack. I rushed through the cottage, grabbing my keys and throwing open the door.

The mist and the fog smacked me full in the face. It had rolled in so quickly that I could barely identify the outline of the rental, though it wasn't far from the door. I stumbled through the fog as it thickened, hauling the luggage into the boot. As I attempted to race back to the cottage, I snagged my shoe on an exposed rock and nearly fell, somehow managing to stagger onward despite the pain radiating through my foot.

I packed my laptop with a bit more care but my hands were shaking so violently that I had to grab one with the other in an attempt to calm myself. All my research notes were computerized, so once I had the laptop in its case, I lurched back to the car and popped it in beside my luggage. I slammed the boot shut, the sound echoing unnaturally. I could barely breathe in this fog. My clothes were permeated with the mist, my hair now clinging to my head in damp folds.

I made my way back to the cottage and grabbed my shoulder bag. My eyes dropped to the table where the pad of paper still sat beside my mobile. Trying to settle my nerves, I dialed the number to the MacGregor B&B. Maurie answered on the first ring.

"Ah," she said when she heard my voice, "so we've everything set for you. You'll be in the big cottage and Eoghan has moved a proper desk in there for you, he has. You'll even have a mini frig and a teakettle."

"Thank you so much." Somehow I managed to get the words out though they sounded like they were

tumbling over one another. "But I don't know the way—
I mean, I know part of the way, but—"

"You'll be driving up the N13, yeah?"

"Yes. I know that far."

"Alright then," Eoghan's voice cut in. "Come off the
N13 at Burt and head into the roundabout. You'll see a
car park on the left. I'll be there waiting to lead you in."

"That's too much trouble—"

"Nonsense. I do it all the time. It's a service of the
B&B. We know we're in the wilds here."

"Okay," I said. "I'm leaving now. I should be there
in—"

"Take your time. The weather is clear up this way
so once you get through the storm there, you've smooth
going. From the looks of the radar, it's only a popup in
your immediate area."

"Alright then," I said. I tried to let out a sigh of relief
but it sounded more like a gasp for air.

"See you soon."

Before I could answer, he clicked off the phone.

A movement caught my eye and I glanced up from
my phone and through the window. Standing just on
the other side, looming so large that he stood above me
in a billowing red jacket and swirling white hair was
Danny O'Ceallaigh.

"Get out!" he bellowed, his face red and contorted,
his bloodshot eyes popping like something otherworldly,
his skin waxy. "Get out!"

I heard a whoosh behind me and I whirled about,
dropping the phone onto the table. The fireplace had
roared to life, the flames shooting upward as though
petrol had been poured upon it. The damper! I rushed
to the fireplace but the flames were scorching. As I tried
desperately to get close enough to reach inside and find
the damper handle, my skin instantly erupted in streams

of perspiration. As my clothing ballooned outward, I realized in horror that my sweater was dangerously close to catching fire. With the door left open, the mist and fog had rolled in to combine with the smoke from the flames. They swirled around me until I didn't know which was mist and which was smoke. I only knew my lungs had begun to ache and I could no longer breathe.

Somehow I managed to teeter through the haze to the front door. I reached the car just as I heard a small explosion inside the cottage. I whirled around to the sight of flames engulfing the interior, the brilliant red and orange undulating through the open door like ribbons.

My hands were quivering as I managed to get the key in the ignition. The car was so close to the cottage that I was terrified the engine roaring to life would further inflame the fire, but miraculously, it didn't. I might have been relieved at this but my heart was beating so wildly that I feared I would faint. I could see absolutely nothing in front of me.

Despite the total lack of visibility, I floored the gas pedal, willing myself to feel the lane beneath the tires, hunched over the steering wheel as if the closer I got to the windshield the better I'd be able to see. I felt the tires slipping and the car careening but I doggedly hung onto the wheel and steered it back on course. The only thought racing through my mind now was to get to the village, alert Fergal and get help.

I was going into the curve just above Danny's cottage when I hit an invisible force that felt as though I had sped straight into a stone wall. The car lurched forward, the nose diving toward the ground and I felt the contents under the hood crumple like an accordion, the foot well collapsing with the weight. A split second later, the car was hurled backward. The world swirled around me as I hit my head with such intensity that it cracked the windshield. Water seemed to be streaming down my face but as it ran onto my clothing, I realized it was my own bright red blood.

I had no control of the car now as it tumbled off the lane and down the embankment, rolling over before coming to rest in the field beyond. I had the hazy sensation of the door opening of its own accord, my laptop case sailing through it and my luggage crushed beneath the weight of the roof. As the car slowed to a gradual spin before stopping completely, I tried desperately to catch my breath. Something was against my chest and I struggled to get loose. I was covered in blood, the sticky sweet smell permeating the car's interior.

I heard the sound of another explosion and my senses rushed back. I could smell the distinct odor of petrol and realized with growing panic that the gas tank had ruptured. The realization that the cottage was engulfed in flames loomed large, and I had no idea how close the car had landed to the uncontrolled fire.

The fog, the mist and the smoke rushed in at me. My dazed brain wondered like one half asleep how the flames could continue in the dampness of the mists. Then in the next instant I was struggling to wrench free of the constraints around me, though I'd been nearly crushed by the metal. I managed to contort myself through to the passenger side, falling out of the open door into the field.

I don't know how long I laid there; it might have been mere seconds or a minute or two. Time felt oddly distorted now. I saw Danny's face looming in front of the window and heard his voice angrily ordering for me to get out. I heard April Crutchley's cries, her voice begging, pleading that her sons would not be shot. Her voice carried over the countryside as it grew in agony like the fabled banshees, screaming for Olivia to get help while she tried desperately to stop the flow of blood gushing from both her boys, facing the nightmare of choosing one over the other in each instant, for she could not help them both simultaneously.

I rolled onto my stomach, coughing in agony, my lungs filling with smoke. As I forced myself onto wobbling legs, I spotted a throng of people coming from the village along the lane. Rather than rushing forward to help douse the flames, the group moved with slow and measured precision, almost shoulder to shoulder, their bodies appearing to move as one. Each of them carried a torch, the flames reaching upward to become churning black clouds of smoke eerily unchecked by the storm.

I could not stop the panic from rising through my body and soul. I felt as though I had been electrocuted; every nerve was standing on end, my breath caught in my throat. I remained motionless like a lifeless statue frozen in time. Then in the next instant, adrenaline coursed through me, pounding against my temples, my heart pummeling in my chest, my breath coming fast, ragged and shallow. A momentary flash of faces flooded through my mind—villagers crowding the pub, demanding to know what I was writing. Isabella Crutchley's face as she told me the entire village knew of the attack. Michelle's voice over the phone, informing me the killers had been Danny O'Ceallaigh's grandfather and great-uncle.

I had to escape.

I could see nothing now through the thick fog and smoke except the flames shooting from the cottage, mixing with the atmosphere so it appeared like a watercolor painting bursting into life—and the flames of the villagers' torches looming ever larger along the lane, their voices rising now in mounting rage.

The carriage house was on my left and fully engulfed in flames; it would provide no sanctuary. Danny's cottage was just below, between the carriage house and the angry mob. The fields were to my right but as I began to run, I stumbled on the rocky, uneven terrain. As I lurched onward, I realized every field was separated by impassable hedgerows and stone walls, the latter low enough for me to attempt to scramble over but not fast enough to outrun the villagers. Danny was somewhere out here as well and he posed an even greater threat as he was closer.

I had no choice. I had to go up. I had to climb the hill between the carriage house and the ruins and though I'd find no refuge in the skeletal remains, I could continue to the cliffs and then down to the British barracks. I'd figure something else out by the time I got that far.

I stayed off the lane the villagers were using, choosing to remain instead on the other side of the deep ditch that ran alongside it. Twice I lost my footing in the mud and slid down the embankment, instinctively clawing at the air and willing myself not to fall into its depths. I lost a shoe somewhere along the way and I scrambled out of the other.

I managed to find the old gate and clambered through it, leaving it screeching on rusty hinges behind me. My breathing grew more labored as the terrain grew ever steeper and soon the carriage house and its flames were somewhere behind me in an eerie red-orange mist. The villagers' voices had grown more remote as I put distance between us. With every step I took, I knew that Danny's face could pop into view through the mist and the fog, and yet those very mists, the fog and the smoke were now my allies. I trusted them to conceal me even while they swirled around me and sucked the breath out of my body.

My bare feet bumped and snagged across brambles and stones and I stumbled across a large boulder with jagged edges, ripping the skin on both my knees as I fell. I was covered in blood from the car accident and my head throbbed, and now my legs were screaming with the agony of deep cuts.

I was almost upon the ruins of Crutchley Manor before I even saw it, halted with a vengeance by the stone carriage post. As I ran into it, I grabbed it with both hands, nearly wrapping my arms around it while I tried valiantly to catch my breath and steady my legs. The mad dash upward had almost completely winded me; my chest ached and my lungs burned.

Through the fog, I heard Danny's voice calling me. He sounded insistent, demanding. He was a killer, my entire body shrieked within me. His family was a gang of stone cold, merciless killers.

I staggered past the carriage post, climbing ever higher until I was lurching past the ruins, one knee now determined in its demand that I stop. I reached down with both hands, pulling my leg forward, knowing all the while that I was slowing while Danny's voice grew ever closer.

I would have to jump off the cliff.

The thought occurred to me halfway between the ruins and the cliffs. There was no other means of escape. I would fall two hundred feet to the sandbar below, pick myself up and get to the British barracks as quickly as possible. He would never see me once I'd gone over the edge. The mists would obscure me from view.

I was only a few yards from the cliff when I heard his voice yet again, but this time he was not calling my name. I stopped barely two feet from the edge. I could not see below; clouds of fog cloaked everything beneath me. The cliffs were sheer; I knew that from my earlier ventures, but I did not remember whether any rocks protruded from the sandbar below. I would have to leap forward to clear the cliffs. I backed up a few feet. The only way to do that was to get a running start.

Danny's voice came to me once again, and this time I could decipher his words as they echoed across the eerie landscape. "The cows!" he was shouting. "The cows!"

I felt as though the entire world had gone insane. Why, at a time like this with the carriage house in flames and the villagers marching toward me with torches and vengeance in their voices was he shouting about cows?

I backed up a few feet further and tried to take a deep breath. Oh my God, my mind shouted. The cows! I took two running steps and my mind's eye saw the cattle running for the cliffs, jumping from them to their deaths below.

I stopped myself just feet from the edge, pivoting off to the side. The path. Where was the path I had taken before? With Danny's voice growing ever louder, I slipped and blundered my way forward. I couldn't make it. He was gaining on me.

I threw myself off the path and into a copse where I slipped around a giant tree. I slid to the ground, bringing my bloodied knees up to my chest, keeping my head lowered, trying to force myself into the smallest and most invisible bundle I could manage. And there I sat with both hands over my mouth and nose in an attempt to keep my gasps from escaping as he grew closer.

He stopped at the edge of the cliffs and shouted my name, his voice echoing into the distance.

Then he was silent.

I had nowhere to look but the ground in front of me and in horror I realized I'd left a trail of blood behind me. My first impulse was to jump up and begin to race forward, find the path downward and get to the barracks. But a voice rose inside me, ordering me to remain where I was and I could only hope it was the sane part of my psyche that I struggled to listen to. I could hear his footsteps shuffling through the underbrush now. I pressed myself against the trunk of the tree, praying against all odds that the mist would keep the ground obscured from his view.

Then I heard him calling my name. His voice was softer now, cajoling. "Don't be afraid," he called out. "I'm not here to hurt you." Oddly, I realized it was the first time I'd heard his voice when he wasn't slurring his words.

I leaned forward as silently as I thought possible and allowed my fingers to search through the underbrush for anything I could use as a weapon. My hands closed around a small rock and then a larger one.

"I begged Fergal not to restore the carriage house," he was saying. "I was born in the shadows of those ruins. I was raised with the telling of the Crutchley executions."

His voice was drawing closer. I pictured him in my mind's eye feeling his way along the path at the edge of the cliffs, peering downward at my trail of blood.

"Heroic, they called it. You have to understand it was wartime. It was the best chance Ireland had for breaking free of England's oppression. And yes, my entire family fought for Ireland's independence—even the women were spies and damn proud of it."

His voice stopped and I listened intently for the sound of his breathing, terrified he would grab me unexpectedly and before I could react, he would throw me over the cliffs to my death below. But had he warned me? Had his shouts about the cows stopped me from certain doom? A short moment later his voice began again, this time off to my left as though he was circling me.

"My family told of crossing the Crutchley land to spy on the movements of the British below. They passed information to the IRB, which led to successful ambushes of the RIC and Black and Tans, for which I'm as proud as my ancestors, I am. You must understand they were killing the Irish, burning whole villages, executing without trials. Immediate justice, they called it."

The voice had moved in front of me now, somewhere into the woods, as if he hadn't seen the blood after all— or perhaps it was a trap.

"Then my grandfather discovered the Crutchley women watching them from the big house. They had to stop them, don't you see? The IRB ordered the house burned and the men killed." He had circled to my right. "But my grandfather and his brother botched it all damn them, and the whole village was mortified at what they'd done. They were supposed to execute them, you see. Line them up against the house and shoot them dead. But in an act of vengeance, they deliberately did not make it clean and fast. They wanted them to suffer."

My hand tightened around the stone.

"What was far worse was they left witnesses to tell the tale."

A strange sense of calm crept over me as time seemed to slow. Now I heard every rustle in the leaves acutely.

"They couldn't kill the women, you see," Danny continued. He'd moved in a full circle; I was sure of it. He had to be standing on the path now adjacent to the cliff edge. "My grandfather said the youngest in particular; she was too pure to be shot, despite her family's loyalty to the Brits. And the mother—well, she never left, did she?"

The acrid odor of the carriage house in flames had reached the woods now and I looked upward through the canopy of trees. I could not tell the difference between the roiling black clouds and the angry smoke. I wondered where the villagers with their torches had gone; whether they assumed I was trapped inside and were helping to burn me along with the cottage, or whether they had fanned out and were searching for me now.

"My great-uncle used to tell the story of going to the priest afterward and confessing to their murders. After he told of the circumstances, the priest asked, 'So they were Protestants, were they?' To which he replied, 'Why yes they were.' 'Then you did not sin,' the priest responded. 'Go and despair no more.'

"I grew up with the Crutchley ghosts," Danny continued. His voice was closer. "I used to watch the boys every evening taking their cattle home to the barn; boys and livestock that were dead decades before I was even born. But it was the mother that haunted me, the mother that awakened me every night of my life, sobbing for the two boys my family had killed. I had nothing to do with it," he finished. "But the sins of the father, you see…"

The hand shot through the fog and grabbed my arm. With my other hand, I hurled the stone with all the strength I had left in my body, the force hauling my torso upward and wrenching free of his grasp. I was on my feet in an instant.

He stood only an arm's length away. His eyes were wide, his mouth slightly open, his expression stunned. A trickle of blood grew into a stream, winding its way down his forehead to his chin. He stumbled backward a step before appearing to gain his balance. And then he staggered as if drunk onto the path and then off the other side.

As he lost his footing, his arms flailed at the air. I briefly lost sight of him as he fell but instinctively, I threw myself forward. Grasping at him, my fingers tightened around his shirt as he went over. I slung both hands around his arm, my fingers digging into his skin even as his weight pulled me forward. I fell to the ground, my belly raking across the uneven path.

"Let me go!" he yelled. "I deserve to die!"

My toes snagged on a stone embedded in the earth, momentarily halting the forward momentum. "Find a foothold!" I heard myself yelling, my voice not even sounding like myself. "Find a foothold!"

From somewhere in the distance I heard someone shouting my name.

"Let go!" he screamed at me. "Let me die!"

I could not hold onto him, and I knew in the next instant I could be pulled over the cliff with him. Yet I couldn't relinquish my hold on him; it was as if we were joined together now. "What if your soul becomes trapped with the Crutchleys?" I shouted in desperation.

"My soul is already trapped with them." He was sobbing now. "Let me go!"

"But you didn't kill them!"

His struggling stopped. I felt my foot slipping away from the stone that had held me, and the arm I had doggedly held onto was slithering through my hands, his shirt torn and his skin so wet that I could not maintain my grip.

Then his slide stopped. He seemed to be pressed now against the side of the cliff and I realized he must have found a foothold. He was trying to haul himself upward.

I repositioned myself and as he reached out for me, I grasped him under one arm. I heard my name shouted again and with a flood of relief I recognized Shay's voice. "Over here!" I shouted.

Danny had managed to find a handhold and another foothold, his torso barely clearing the cliff's edge when Shay appeared. He rushed forward, grabbing me and hauling me backward. With my hold still on Danny, I was able to drag him with me until he collapsed onto the path. He lay there sobbing as though expelling a lifetime of pain.

"Are you alright?" Shay asked, pulling me to my feet. As he held me, I could feel his heart pounding in his chest and I knew my heart was matching the ferocity.

"Where are the villagers?" I asked in panic.

"They're trying to put the fire out. Don't you hear the firetrucks?"

"But—" I had been so focused on Danny that I hadn't heard them before now but as I fought to catch my breath, I heard a myriad of voices and more than one firetruck's siren. "The villagers—they had torches. They were coming after me."

Shay pulled slightly away to peer into my eyes. "They don't have any torches. They're trying to put out the fire, not start one."

"But—"

"I know what you saw," Danny interjected. He rolled onto his back. "I have seen them every night of my life. They're the spirits of every villager that marched to Crutchley Manor to set the big house afire."

My knees buckled under me and Shay clutched me to prevent my fall. "They're ghosts?" I managed to say.

"I've been haunted by them all my life," Danny said. "I could feel them coming; the air changes. I tried to warn you." He struggled to his feet. "I'm the last of the O'Ceallaigh's. Let my family's sins die with me."

Before we could react, he'd spread his arms wide and stepped off the edge of the path. We rushed to the edge, Shay trying to keep me back but I was doggedly determined to peer below. The mist stopped abruptly and the fog began to part. Danny's body lay at the base of the cliffs, his back bent unnaturally over the rocks, the ocean spraying his lifeless body.

27

Eight months later

It was an uncommonly cold day in early December. I gazed out the kitchen window at the snow falling in large, graceful flakes that caught on the wind and traveled to the skeletal branches of trees that would remain dormant until spring. There were already several inches of snow on the ground, turning Ireland into a pristine white wonderland. Somewhere in the distance I heard children laughing and screaming as they careened down neighboring hills on their sleds.

The teakettle began to whistle and I reluctantly pulled myself away from the idyllic scene. I shut off the stove and poured two cups, gathering a snack of assorted sweets while the tea steeped. The home carried the aroma of freshly baked gingerbread and a traditional Irish Christmas cake containing fruit and Irish whiskey.

I arranged it all on a tray and carried it into the adjacent room where Shay was turning on the Christmas tree lights. The room sprang to life in crystal lights, the occasional blue, red and green bulbs he'd added providing a merriment of color amid all the white.

"It's beautiful," I exclaimed, setting the tray on the coffee table. He stepped toward me, wrapping an arm around my shoulder as we both soaked in the ambiance. A pine bough graced the mantle, candles of pine and cranberry filled the air with their scents, and an assortment of miniature Christmas figurines covered the sofa table. This Christmas would be a special one; I could feel the warmth of Ireland—and Shay—embracing me.

I'd returned to America at the beginning of May, passing by long lines of tourists arriving in Ireland as I was departing. From their accents and height, I surmised they were primarily Scandinavian, but Americans would be arriving soon enough. Dublin was already a melting pot of Europeans, the city more of an international presence than an Irish one, and in the weeks ahead the island would be bustling with tourists from around the world.

It was sad leaving, especially saying good-bye to Shay, but I knew my absence would be short-lived. I returned to Massachusetts, submitted my book to my editor and immediately began planning my move. With Shay's help, I secured a one-year lease on an adorable cottage. It was nestled just outside of Galway with an amazing view of Lough Corrib, a lake connected to the Atlantic Ocean by a river. Each morning I awakened to the sight of horses, cattle and sheep on the rolling hills as well as the calm blue waters of the lough. Though I truly felt as though I was at the back of beyond, I was only minutes away from Shay's home and all the sights and sounds of Galway.

As we admired our Christmas handiwork, the doorbell rang. "Were you expecting anyone?" I asked.

Shay shook his head, his brows knit in puzzlement. As he made his way to the door, I stood at the other end of the hallway and watched out of mild curiosity.

"Fergal," Shay said in surprise as he discovered the man on his stoop. "Come in, won't you? What a pleasant surprise."

"And a grand hello to you both," Fergal said as he entered. "I suppose I should have phoned you up first but I was in Galway on some business and thought I'd pop by."

I met him in the hallway and gave him a hug. "Come in, won't you?" I asked. "I just made some tea."

"Ah, that sounds grand. It's a bit nippy out, you know?"

As Shay led him to the living room, I made my way to the kitchen to retrieve another cup and saucer. I found them chatting amicably, having already sampled the sweets while they chatted.

"So I've heard correctly," Fergal said as I entered, "I understand you're now living in Ireland, 'ey?"

"I am," I answered. "News travels fast on this island," I chuckled.

"Well, it's a small place, 'ey? Anyway, I can see you're quite busy, you are, with the holidays and all," he continued as I poured him a cup of tea, "but I was wondering if you'd be kind enough to do a book signing at the pub?"

"Oh?" I settled into the chair across from him.

"Aye, the villagers thoroughly enjoyed your talk this spring last about the book on your ancestors, and now that it's been released a number have purchased it, they have. They'd like to know if you'd be kind enough to sign their books, and perhaps sell a few more while you're here, 'eh?"

My eyes caught Shay's, who smiled encouragingly. "I'd love to," I answered. "When were you thinking?"

"This coming weekend, if that's not too soon for you?"

"I don't know if I can get copies of the book that quickly."

"Oh, not to worry. I've sorted it. I have already ordered a few dozen books from the village bookstore to have on hand during your talk and they assure me they will arrive in time."

I chuckled. I suppose it was the Irish optimism that had him two steps ahead of me. "Sounds great. It's a date then."

"I like to plan ahead, you know. Come early on Saturday and we'll treat you and Professor Macgregor here to a delightful Christmas spread. The village is all decked out for the holidays, you see, and we're celebrating it all month long at the pub..."

"We'd love to," I said as Shay nodded his head in agreement. "Thank you so much for the invitation."

"My pleasure, it is indeed. Oh, and by the way, I've a story to tell you twos if you have the time?"

"Of course," Shay said. He leaned back in his chair, his cup of tea perched precariously on one armrest while a plate of fruitcake balanced on his knee.

"I've been caring for Danny's cattle I have," Shay began, his voice growing excited, "while his property is tied up intestate, you see. So a few days ago I brought the cattle into their normal field and closed the gate solidly behind them. Well, I returned early evening to drive them home and the gate was standing wide open, it was, and the cattle were all in the Crutchley field with the gate there closed and locked."

"No." I pictured the old gates, one side beginning to teeter, propped open by craggy roots that had no doubt held it in place for decades.

Fergal laughed. "It was the most mind-boggling thing I ever saw, as the gate was closed big as you please but the stone wall had long since been removed. Yet there they were as if the wall was still there and they were completely and securely confined."

"Are you serious?" Shay asked.

"I am indeed. Danny's two dogs were even in there with them, they were, and we all scratched our heads, not knowing how the animals managed that on their own."

"And no one from the village moved them?" I asked.

"No one would've done that, no indeed." He took a deep, satisfying gulp of tea.

I pictured Danny's spirit unlatching the gate and whistling to the dogs to drive the cattle up the hill to the Crutchley fields. They would have passed right by the grave at the base of the hill dug just last April, and past the tombstone bearing his name followed by "*At Peace At Last*" in Gaelic.

"And the cattle and the dogs were not spooked on the Crutchley land, as they had been," Fergal was saying. "It's the first time in a hundred years that the Crutchley lands have been grazed."

"Do you suppose April and her sons have crossed to the other side now?" I asked.

"I'm sure of it, I am." He fell silent, slightly shaking his head in disbelief at his own story.

"Will you rebuild the carriage house?" Shay asked.

Fergal was quiet for a moment longer. "I don't know if that's the right thing to do, 'ey?"

"But you put so much effort into it," I protested. "And it was lovely and in such a beautiful place."

"Aye, and it's a bit sad, it is. But wouldn't you know everything I did to upgrade it was burned beyond recognition. All the wiring is gone, all the new furniture... Even the new plumbing was melted like lava." He shook his head. "The new metal roof with the skylights caved."

I kept my eyes downcast as I remembered the sight the following day when I met with the fire inspectors to give my account of what had transpired. Even the glass windows had been blown out. The fire had started in the fireplace and despite my adamant protestations that I had not started the fire myself and failed to properly open the damper, I was certain that was precisely what they put on their report.

"It was not your fault, you know," Fergal said as if reading my mind.

"I would not have done that to you," I said quietly.

"I know it was April and her boys," he said. "The time had come for them to move on."

"Do you suppose they resented the use of the carriage house as a tourist rental?" Shay asked.

"I thought of that myself, I did," Fergal said. "Perhaps it was disrespectful of me." He slapped his knee. "Anyway, I've plans for the place, I have."

"Oh?" I leaned forward.

"I've petitioned for the bodies to be exhumed and buried properly. You see, I was told the boys had not been buried in coffins because no one would sell them to the family, on IRB—"

"—IRB orders—," I interjected.

"—and the family did not even have a blanket in which to wrap them, on account of their house burning."

"So they simply put them into the ground?" Shay asked.

"That would have traumatized a mother all over again," I shuddered, "watching the dirt shoveled onto their faces like that."

"What else could they do?" Fergal answered, shrugging his shoulders sadly. "Anyway, I have ordered fine coffins and new headstones as well as a Celtic cross—they were as much Irish as anyone—and come spring, perhaps next April, we'll have a ceremony."

"Where will you rebury them?" I asked.

"Why, exactly where they are," he answered. "It's a fine view of the countryside, it is, and the ocean as well." He pulled a slip of paper out of his pocket. "Besides their names and dates, I asked for the engraving *'Never a boy was loved more by a mother'*." He'd read the last part and now dabbed at his eye as he returned the paper to his pocket. "In Gaelic, of course."

"That's beautiful," I said.

He nodded, his lips pursed as if he was attempting to control his emotions. "It will be on each headstone." He cleared his throat. "Anyway, I understand you've been in touch with the Crutchley descendants? If you'd be so kind to share their contact information with me, it would be nice if they could join us for the ceremony, don't you think?"

"I think that's a fine idea."

We each fell silent, perhaps with our individual thoughts and memories. I broke the hush that had descended over us, my words soft. "Danny wasn't guilty of anything."

"I know," Fergal said quietly. "I know."

Before I could say more, Fergal continued, his voice a bit reluctant, "I must get on my way, I do. Customers will be arriving at the pub soon, you see. They'll expect me to be there to attend to them."

"Of course. We'll see you Saturday."

We all rose, setting our plates and cups on the tray before making our way down the hall to the front door. I kissed Fergal on the cheek and gave him a good strong hug.

"Looking forward to your talk," he said as he set his cap on his head. We watched as he pulled his scarf tighter about his neck and made his way to his car, waving as he drove away.

When we closed the door, I leaned against it and looked at Shay.

"Do you think Danny's spirit herded them onto the Crutchley land?" he asked quietly.

"I hope so," I said wistfully. "It would mean April and her two boys have finally crossed over."

"It's unlikely the boys herded them."

I thought of Anne, her spirit strolling through a stranger's house even as her body slept half a world away. There were things we might never know about the resiliency of the spirit, I thought. I knew in my heart that April had remained on the old Crutchley estate to be close to her boys, and I recalled the repeated sensation I'd had that April was listening to my conversations. I was certain it had been her, as sure as I was that with the burning of the carriage house, April and her boys could finally move through that veil separating this life from the next.

"You're right," I said thoughtfully, "I think it was Danny, looking out for his cattle still. It's truly sad; after all, Danny had done nothing wrong. He'd simply been born into the family, but long after the two boys were murdered."

Shay took my hand and led me back down the hall where the Christmas lights twinkled. "Let's put it behind us now, shall we?" Shay turned toward me, wrapping his arms about me. "We've still to go to the Christmas Market in Galway; I can't wait to see your eyes light up when you see it. It will be dark soon and the whole market will be lit up spectacularly."

As if in agreement, Sadie bounded up from her bed in the corner and barked excitedly.

"Yes," I said, laughing. "I've been looking forward to it."

"I'll get our coats," Shay offered. He disappeared back down the hall and returned with our heavy overcoats. Our scarves, ear muffs and gloves were stuffed into the sleeves, just as I used to do when I was a child.

"Tomorrow we decorate my place," I said as I dressed.

"Absolutely. That was our agreement," Shay said, smiling. "I'll get the car and you lock up?"

I watched him on his way to the door before turning back to the room. The tree lights which had been shining solidly began to twinkle in an on/off pattern that illuminated the walls in warm flickering colors. Reluctantly, I made my way to the outlet strip and unplugged it from the wall, casting the room in shadows as the tree and decorations grew dark. I consoled myself with the knowledge that we would return in a few hours and the room would be aglow again.

I was halfway down the hall toward the door when the walls began to twinkle. Startled, I turned around to find red, green and white colors pulsating. I made my way back down the hall to the living room to discover it bathed once more in glimmering lights. The tree was sparkling, the lights racing on and off along its boughs, and the mantle bough was twinkling as well. My eyes followed the cords to the outlet strip. It was still unplugged, just as I'd left it.

The car horn honked in the driveway.

"Merry Christmas," I said to the room.

I hurried to the front door. I was standing on the stoop ready to close the door when the lights flickered once more before plunging the house into darkness. I closed and locked the door and rushed to the car where Shay and Sadie were waiting.

Author's Notes

Like many of my books, *April in the Back of Beyond* was inspired by true stories interwoven into one.

While researching Irish history for a series on my Neely ancestors, I came across the story of two teenage boys who were murdered in Ireland in 1919. Their family had been in the country for generations and by all accounts, they were admired and valued in their original home, but they relocated to a larger estate in what would turn out to be a horrifically fatal mistake.

Unlike their original home where Catholics and Protestants coexisted, their new home was in the middle of a war zone. The Royal Irish Constabulary (RIC) and RIC Special Forces (better known as the Black and Tans for their mismatched uniforms) were fighting against those campaigning for Irish independence, such as the Fenian Brotherhood and the Irish Republican Brotherhood (IRB), the forerunner of the IRA (Irish Republican Army). Their new home, like the one portrayed in this book, overlooked British barracks and when the two teenage boys informed their neighbors they were not allowed to trespass on their property, they were shot and killed and their home burned to the ground.

The story, however, did not end there; it was only the beginning of a nightmare that would culminate in their mother suffering from severe emotional trauma, having tried vainly to save her sons from bleeding to death while their home and all their possessions burned. The true attack was particularly vicious, the shots delivered so they would suffer at least a day before dying; it was so imprinted on my mind as I learned of it that I was unable to replicate the savagery in this book out of respect for my readers. The information regarding the sale of their home is accurate as well as their migration to Australia, where the family's descendants continue to live today.

I did not feel comfortable placing the home in this story in the same county as the actual events took place, so literary license was used to move the location of the house, carriage house and British barracks. Only the barracks survive today as an abandoned property, a relic of World War I. The names have also been changed for both the victims and the perpetrators for obvious reasons.

Throughout this book is another story inspired by fact. The main character, Hayley Hunter, is a writer that is researching her family's history, beginning with her ancestor's migration to Ulster from Scotland and became involved in O'Doherty's Rebellion. These scenes are based on my creative nonfiction book, *Checkmate: Clans and Castles*, which was released in 2017 by Drake Valley Press. In *Checkmate*, my own ancestor, William Neely, arrived in Ulster with William Stewart. Their land bordered on Cahir O'Doherty's Inishowen Peninsula, separated only by the lough. When Cahir set fire to Derry and began O'Doherty's Rebellion, it would require my ancestor to make a choice: whether to fight for King James against the uprising or side with the Irish that had lived and ruled that region for over a thousand years. *Checkmate* was the result of years of painstaking research and I attempted to remain faithful to the facts.

Though the battle of Derry depicted in *Checkmate* occurred in 1608, it would not be the first and far from the last. The city was rebuilt through London private donations and renamed Londonderry. Today, more than 400 years later, it continues to be a city divided between those loyal to Britain and largely Protestant (unionists or loyalists) versus those fighting for a united Ireland that are largely Catholic (republicans or nationalists). The ideological war between the two factions was originally those loyal to Britain versus those loyal to Ireland, but it became a religious war as well, fueled by zealous ministers and priests. The city is often referred to as the "slash city" Londonderry/Derry because the republican/nationalist Irish do not recognize the name "London" in their city, it having been named Derry centuries earlier, prior to England's invasion.

During the writing of this book, tensions increased in Ulster—most notably Derry and Belfast. A journalist was killed covering a violent uprising in Derry and several Catholic churches were burned. The increase in violence was attributed to Brexit, which could possibly lead to checkpoints and guard posts between Northern Ireland and the Republic of Ireland, which had unfairly targeted Catholics in decades before the Good Friday Agreement and the removal of those border walls.

Anne's story is also based on a true story, in which a woman dreamt of a very specific house for several years before deciding to vacation in Ireland and look at properties to purchase. When she visited a particular house for sale, the owner promptly fainted. When he was brought to, he told the story of a ghost that had been frequenting his home for several years, wandering the halls at night and eventually frightening him and his wife so badly that they placed the house on the market. The ghost, as it turned out, looked identical to the woman looking at properties for sale. She purchased the property and lives there still. Sometimes truth really is stranger than fiction, and I appreciate her permission as well as the permission of the now-grown children of the original owners to tell the story here.

The romance between the writer Hayley Hunter and the historian Shay Macgregor is purely a work of fiction. Even mysteries and ghost stories are made better with a touch of romance, don't you think?

About the Author

p.m.terrell is the pen name for Patricia McClelland Terrell, the award-winning, internationally acclaimed author of more than 23 books in multiple genres, including contemporary suspense, historical suspense, computer instructional, non-fiction and children's books.

Prior to writing full-time, she founded two computer companies in the Washington, DC Metropolitan Area: McClelland Enterprises, Inc. and Continental Software Development Corporation. Among her clients were the Central Intelligence Agency, United States Secret Service, U.S. Information Agency, and Department of Defense. Her specialties were in the detection of white collar computer crimes and computer intelligence.

A full-time author since 2002, *Black Swamp Mysteries* was her first series, inspired by the success of *Exit 22*, released in 2008. *Vicki's Key* was a top five finalist in the 2012 International Book Awards and 2012 USA Book Awards nominee, and *The Pendulum Files* was a national finalist for the Best Cover of the Year in 2014.

Her second series, *Ryan O'Clery Suspense*, is also award-winning. *The Tempest Murders* (Book 1) was one of four finalists in the 2013 International Book Awards, cross-genre category. *The White Devil of Dublin* (Book 2) was released one year later.

Her historical suspense, *River Passage*, was a 2010 Best Fiction and Drama Award Winner. It was determined to be so historically accurate that a copy of the book resides at the Nashville Government Metropolitan Archives in Nashville, Tennessee.

Songbirds are Free remains her bestselling book to date; it is inspired by the true story of Mary Neely, who was captured in 1780 by Shawnee warriors near Fort Nashborough (now Nashville, Tennessee).

Inspired by the vast number of Neely descendants that contacted her after the publication of *River Passage* and *Songbirds are Free*, she researched her genealogy back to 1608 Scotland, resulting in a book of her ancestor William Neely entitled *Checkmate: Clans and Castles*.

She was the co-founder of The Book 'Em Foundation, an organization committed to raising public awareness of the correlation between high crime rates and high illiteracy rates. She was the founder of Book 'Em North Carolina, an annual event held in Lumberton, North Carolina, to raise funds to increase literacy and reduce crime, serving as its chairperson and organizaer for its first four years. Robeson Community College now chairs and hosts it.

She also served on the boards of the Friends of the Robeson County (NC) Public Library, the Robeson County (NC) Arts Council, Virginia Crime Stoppers and became the first female president of the Chesterfield County-Colonial Heights (VA) Crime Solvers.

For more information, visit the author's website at www.pmterrell.com.

Books by p.m.terrell

Historical Suspense
Checkmate:Clans and Castles
River Passage
Songbirds are Free

Black Swamp Mysteries Series
Exit 22
Vicki's Key
Secrets of a Dangerous Woman
Dylan's Song
The Pendulum Files
Cloak and Mirrors

Ryan O'Clery Mysteries
The Tempest Murders
The White Devil of Dublin

Stand-Alone Suspense
A Thin Slice of Heaven
The Banker's Greed
Ricochet
The China Conspiracy
Kickback

Visit www.pmterrell.com for more titles, to view book trailers, read excerpts and more!

Made in the USA
Columbia, SC
30 June 2019